# FAKING MS. RIGHT

A HOT ROMANTIC COMEDY

DIRTY MARTINI RUNNING CLUB
BOOK 1

CLAIRE KINGSLEY

Always Have LLC

Published by Always Have, LLC

Edited by Elayne Morgan of Serenity Editing Services

Cover by Lori Jackson

ISBN: 9781099282096

www.clairekingsleybooks.com

❀ Created with Vellum

*To the girls in my circle of trust.*

# ABOUT THIS BOOK

*"When I kissed you last night, I wasn't pretending."*

Everly Dalton is a walking, talking, martini-drinking dating disaster. Forget kissing frogs. She can't even get past the first date. But at work, she's a badass—the longest-running assistant billionaire Shepherd Calloway has ever had. Her coworkers wonder how she handles the big bad wolf—and never gets bit.

Shepherd Calloway isn't interested in being anyone's sugar daddy. Tired of women who only want him for his money, he swears off dating, determined to focus on running his empire. Until his gold-digging ex hits him where it hurts, putting him in a difficult position.

His solution—to have Everly pose as his live-in girlfriend—is obviously crazy. But the timing is uncanny. It just so happens Everly needs a favor from her boss—a big and awkward one—and this could ensure everyone gets what they want.

Besides, Everly can totally survive a few months of faux romance.

Except there's a problem. Shepherd is supposed to be a

single-minded, unemotional robot boss. Not an actual human with a heart and morning wood. Between the awkward bed-sharing and tingly fake dates, lines are blurring. And as Everly gets to know the real Shepherd, she discovers there's more to the man behind the bank account.

And faking it gets all too real.

# 1

## EVERLY

*C*all me weird, but I didn't hate Monday mornings.

Every Monday was a fresh start. A chance to shake off the previous week—or in my case, the disastrous events of the weekend—and move forward.

I didn't want to think about how many Mondays over the last several months I'd felt the need to put a bad first date behind me. But now wasn't the time to ponder my terrible dating luck—even though it was pretty horrific. I'd dish to my girlfriends about it tonight. Over martinis, of course.

For now, I had work to do. And here, in this office, I wasn't Everly Dalton, serial dating disaster. I was Everly Dalton, executive assistant. And I was damn good at my job.

"Good morning, Everly."

I smiled at Nina, the front receptionist. "Good morning. I love your hair today."

Her smile brightened. "Thank you."

I walked down the hallway, smiling and greeting my coworkers. They all said hi and smiled in return. Even Leslie —who hated mornings more than anyone I knew—cracked a little grin over her coffee.

"Morning, sunshine," Steve said. He was dressed in his usual plaid button-down shirt and brown cardigan. He wasn't that much older than me—maybe five or six years— but his clothes made him look like a grandpa from the fifties. I was pretty sure that after work he changed into another cardigan that had a zipper, and probably brown slippers. But he was super nice.

"Morning, Steve," I said. He liked to think he'd nick-named me *sunshine*, but he was probably the tenth person to do so over the course of my life. Maybe it was because I wore so much yellow—my favorite color—or because I smiled a lot. His desk was near mine, just across the aisle, so we chatted pretty often. "How's Millie?"

"I think I need to modify her diet again. I might elimi-nate fish to see if it helps improve her mood."

Millie was Steve's cat, and he was forever tweaking her diet, hoping it would make her be less of an asshole. I'd never had the heart to tell him that Millie was just an old cranky cat, and no special diet would ever make her nice. But it would have crushed him to hear that his cat hated him and probably wanted to murder his face.

"Sounds like a good plan. Keep me posted."

"I sure will," he said and went back to his desk.

Did I really want to hear all about Millie's diet? Not particularly. But it made Steve happy to have someone who listened, so I endured a little bit of cat conversation now and then. I figured if more people made an effort to be friendly, the world would be a much better place.

The truth was, I liked making people happy. It was my catnip. Getting someone grouchy to smile? Best high ever. Like Leslie, Miss I-Hate-Mornings. She'd been resis-tant to my drive-by *good morning*s for a while. But eventu-ally I'd worn her down. Stopping by with breakfast muffins and strong espresso a few times had done the trick.

Everyone had a chink in their armor—a place I could get in to find their happy side. Even the grumpiest people were no match for Everly Dalton's sunshine.

Except one man.

Like a cloud passing in front of the sun, casting a dark shadow, a chill spread across the office. I glanced at the time. Eight twenty-seven. Right on time.

His entrance onto the floor created a ripple, like tossing a rock into still water. It radiated out ahead of him, warning everyone of his arrival. The only person I'd ever met who was impervious to my happy-making. My boss, Shepherd Calloway.

Steve looked up at me and winced. I pretended not to notice. I knew he felt sorry for me. Working for Mr. Calloway was not easy. He was cold, harsh, and demanding. He never said thank you, or gave any sort of praise. I'd lived in terror for the first few months I'd worked for him, positive he was going to fire me. He always seemed so angry.

But after a while, I realized that was just the way he was. He wasn't angry at *me*. In fact, he barely noticed me. Sometimes I wondered whether he'd recognize me if he had to pick me out of a police lineup. He so rarely looked directly at my face that I wouldn't have been surprised to learn he didn't really know what I looked like.

I was pretty sure he knew my name, although he never called me Everly. He never called me anything, really. Just said what he needed to say, without addressing me first. No greetings. No goodbyes. Just, *what's on my calendar today*? Or, *send me the files before my meeting*.

The ripple strengthened and I heard his footsteps over the sudden hushed silence on our floor. I stood, grabbed a stack of paperwork and his coffee—black, just like his heart —and waited.

He didn't look at anyone as he walked down the hall toward his office. No side glances or nods at his employees. Just his steady gait—a man in a perfectly-tailored suit striding toward his office. His dark hair perfectly styled, his stubble perfectly trimmed.

Without so much as a glance in my direction, he walked past my desk. I fell in step behind him as the clock ticked over to eight twenty-eight.

I followed him into his office and set his coffee on his desk, six inches from the edge and slightly off-center, where he wouldn't knock it over when he took off his jacket or bump it when he set down his laptop. I picked up a remote and opened the blinds, stopping them before they let in too much light. He took off his suit jacket, and I was there to take it and hang it on the coat tree near the door.

"Good morning, Mr. Calloway," I said, my voice bright.

He didn't answer. He never did. Not once had he said good morning in return. But I still did it. Every single day. It was part of our routine, so it would have felt weird not to say it.

He sat and opened his laptop. Grabbed his coffee without looking for it and took a sip.

"Did the lawyer from Duggan and Nolan send over what I asked for?" His voice was smooth and even, without a hint of emotion. Everything he said was delivered in that same tone. People were terrified of Shepherd Calloway, but it wasn't because he yelled. He didn't get loud and berate people when they made mistakes. He froze them. His ice-blue eyes and low voice were more chilling than any tirade could have been. He was a man who could make your heart stop with a glare.

"Yep, no issues there." I placed a thick manila envelope on the side of his desk.

He touched it with two fingers and shifted it up about an inch.

"I also have something for you from Mark in Accounting." I set a file folder directly on top of the envelope, making sure the edges lined up nicely.

"Why didn't he give it to me himself?" he asked.

*Because everyone is afraid of you, so they come to my desk early and pretend they didn't realize you wouldn't be in your office yet.* "I suppose because you weren't in."

He didn't respond.

"You have meetings at ten, noon, and three." I quickly flipped through his calendar—synced with mine—on my phone. "The noon is at McCormick and Schmick's, and I already ordered for you. I moved your dentist appointment to next week because it was going to be too close to your three o'clock. I didn't want you to have to rush. But check with me first before you schedule anything for next Tuesday afternoon, because we shouldn't put that off again. Oral health is important."

I paused, although I knew he wouldn't reply. And he didn't.

"I spoke with Leslie about those reports you needed, and she'll have them for you this afternoon. The painting you bought at the Hope Gala last weekend is being delivered to your place later today, so I'll run over there and sign for it. That means I'll be out of the office for an hour or so."

"I need dinner reservations for tomorrow," he said, still not looking up. "For two. Tulio or Assiaggo are acceptable. Not Canlis. And book a room on Maui for ten days, beginning Saturday. One of the usual resorts. Doesn't matter which one."

I probably could have indulged in the smug smile I tried to hide. It wasn't like he was looking at me. But I nibbled my lip to stop myself anyway. Dinner for two at Tulio or Assiaggo, but not Canlis, and a last-minute trip to Maui meant he was breaking up with his latest gold-digger, Svetlana.

"Should I clear your calendar?" I asked, knowing he was going to tell me he wasn't going. He'd send Svetlana on the trip to appease her for breaking up. But I had to pretend I didn't know that, and ask anyway.

"No, I'm not going."

"Okay." I indulged in the smug smile. I hated Svetlana. She was a ridiculously gorgeous Bulgarian model—tall, slender, big boobs. A woman that heartless should never have been granted such phenomenal beauty. But the fact that she was stunning wasn't why I hated her. I loathed her because I knew she was only with Mr. Calloway for his money.

She didn't even try to hide it. Strutted around here like she owned half the company—which you could tell she thought was a forgone conclusion. As if he'd *marry* her. Ugh. The very thought made my skin crawl.

Granted, she wasn't the first gold-digger he'd dated. He attracted them like a super-powered electromagnet. Most of the women he dated were similar: insanely beautiful, of varying intelligence, and primarily interested in the extravagant lifestyle they assumed dating—and even marrying—Shepherd Calloway would give them.

They were in for a rude awakening when they found out Mr. Calloway was not the type of billionaire businessman who lavished his girlfriends with luxurious gifts. Nice dinners, perhaps. And they could attend exclusive events among Seattle's elite perched on his arm. He was certainly a means to being seen.

But from what I could tell, he was just as cold and unemotional with his girlfriends as he was with his employees. And he never spent a lot of money on them. They undoubtedly went into it picturing limo rides to romantic dinners, beautiful jewelry, and fancy vacations. What they got was a man who ignored them almost as much as he ignored me, and who didn't buy them presents—probably because it never occurred to him to bother.

Svetlana hadn't lasted long, but that wasn't a surprise. He'd been seeing her for a couple of months—not that I kept track, really—and it seemed she'd already chafed his nerves more times than he was willing to live with, regardless of what she looked like. And boy, was I glad.

I had no reason to care. Mr. Calloway and I weren't friends. So it shouldn't have mattered to me whether some woman was trying to latch onto him for his money. But it did. I did care about him, even though I knew better. I couldn't help it. I figured I was just built that way and tried to ignore it.

Except for moments like this, when I could privately gloat.

"That's it," he said.

"Sounds good, Mr. Calloway. I'll be at my desk if you need anything."

I said that to him every day, too. And he never replied. But it had become part of our routine, so I said it anyway.

Back at my desk, Steve gave me a reassuring smile. "You sure are tougher than you look."

I shrugged and grinned, feeling a little glow of satisfaction. I always felt that way when people commented on my job. I'd lasted longer than any other assistant Shepherd Calloway had ever had. And I wore that distinction with a great deal of pride.

Only two types of people lasted at this company: people who were close enough to being his peers that they weren't intimidated by him, and people who didn't have to interact with him.

Anyone else usually lasted six months—maybe a year if they were tougher than average.

I'd worked for him for three years—a company record. Before me, he'd gone through assistants like some women went through purses. In one season, out the next. But me? Miss Everly Dalton? I was the only assistant he'd ever had who could actually handle him.

Really, I kind of got off on it. I liked having access to the man everyone was afraid of. The man with the power in this place. I liked the respect my position earned me. Outside these walls, people took me for a sugary-sweet, plain as vanilla, boring blond girl with a big smile.

But my coworkers saw me as something else entirely. They looked at me in awe, wondering how I could possibly handle the big bad wolf. How I never got bit.

It wasn't as hard as they all thought. Once I got to know him—as well as I could, considering he didn't speak to me very much—it was easy to get along with him. Learn his routine. Make sure anything within my control was executed on time. Stay out of his way.

And it worked. I didn't rock the boat. I didn't expect anything I knew he wouldn't give. He wasn't going to be friendly. No asking about my day or thanking me for a job well done. Which was fine. I knew I did my job well, and my pay reflected that.

The situation worked for me, and whether or not he'd ever acknowledge it, I knew it worked for Mr. Calloway too.

I winked at Steve, and grabbed my phone. I had work to do.

## 2

## EVERLY

*M*y shoes hit the pavement in a steady rhythm, and I tried to concentrate on my breathing. Running wasn't my favorite activity—I'd never been what you'd call an athlete—but something happens when you turn thirty. You just can't recover the same way.

My girlfriends and I couldn't, at least. Not from any of the things we used to do without batting an eyelash—or gaining a pound. Martini Mondays. Taco Tuesdays. Wine Wednesdays. Thirsty Thursdays. Fast-food Fridays (don't judge). Not from binging on cheap pizza and chocolate ice cream because one of us had an epic breakup. And let's be honest, best friends *cannot* shirk their gorge-on-crap-food-and-get-drunk duties just because said breakup occurred after the age of twenty-nine.

"Are we done yet?" Nora asked. She jogged beside me in full makeup, looking gorgeous as always. Her thick, dark hair was in a beautifully curled ponytail that swished and swayed as she moved.

Hazel looked at her high-tech watch. "Almost. We're at two-point-seven miles. We're doing three today."

"Ugh," Nora said. She was acting put out, but she didn't even sound winded.

"Nora…" *Breath.* "You're doing awesome." *Breath.* "You're not even breathing hard."

"Her metabolic rate has improved," Hazel said, pushing her glasses back up her nose.

I'd been best friends with Hazel and Nora since forever. The three of us lived in the same apartment building now, but we'd met in middle school and could have been voted *girls least likely to be best friends*. We were all so different. Nora had always been exceptionally beautiful—and popular. Men loved her, and women wanted to be her. Hazel was gorgeous in her own way, but she tended to minimize it. Plus, she was brilliant—an actual, bona fide genius. I think she even had a plaque somewhere.

And then there was me. People usually called me cute, rather than beautiful. Being blond and admittedly a little bit bubbly added to the cute factor. I had a reputation for being an optimist, and it was true. I tended to see the good in everything, and everyone—which occasionally got me into trouble.

Okay, maybe not *occasionally*. Maybe it *often* got me into trouble.

"You realize I'm only doing this to offset the copious amounts of vodka I'm planning to drink this week, right?" Nora asked.

"Nora, we've been over the benefits of regular exercise," Hazel said. "For starters—"

"Stop," Nora and I said together. We both loved Hazel, but once she got going on a topic, it was hard to shut her up.

"We've heard your statistics-laced lecture at least a dozen times," Nora said.

"It's really good," I said between breaths. "Good information, I mean."

"I'm just saying the facts are well-documented," Hazel said.

The park where we'd started our run came into view, so we slowed to a walk to cool down. Streetlights winked to life above us. We usually ran in the evenings, and the sun would be setting soon. I put my hands on my hips and took deep breaths. Hazel pressed her fingers to the side of her throat, taking her pulse. She always recorded it at the start and end of every run. Nora pulled her phone out of her sports bra and checked her messages.

"Good job, ladies," I said. "That was a great run."

"It was," Hazel said. "But I think we're reaching a plateau. We might want to start incorporating fartleks."

"I'm sorry, what?" Nora asked. "You didn't say fart-something, did you?"

"Fartleks," Hazel said. "It's a Swedish term meaning speed play. It blends continuous training with intervals— periods of fast running broken up by recovery periods at a slower pace."

Nora laughed. "I don't see how running at any pace is considered a *recovery period*. It's still *running*."

"I don't know, it sounds good to me," I said. "Hazel can map out the program and tell us what to do."

We made it to the parking lot and stood behind Hazel's car to finish cooling down and to stretch. When we were all finished, we walked across the street to Brody's Brewhouse.

It was possible we always came here to start our runs because Brody's was right across the street. Their bar was one of the best in Seattle, and the bartenders never minded us coming in all sweaty. In fact, it was Jake, one of the regular bartenders, who'd given us our nickname—the Dirty Martini Running Club.

Jake was working tonight and gave us a nod when we came in. We chose a tall table with high-backed stools in the bar section. Brody's had a nice casual vibe with wood paneling and comfortable seating. Their food was top-notch, too, especially their homemade potato chips. Not that we ordered those very often.

"Ice waters to start?" Jake asked.

"You know the drill, baby," Nora said, curling her pouty lips in a smile. She winked at him.

He winked right back, but Jake was only playing. Nora knew it, too. He was devilishly good-looking, but the big fat gold ring on his left hand was a constant reminder that Jake was not available.

Nora was never serious about men, anyway. But she did love to flirt. It was probably her favorite hobby, besides running and drinking. And she really only ran because we made her.

Jake brought us each an ice water with lemon, then asked for our orders. We all ordered salads and dirty martinis, as usual. The salads were another concession we'd all had to make to the reality of post-twenties life.

We weren't willing to give up the martinis.

Our drinks and salads came out quickly—another reason we loved this place—and we started eating.

"How was your weekend?" Hazel asked. "Do anything exciting?"

Nora shrugged. "I went out with Max again, but I think I'm over it."

"But you guys have only been seeing each other for a month or so," I said. "I thought you really liked him."

"He's not bad," she said. "But if I keep going out with

him, he's going to get attached. I do *not* want that happening."

"Would it be so terrible to have a real relationship?" I asked.

"I'm just not interested," she said. "I like my life the way it is. A man would only complicate things."

I didn't push the issue. Nora always said things like that when one of her temporary boyfriends seemed to be getting serious. Anytime she thought a guy was developing feelings for her, she'd fly out of there faster than my ex-boyfriend's buddies when the bar tab was due.

"What about you, Hazel?" I asked.

Hazel adjusted her glasses. "Well, a certain someone published another article. I don't understand why the scientific community doesn't run him out of town, metaphorically speaking. He's a menace."

In addition to being a genius, Hazel was a psychology researcher at UW. She'd been embroiled in what was becoming a vicious rivalry with another psychologist for months. It was all she could talk about.

"Did you read his article?" I asked.

"Of course. Every unsubstantiated word. He has no business calling himself a scientist."

Nora and I shared a look. Genius or not, Hazel tended to have a one-track mind. Once in a while, we used the word *obsessive*, although she denied it. But she was definitely becoming obsessed with this guy and his supposedly bad research.

"I know how you should deal with him." Nora smirked behind her drink.

Hazel pursed her lips and raised an eyebrow. "I'm not sleeping with Corban Nash."

"I actually agree with Hazel," I said. "That's a terrible idea."

"I never said anything about *sleeping*," Nora said. "I was thinking more along the lines of blowing his mind by fucking him senseless a few times."

My cheeks flushed hot and I glanced away, clearing my throat.

Nora laughed, a light tinkling sound. "Everly, you're the cutest. I love making you blush. It's so easy."

"No, it's not," I said. But she was completely right. It was very easy to make me blush.

"Come on, Hazel," Nora said. "You have too much repressed sexual energy. All that beautiful womanhood needs an outlet."

"I disagree," Hazel said. "I've decided I'm no longer dating. Or having sex. Or engaging in any sort of relational exchanges with men."

"Why would you do a silly thing like that?" Nora asked.

Hazel pushed her glasses up her nose. "To use a common colloquialism, I've been there, done that. I've dated casually. I've been in a long-term relationship. Neither worked well for me, and I have other things in my life that are taking my focus right now."

"If that's what you think is best," I said.

Nora scrunched her nose. "No men? At all?"

"I don't need a man to be satisfied with my life," Hazel said.

"Of course you don't *need* men," Nora said. "But they're very nice to have around. They can fix things, and lift things that are heavy. And when it comes to sex, I will admit there are a multitude of ways to keep yourself satisfied—but let's be honest, nothing beats the almighty cock."

I put a finger to my lips. "Nora, not so loud."

"Speaking of," Nora said, turning to me. "What am I thinking? You had your date with Gunnar on Saturday. How was it?"

I sighed. "It wasn't good."

"Oh no. Do you want to tell us about it?" Nora asked. "I mean, obviously you have to; I'm just trying to be nice."

After a string of bad first dates, I'd been ready to side with Hazel and give up on dating. Or at least take a good, long break. But Nora had offered to pick my next date. Her theory was that we could outsmart my bad dating luck by having someone else choose who I went out with.

She'd found Gunnar, a guy she deemed Everly-date-worthy, on a dating app. I'd messaged him, hoping her theory was right.

Her theory had been wrong. Very, very wrong.

"First of all, I thought we were going to lunch, but he took me to a wedding."

"On your first date?" Hazel asked.

"Yes, and he was a groomsman," I said. "He didn't tell me until we were in the car, already on the way. He had some excuse about thinking the wedding was next weekend and he didn't want to break our date. I should have gone home right then. But I thought maybe an unconventional first date was a good sign."

"That's fair logic," Hazel said.

"You'd think. It was two hours away, at a winery in the mountains. The wedding itself wasn't terrible, but as soon as we got to the reception, everyone started guzzling tequila like they were at a club in Mexico over spring break. I wound up on the dance floor among a bunch of drunk people twerking. A bridesmaid rubbed her boobs all over me like a stripper giving a standing lap dance, and then a cake fight broke out. I barely made it out of there alive. And that's still not the worst part."

"What could be worse than all that?" Hazel asked.

I shuddered, the memory of my awful Saturday burned into my brain. "Oh my god, I don't know if I want to tell you."

"Come on, sweetie," Nora said. "Circle of trust."

Nora clasped hands with Hazel on one side, then offered me her other hand while Hazel did the same.

I took both their hands, forming our sacred circle of trust. "Okay. I went outside to figure out what to do, and Gunnar came out with one of the drunk bridesmaids. She was hanging all over him, basically humping his leg."

"Oh god," Nora said.

"So then he invited me to come with them to the hotel next door for a threesome. He said he had enough for both of us, and then she made some very graphic comments about what she'd do to me, if I was willing to do the same to her."

"She said she'd eat you out if you ate her out, didn't she?" Nora asked, completely nonchalant.

I rolled my eyes. "Yes, but did you need to say it out loud?"

"I was just clarifying."

"Obviously I said no. I took a picture of him with the drunk bridesmaid and texted it to him so he'd see it when he sobered up, and told him it was why I was blocking his number."

"Good," Hazel said.

Nora let go of my hand and held hers out. "I need to see this."

I got out my phone and showed her the photo. The lighting wasn't great, but it showed a disheveled, cake-smeared Gunnar, with a woman in an ugly peach brides-maid dress groping him on the front porch of the winery.

"Wow," Nora said, holding the phone by her fingertips, as if the photo itself would soil her. "That's horrible."

"It was exactly as bad as it sounds. Even I can't sugar coat it. I was stuck at a stranger's wedding two hours from home where basically everyone was drunk. My date ditched me because I wouldn't go to a hotel for a threesome. And I didn't even get any cake because they ruined it with the food fight."

"Honey, I am so sorry." Nora put my phone down and squeezed my hand. "This is all my fault."

"No, it's not. I know he was your pick, but it was just a guy on a dating app. It's not like you could have known."

"How did you get home?" Hazel asked.

"Oh, well, that's the good part, actually. I met the family that owns the winery. They're the sweetest people. They offered me a guest cottage for the night and I ended up having dinner with them. I would have called one of you to come get me, but they insisted on driving me home yesterday. And before you freak out because I'd just met them, they're all married adults and most of them have kids. I drove back yesterday with two of the couples. Honestly, they were all so great, it was hard to say goodbye."

"I'm glad for that, at least," Hazel said.

"Can I have that photo?" Nora asked.

"Why?"

"Because I want to plaster it all over social media."

I snatched my phone off the table. "No."

"Come on, Everly. I hate him for what he did to you, and it's my fault because I chose him. I still don't know how my instincts were so off."

"I don't think it's you, I think it's me," I said. "We tried to fool my bad luck and it didn't work. I'm cursed."

"There's really no such thing as luck," Hazel said. "Or curses."

"Disagree," Nora said. She tossed back the rest of her drink and waved her empty glass at Jake for another, tapping mine with her other hand. "Everly does have terrible luck with men."

"Luck has no basis in reality," Hazel said. "You can't predict or prove its existence."

"Exhibit A, Gunnar," Nora said. "I don't even need to explain how he proves my point."

"I agree, that was bad," Hazel said.

"Exhibit B, the guy who interviewed her, including questions about her medical history to determine whether she could deliver healthy babies. And his mom showed up to review his notes."

I winced. "Jerry. Yeah, that was pretty bad."

"Exhibit C, the gay guy who'd been through a recent break-up and was trying to get out of a rut by taking a woman on a date."

"To be fair, that was his friend's idea," I said. "And despite not being compatible, we had a nice time."

"I don't think additional evidence is needed," Nora said. "Although I could go on and on. Do you remember Nick from a few years ago?"

I groaned.

"She dated him for a few months until she found out he was dealing stolen prescription narcotics."

Jake brought a fresh round of drinks and I took a long swallow of mine. "That police raid was so stressful."

"See? Bad luck," Nora said. "Terrible, actually. It's not like you could have predicted any of it. We all have things we watch out for in men, but no one has their radar tuned to the kinds of men you seem to attract."

"There's something wrong with me," I said. "Do I have a sign on my back that says *desperate*?"

"Of course not," Nora said. "That's what I mean about bad luck. It's not your fault."

"I guess not," I said. "But look at me. I'm thirty years old and still single. I might as well get a cat."

"I have a cat," Hazel said. "What's wrong with cats?"

"Nothing; cats are fine. I just mean I'm pretty sure I'll be single forever. I might as well get used to it."

"Single has a lot of advantages," Nora said. "But I know you want to find the right guy. He's out there, sweetie. And one of these days, he's going to look into your big, blue eyes and see that sunshine smile and fall desperately in love with you. In fact, he'll wonder how he ever lived without you. And then you'll make me wear an ugly dress at your wedding and I'll fuck one of the hot single groomsmen to make up for it."

"I don't see the connection between someone falling in love with Everly and an ugly dress," Hazel said. "Bridesmaid dresses aren't all unattractive. Everly has good taste. She could choose something—"

"Kidding, Hazel," Nora said with a smile. "I was just making a joke."

Hazel's confused expression softened. "Oh, I see. In that case, I also hope you find the right man and it results in bridesmaid dresses and... whatever else."

"Thanks," I said. "But I think I need to join you on your dating hiatus. Maybe some time away from men will break my curse."

"It pains me to agree with you," Nora said. "But maybe

you're right. Have you considered whether you're gay? Should we try a woman?"

"I asked my sister about that once." My sister, Annie, was happily married to a woman, Miranda. "She described how she feels and I didn't identify with any of it. I'm not gay. I like men. I just keep dating terrible ones."

Nora squeezed my hand again. "Honestly, Everly, I'm baffled. You're literally the sweetest person I know. You're smart, beautiful, and successful. I'm telling you, he's out there. One of these days, you're going to meet a man who wants to spend the rest of his life basking in your sunshine."

I smiled and squeezed back. "Thanks."

"I agree with Nora," Hazel said.

"I love you guys."

"I'd like to propose a toast." Nora lifted her glass. Hazel and I did the same. "To Everly. May this time of singlehood be as long or as brief as she wishes. And may the next man in her life be the one to sweep her off her feet, and may he also have a big dick."

"I'll drink to that." I lifted my glass to clink against theirs, and we all took a sip.

*Sweep her off her feet.* I didn't see that happening anytime soon. But I was nothing if not a perpetual optimist, and a girl could still dream.

## 3

## SHEPHERD

*M*y assistant came into my office. She didn't knock, but she was the one person who could get away with it. Probably because she never interrupted me when I was on a phone call or in a private meeting. She took my coat off the hook and draped it over her arm.

"You should get going or you'll miss your reservation," she said.

I glanced at the time. I did need to leave. Lateness was something I could not abide. I didn't allow it in myself any more than I allowed it in others. But I'd been distracted, caught up reading a proposal.

I closed my laptop and put it in my briefcase, then stood, my mind already on the unpleasant dinner ahead of me. This had the potential to go very badly. Breaking things off with Svetlana in public was a risk. I hadn't been seeing her for very long, but she had a flair for drama. I hoped I'd made the right call in taking her to a restaurant.

"I confirmed your reservation at Tulio," she said,

handing me my coat. "Do you want me to send you the menu?"

"No." I slipped on my coat and pocketed my phone. I hadn't finished reviewing the proposal. Tomorrow was going to be busy with meetings, so I'd have to go over it tonight. The sooner I finished this dinner, the better. Maybe I wouldn't stay to eat. Get in, get out. Move on.

I fixed the collar of my coat and took my briefcase off the desk.

"Goodnight, Mr. Calloway," she said as I walked out the door, heading for the parking garage.

This Svetlana thing had me distracted. I probably could have blown her off without seeing her in person again, but she struck me as the sort of woman who'd try to make trouble. If there was anything worse than a shitty breakup, it was a shitty breakup that made it into the press. She knew how private I was—how closely I guarded my personal life. If I pissed her off now, I was certain she'd make it as public as she possibly could. My best bet was to mollify her with money.

Not a direct bribe. I wouldn't insult her by treating her like a prostitute. But I knew the sort of currency that had the potential to satisfy a woman like Svetlana. After all, that was why she'd been dating me in the first place.

I should have seen it in the beginning, but the woman's acting ability deserved an Oscar. She'd approached me at a fundraiser, and her smile had caught me. To look at her, you'd think it would have been her body—because honestly, her body was insane—but it had been her smile. She'd smiled at me, wide and bright, and I'd known I was taking her home with me.

But at thirty-six, I was apparently still shit at judging authenticity, because her smile was as fake as her hair color.

Beneath that incredibly hot exterior, Svetlana was a nightmare. She was territorial, demanding, and whiny. She wanted a billionaire sugar daddy—a role I had no interest in playing—which was clearly why she'd set her sights on me.

Just like Brielle. And Sasha. And Marissa before her.

Clearly, I had a problem.

I was beginning to think I might be cursed. I wasn't stupid. I knew it was normal for a man like me to attract a certain type of woman. In my younger days, I wouldn't have dreamed I'd ever tire of the string of gorgeous women beating down my door. But they were all the same. A beautiful face and a hot body only went so far. It wasn't that I was looking for something serious. I barely had room in my life for a casual relationship, let alone anything long-term. But spending time with a woman who wasn't a viper disguised as a kitten would be a nice change.

My black Mercedes was parked near the elevator. I got in with a sense of resignation. I'd let her down easy, which would hopefully minimize the fallout. And if she did come after me, I'd handle it. As with any business deal, there were always work-arounds. Ways to cope with challenges and unforeseen problems.

Tulio was an upscale Italian restaurant. Small. Nice atmosphere. Good food. Svetlana wasn't here yet, so I waited near the front.

I didn't need to look up from my phone to know she'd arrived a few minutes later. The stir she caused wherever she went heralded her entrance.

Svetlana was beautiful in every sense of the word—physically, at least—and people noticed her. She'd been blessed with the best of nearly every feature, and had bought the rest. Perfect facial symmetry. Large eyes. Sleek nose. Full lips. Stunning curves. Just enough of her

Bulgarian accent remained so she sounded pleasantly exotic.

She smiled at me, but I didn't return it. Just nodded to the hostess that we were ready to be seated. We followed her to a table near the back. Svetlana paused while I pulled out her chair, but I didn't kiss or touch her.

Her lower lip protruded as she took her seat. "You're especially cold tonight."

She hadn't asked me a question, so I didn't give her an answer. Just took off my coat and sat across from her.

"I have no idea what to order here," she said, looking at the menu. "Everything has carbs."

"Hmm," I said, ignoring her thinly veiled complaint about my restaurant choice.

The waitress came back and asked if we'd like something to drink.

"Should we get a bottle of wine?" she asked.

"Nothing for me."

She scowled and plucked the drink menu off the table. "Pomegranate martini, then."

"I'll be back with your drink," the waitress said. "Then I can take your order."

I decided I wasn't ordering dinner. I had too much work to do.

"Svetlana, I've booked a ten-day vacation for two at an all-inclusive resort in Hawaii." I reached into my jacket and pulled out an envelope with the information she would need. "Everything will be taken care of. Flights. Meals. Drinks. Even entertainment."

Her eyes widened. "Oh, Shepherd, are you serious?"

"Yes, but I won't be joining you." I put the envelope in front of her. "You're welcome to take anyone you'd like. Get in touch with my assistant to finalize the details. I've enjoyed your company the last couple of months, but we won't be seeing each other anymore."

Her mouth dropped open and she stared at me. "You're leaving me?"

*Leaving me.* It wasn't the fact that English was her second language that made her choose that phrase. It made it sound as if I were divorcing her, not ending a casual fling.

"This has run its course," I said.

"And what is that?" she asked, gesturing to the envelope. "You never take me anywhere, and now you're getting rid of me by sending me on vacation by myself?"

"I said you can take whomever you like."

"I can't be bought, Shepherd."

I raised an eyebrow. That was a fucking lie if I'd ever heard one. "Indeed. I thought it might be a pleasant distraction." I plucked the envelope off the table. "But if you think I've insulted you, apparently I judged wrong. My apologies."

Knowing she'd ask for it back, I made a show of tucking it back into my pocket.

"Well..." She paused and rolled her eyes. "I might as well use it, if it's already booked."

I set the envelope in front of her just as the waitress came back with her martini. I looked at the waitress. "Her dinner is on me. She can order whatever she'd like."

"Of course, Mr. Calloway," the waitress said.

I stood and grabbed my coat. "Good night."

Without waiting for a reply from either Svetlana or the waitress, I turned and left.

That had gone much better than expected. In a few days, Svetlana would be off to Hawaii. When she returned, I had no doubt she'd find someone new. A woman like that wouldn't be alone for long.

I would be, however. Having a woman in my life had never been anything but a complication. A distraction.

A disappointment.

Pushing aside the thoughts of Svetlana—and my dissatisfaction with dating in general—I went to my car. I had work to do tonight.

## 4

## EVERLY

*T*he little bistro my sister and sister-in-law had chosen for dinner was adorable. It was colorful, with funky decor and a great menu. I found them already at a table, leaning in close together and laughing about something.

Annie was three years younger than me, but always seemed to have her life together in ways I didn't. She was very goal-oriented and driven. She'd graduated both high school and college early. Passed her CPA exam with flying colors. She was brilliant, successful, beautiful. Married to Miranda, the coolest woman ever. They were remodeling their second house together, because both of them were freaking overachievers.

It wasn't that I was jealous. Jealousy was so negative. But I did tend to feel a bit inferior next to my baby sister. I still lived in an apartment I rented. My job was great, but *executive assistant* didn't sound nearly as impressive as *CPA*. Not even if I was an assistant to one of the most prominent businessmen in Seattle.

"Hey, sis." Annie stood and hugged me. She looked a lot

like me, except her hair was a little darker and cut in a sleek bob. As usual, she looked stylish in a blouse and slacks.

Miranda stood for a hug. She wore glasses and never fewer than four colors at a time. She was breezy and artistic, and it showed in her wavy hair and eclectic style. Although she and my sister seemed so different, they were great together.

"Hey, you two," I said as we all took our seats. "How's everything?"

"Good," Annie said. "How about you? I feel like it's been ages since we've seen you."

"Yeah, I guess so," I said. "I'm good. Work is busy, of course."

"Isn't it always?" Annie asked. "What about your personal life? Anyone special you need to tell us about?"

I shook my head. Annie was great, but she'd never been the person I confided in. I didn't really want to tell her about my latest adventures in dating. "No, I'm not seeing anyone."

"Why not?" she asked. "Honestly, Everly, I can't believe you're still single."

Miranda nudged her. "Annie."

"I'm sorry. I didn't mean it like that. I just know how great you are, that's all."

"Thanks. And it's okay. I'm taking a break from dating for a while."

"That's wonderful," Miranda said. "I think it's smart to focus on you. I did that a few years ago and it was the best decision I ever made."

"You hardly took a dating break," Annie said. "You met me a few weeks in, didn't you?"

"Exactly," Miranda said. "I'm a firm believer that the right person comes into your life only when you stop looking for them."

"Hmm," Annie said. "She might have a point."

"Yeah, maybe," I said. "I'm in a good place with everything. Work is fine, and being single isn't so bad."

"Of course not," Annie said.

"So what about you guys?" I asked. "What's new?"

"Well," Annie said, glancing at Miranda, "we actually have news."

"Yeah?" I asked. "Oh god, please don't tell me you're moving out of state or something."

"No, we're not moving," Annie said. "Actually, we're going to try for a baby."

"Aw," I said, squashing the nasty little flare of envy that tried to take root in my tummy. So what if I was older than her and single? And so what if Annie was happily married, and about to make our mother's dreams come true by giving her a grandchild? That didn't matter, and I wasn't going to rain on Annie's parade. "That's amazing. I'm so happy for you both."

"Thanks," Annie said. "We've always known we want kids, and the timing just feels right."

Miranda took her hand and squeezed it. "Exactly. It's a big decision, but we're ready."

"You two will be the best parents," I said. "How are you going to go about it? Will you adopt?"

"Well, we will if we decide we want more than one," Miranda said. "But Annie really wants to experience pregnancy."

Annie nodded. "I do. I know it's probably going to give me stretch marks and ruin my boobs, but I don't care. I want to do it anyway."

"It's not going to ruin your boobs," Miranda said. "And I'm going to love your body even if you get stretch marks."

Annie beamed at her.

"I think this is great," I said.

"You do?" Annie asked.

"Yeah. Why, did you think I wouldn't be happy for you?"

"No, we knew you'd be happy," Annie said. "Aren't you always?"

I shrugged. "Not literally always. But of course I'm happy about this. I get to be an auntie. What's not to love?"

Annie took a deep breath and exchanged another look with Miranda. "We were really hoping you'd be supportive."

I narrowed my eyes and tilted my head. "Yeah, of course I am."

"Good," Annie said, "because we need your help."

"I'm not sure how I can help in this situation. I have ovaries and a uterus, but you have two sets of those between you. I think you need someone with the other parts to make this baby thing happen."

"That's what we need your help with," Annie said. "We'd like to use donor sperm."

"Okay," I said, still not sure what she was getting at. "But what do you need my help with? Don't you go to a sperm bank or something for that?"

"Well, we could," Annie said. "But we have a donor in mind, so this would need to be a private exchange. We've spoken to a lawyer and we have a contract all drawn up and ready to go."

"Who do you have in mind?" I asked. "And what does it have to do with me?"

Annie took another breath. "Shepherd Calloway."

"What?" I asked, not even trying to hide my shock. "What the hell are you talking about?"

"Everly, he's perfect," Annie said. "He has all the traits we're looking for. Height, build, coloring, intelligence. And I know that makes it seem like we're trying to custom-build a baby, but when you're working with donor sperm, that's how it works."

"Sure, he has all the traits you want... except a *soul*," I said. "You realize you'd run the risk of giving birth to a robot, right? I'm not convinced he isn't a cyborg."

"Come on, you've worked for him for years," Annie said. "He can't be that bad."

"The man has no feelings," I said. "If you'd like to have a baby with the emotional range of a rock, then yeah, he'd be a great choice."

"We've done our research," Miranda said. "We made a very thorough list of traits we want to target, and traits we want to avoid. Shepherd Calloway fits in every way."

Annie looked at me with her eyebrows raised, her eyes big and round. She scrunched up her shoulders and gave me a tentative smile. Oh my god, she wanted—

"No," I said.

"Everly," Annie said. "We haven't asked you anything yet."

"I know what you're about to say. And the answer is no. I'm not asking my boss to donate his sperm to you. No freaking way."

"Come on, Evie," Annie said. *Damn her for invoking my childhood nickname.* "It's impossible to contact the man if you're not in his inner circle. He's built the modern equivalent of a medieval fortress around his life. And we realize he has a certain... disposition. That's why we need you to butter him up for us."

"Exactly," Miranda said. "You can start planting the seeds—pun intended—and slowly work your way up to asking him."

"And how do you expect me to do that?" I asked. "You guys have the wrong idea about my job if you think I can sit down and have a conversation with him. He doesn't *talk* to me."

"You're his assistant," Annie said. "Of course he talks to you."

"No, he talks *at* me," I said. "There's a difference."

"You're one of the only people in the entire world who has access to him," Annie said. "His whole life is so closely guarded, it was hard to even get information about him. But you see him every single day. You're in his office, alone with him."

I knew she was right, and there was that thing I liked— being the one who had access to him. I shouldn't have let that tempt me, but it was irresistible. "Yeah."

"Just see what you can do," Annie said. "We don't expect a miracle. He might not be interested in this sort of arrangement, and that's fine. We wouldn't want to put any pressure on him. We just want a chance. And you, my sweet big sister, are that chance. Don't you see? You're the key. You're the only way this works."

"Oh my god, you're laying it on thick," I said.

"Is it working?"

I groaned, my shoulders slumping. "I don't know. Maybe a tiny bit. I'll think about it. But I'm not making any promises."

Annie grabbed my hands. "Thank you. Really, thank you so much. This means the world to us."

"Don't get too excited," I said. "I didn't say I'd do it. I said I'd *think* about it."

"That's all we're asking," Annie said. "Just consider it."

I picked up the menu and looked at the choices, feeling grumpy. Ask Mr. Calloway to be a sperm donor? How did one even start a conversation like that? Especially with someone you didn't have real conversations with.

*Good morning, Mr. Calloway. You have a nine o'clock meeting with your lawyer, and by the way, would you consider donating sperm to my sister so she and her wife can have a baby with the right genetic traits?*

Kill me. There was no way.

But my sister looked so happy. I loved my sister, and I loved making people happy. Was there a way to do this that wouldn't be totally mortifying? I had no idea, but maybe I could think of something. Although I wondered if my time would be better spent searching for an alternative donor who had the genetic traits they were looking for. Because the thought of asking my boss to donate his baby batter made me want to crawl under the table and die.

## 5

SHEPHERD

Straightening the sleeves of my tux, I walked over to the bar at the Four Seasons Hotel. Soft music played in the background and a handful of other people conversed nearby. Tonight's event was in the ballroom, but I wasn't ready to make an appearance yet. I was here alone—dateless for once—and I wanted to take my time.

Truth be told, I didn't want to be here at all. I wasn't a fan of these events. Giving to charity was fine, but I could do that by having my assistant send a check. These things were for networking. Rubbing elbows. Showing off.

I didn't need to show off. But I was here anyway. The Seattle Philanthropic Society was presenting my father with an award, and he'd hounded me into being here to see it. Somehow my brother, Ethan, had managed to get out of attending, which meant I really couldn't leave.

I took a seat at the bar and caught the bartender's eye. Ordered a Manhattan.

Being here alone was pleasant. No fussy date to attend to. I could arrive late—which I had—and leave early—

which I planned to. And I didn't have to listen to my date's endless stream of chatter.

I was going to stretch out this period of singlehood. No women for a good, long while. Maybe I'd take that vacation my brother was always bugging me about. Go alone, to a city where no one knew me. Spend my time any way I wanted, my only obligations to myself. It was tempting enough that I almost had myself convinced I'd do it.

But I probably wouldn't. Time away from the office wasn't relaxing for me. There were always too many things happening, and I didn't trust anyone else to run my company.

I didn't trust many people, to be honest. Not with anything.

Trusting others got you into trouble. People always had ulterior motives. My money and influence made me a target. It was tough, sometimes, feeling like I had to go it alone. But I didn't see any alternatives.

My mother had taught me that. Hammered the lesson into my head more times than I could count. Then she'd demonstrated it by having an affair and leaving my dad. He'd trusted her, and look where it had gotten him. My mother was wealthy in her own right, but she'd still taken my father for as much as she could, even though it had been *her* infidelity that had ended their marriage. She was a lawyer, through and through. My dad's trust in her had almost been his downfall.

But despite trusting too easily, my dad was a survivor— smart as hell, and persistent. He'd bounced back just fine.

"Well, hello."

That sultry voice with its slight accent made my back clench. What was Svetlana doing here? Hadn't I sent her on vacation somewhere?

"What are you doing here?" I asked.

"Getting a drink." She leaned against the bar, looking like she ought to have a cigarette perched between her fingers, waiting for me to offer her a light, like some starlet from the forties. "Maui was lovely. It's too bad you didn't join me."

I supposed it had been several weeks since I'd last seen her. "I'm glad you enjoyed your trip."

"It was very generous of you. I never did get to thank you properly."

"No thanks necessary. That was the point."

The bartender came over and she ordered a cosmopolitan. She glanced at me, but I didn't offer to pay.

Why was she here? She'd left me two messages shortly after I broke things off with her, but I hadn't returned her calls. It seemed she'd been happy to spend my money in Hawaii. She was certainly tan.

I'd made it clear we were over. What did she want?

"All alone tonight?" she asked.

"No, my date is running late."

Obviously I didn't have a date. But I wanted her to think I did. Solidify the fact that our brief encounter was finished. I'd moved on.

The bartender brought her cocktail. She held it with her fingertips. "I see. Well, have a nice evening, Shepherd."

"You too."

She walked away and I took another sip of my drink. Svetlana was probably here to case the bar—either looking to 'accidentally' run into me, or simply to meet some other rich asshole who'd fall for her act. This was the place for it, especially tonight.

Finishing my drink, I put her out of my mind.

The ballroom was busy, a low hum of voices hanging in

the air. Men in tuxes and women in evening gowns wandered around or congregated in small groups. Others sat at tables set with white linens. Waiters walked through the cavernous room with trays of hors d'oeuvres and glasses of champagne.

I spotted my father a short distance away. He was dressed in a black tux with a silver tie, his graying hair neatly cut. My father looked like a shark, but he had all the bite of a puppy.

"There he is," Dad said, walking toward me with his arms outstretched.

I endured his hug, patting him on the back. "Hi, Dad."

"It's a shame your brother couldn't be here," he said. "But thanks for coming."

"No problem. Do you have a speech planned?"

He waved his hand, like it didn't matter. "Oh, I'll think of something suitable to say. I'd written one but... well, I have a different perspective on things lately."

"You look good. Tan. Have you been on vacation?"

"I was." His face fell, and for a moment, he looked serious. He cleared his throat, and then his smile was back. "I needed to get away and clear my head. But we can talk about that later. Right now, I have someone I'd like you to meet."

The sparkle in his eye said it all. Dad had a new girlfriend. Or fling. It was hard to say. Unfortunately, he wasn't any better than I was at choosing the right woman—my mother being a prime example. Since their divorce when I was a teenager, he'd been with a number of different women. They'd ranged in age and ethnicity— I had to give it to him; at least he'd been trying different things.

I knew exactly what his problem was. He was too goddamn

nice. Wealthy businessmen had a reputation for being cold and unfeeling. Hell, the term *businesslike* had been coined for a reason. But my dad was a fucking teddy bear. He was a brilliant businessman, but he always saw the best in people—especially beautiful women. It made him an easy target.

"That's great, Dad."

"What about you?" he asked. "Where's your date? I was hoping I'd get to meet this one."

I opened my mouth to tell him that I hadn't brought a date, but nothing came out. My throat felt like there was a hand wrapped around my windpipe, making speech impossible.

Svetlana approached, dressed in a long gold gown with a slit that went almost as high as her fucking belly button. I hadn't even noticed her dress when I'd seen her in the bar, but she sauntered toward us, using every inch of her attire to its best advantage. Her thick hair was down in waves around her bare shoulders, and her sparkling gold heels made her almost as tall as me.

But it wasn't her dress, the amount of thigh showing, nor the look of evil cunning in her eyes that rendered me speechless. It was the way my dad slipped an arm around her waist and drew her against him that cut off my air supply.

"Shepherd, this is Svetlana Genov," he said, his dimples puckering with his wide smile.

Oh my god, she had to be fucking kidding me.

Svetlana smiled, tilting her head slightly, like she was being shy, and held out her hand. "So nice to meet you, Shepherd. Your father has told me so much about you, it feels like I know you already."

Fuck. Dad had no idea I'd been dating her. It's not like

I'd introduced her to my family. I'd probably never even mentioned her name.

How had she met him? And was she going to pretend we didn't know each other? Why the fuck did she think I'd go along with that?

But one look at my dad's face, and I knew I couldn't out her. Not here, in front of an audience. When it was supposed to be his night. That soft heart my dad carried in his chest was going to be crushed. I needed to get through the evening, then see my dad privately.

I took Svetlana's hand for as brief a handshake as I could manage. "How did you two meet?"

"Hawaii," he said. "We were staying at the same resort. She offered to buy me a drink, and then we had a good laugh because we were at an all-inclusive."

"Really?" I asked. *Motherfucker.* "Dad, I had no idea you'd gone to Hawaii recently."

"Like I said, I needed some time to figure things out." He pulled Svetlana tighter against him. "Obviously it was time well spent."

Svetlana batted her eyelashes and nuzzled against his arm.

I swallowed back the taste of vomit. "That's great, Dad."

"So tell me, son, where's your date? I'd love to meet her."

Svetlana's lips parted over her white teeth in a wicked grin. "Yes, Shepherd, where is she? I'd love to meet her as well."

I narrowed my eyes. Fuck her. She wanted to play this game? She had no idea who she was dealing with. I was going to bury her.

"She's just running a little late." I pulled out my phone. "In fact, I should give her a call to see if she's on her way."

"Good," Dad said. "Come find us when she gets here."

"I will." I gave Svetlana a cold smile before turning to walk away.

I kept my pace unhurried until I was out of their line of sight. Then I rushed my ass into a stairwell and started flicking through my contacts. Now I needed a goddamn date. But who could I get down here on a moment's notice?

I scrolled through the names, ignoring my business contacts—which were most of them. I wasn't exactly on friendly terms with any of my exes. The women I dated typically hated me when our brief relationships were over. Somehow they always blamed me for not being what they were looking for—a wealthy man who'd spoil them—and were mortally offended when I had the audacity to dump them.

I scrolled back up, in reverse alphabetical order. I was not letting Svetlana win this round. If I had to call a fucking escort service, I was going to have a beautiful woman on my arm in the next half hour.

A name stared at me from my screen. I'd already scrolled by it twice, not even considering her as an option. But there it was. Everly Dalton, my personal assistant.

She was hands down the best assistant I'd ever had. The fact that she'd worked for me for so long was proof of that. My assistants always quit. Male or female, they always wanted a bunch of goddamn hand-holding and pats on the head. I didn't need a pet who was constantly seeking my approval. I needed an assistant who could do the job I'd hired them to do.

That was exactly what Everly did.

At first, I'd thought she'd be just like the others. She didn't come across as a woman with a solid backbone. She was too cute—smiled too much. But she was tough as nails. Smart, efficient, productive. She was great at her job and I paid her well for it. Very well, in fact. In three years, I'd raised her salary four times.

But standing in as my date? I scowled at my phone. Everly wasn't that sort of girl. She was nice to look at, certainly. I didn't choose my assistants based on their attractiveness, but if I did, Everly would've passed with flying colors. Pretty face, long blond hair. I could almost picture her in an evening gown, but that was a stretch. She was not the sort of woman I dated—not anything like them. Could she pull it off and fool my dad?

Plus, Svetlana had met her. She'd know I was lying.

Or would she? When Svetlana had come to my office, she'd eyed Everly with open jealousy. As if she'd been sure I was fucking my pretty assistant on the side. I wasn't—I never dipped my pen in company ink. But Everly here as my date would dig at Svetlana in a way no other woman could.

That clinched it. I tapped Everly's number and hit call.

"Um, hello?" she said. "Mr. Calloway?"

"I need you at the Four Seasons Ballroom," I said.

"Wait, what?"

"Four Seasons."

"I know where you are, I just don't understand why you need me to come down there. It's nine o'clock at night. What's wrong?"

I glanced at my watch. I needed her here, now. "Text me your address and I'll send a car to pick you up."

"Wait, Mr. Calloway, I don't understand."

"Just get down here," I said. "I'll pay you for your time."

"Well, okay, but I'm confused."

I let out a frustrated breath. She never wasted my time like this. "Everly, listen to me. Address. Car. Four Seasons."

"I... you just... um... okay?"

"And dress sexy. Text me when you get here."

I hung up so I could text my driver, letting him know he needed to go pick her up, and I'd forward the address as soon as I had it. A few seconds later, Everly's text with her home address came through.

Good girl.

I pocketed my phone. Judging by her address, she lived about fifteen minutes away. That meant half an hour before she'd arrive. I'd have to avoid my dad and Svetlana while I waited, but that shouldn't be an issue. This place was crawling with people who wanted a piece of me. I usually kept to myself, so all it would take would be to show a bit of interest in a conversation, and I'd have no shortage of people to keep me occupied and unavailable.

Now, I just had to wait for Everly.

# 6

## EVERLY

*I* stared down at my phone, wondering what had just happened. Had my boss just told me to meet him at the Four Seasons? At nine on a Friday night?

That wasn't even the weirdest part. He'd called me *Everly*.

I had no idea what was going on. I'd never gone to an event with him before. He always either took a date or went alone. What was going on that he needed me down there? And dress *sexy*? What the hell?

The Seattle Philanthropic Society Gala was black-tie. The men would be in tuxes, the women in formal evening gowns. I didn't know if I had a dress that would get me in the door, let alone one that was *sexy*. This was truly an emergency. So I did the only thing I could. I called Nora.

"Hey, love," she said.

"Oh, thank god you answered. Are you busy? I have an emergency, and literally no time."

"Talk to me."

"My boss needs me to come to a black-tie event. His car is on the way to pick me up. And he said *dress sexy*."

"I'll be right down."

I breathed out a sigh of relief, then ducked into the bathroom to glance in the mirror at my flat hair and makeup-free face. I wasn't giving her much to work with. But if anyone could pull this off, it was Nora.

I barely had time to contemplate why Mr. Calloway had put me in this position before Nora banged on my door. I answered and she burst in, a bag slung over her shoulder and a heap of clothes in her arms. She went straight to my bedroom and dumped everything on the bed.

"Thank you so much for coming over," I said. "I'm so lost right now. Were you busy?"

"Max was over, but I told him I had to go."

"Oh god, I'm sorry."

She waved a hand. "Don't be, it's fine. How much time do you have?"

"I don't know, ten or fifteen minutes?"

She rolled her eyes. "Fucking hell. Okay, let's do this. Strip."

I took off my t-shirt and leggings while she tore through my underwear drawer, grumbling things like *practical cotton* and *doesn't have anything decent*. She chose a strapless bra and black panties. I slipped into them while she started holding up dresses.

"No," she said, tossing one aside. "No. Also no. No." She threw another down and picked up a long red gown. It shimmered in the light. "Oh, this one. This might be it."

"Red? I don't know."

"Are you kidding me? You can rock this. Put it on."

She helped me into the dress and zipped it up the back. I stood in front of my full-length mirror and cringed. It was strapless and so form-fitting I felt naked. The bottom of the skirt widened just enough for a hint of a mermaid silhouette, and the slit up the leg was the only way I'd be able to walk in this thing.

I smoothed it down, running my hands from my waist to my hips.

"Don't utter a single word." She sounded a little breathless. "I'm never wearing it again because this is magnificent on you. But the panties have to go."

"Excuse me?"

"You'll have to go commando. You don't want a line."

"But—"

"Nope, no time." She hiked the dress up and yanked my panties down before I could get out another word.

I fixed the dress, smoothing it down over my backside, but I felt even more naked than before. She threw a towel around my shoulders, pushed me onto the edge of the bed, and attacked my face with makeup.

Ten minutes later, I stood staring at a stranger in the mirror. The dress was... well, it was incredible. The red was deep and rich, and the fabric had something that sparkled. Nothing bold, like sequins. It was subtle, shimmering whenever I moved. She'd done my makeup flawlessly, especially for how fast she'd worked. It looked like me, just *formal me*. Soft eyes and bright red lips to match the dress. My hair was up—she'd complained that she needed more time to do it properly—but with the strapless dress, it worked.

"A manicure would have made the whole thing really pop, but your nails look decent at least," she said. "Do you have shoes?"

My phone buzzed with a text from Mr. Calloway's driver, saying he was outside. "Yeah, I think so. Can I wear black? I don't have red ones that match."

"Black is fine."

I dug out a pair of black heels and stepped into them.

"Those are adorable," Nora said.

I took a deep breath and glanced in the mirror one last time. "Okay, I have to go. Do you think I'll fit in with everyone there?"

"No," she said, shaking her head with a smile. "You're not going to fit in. You're going to blow everyone away. You're a knockout."

A rush of nerves made my stomach feel queasy. "This is crazy."

She tucked my phone and the red lipstick into a little black clutch and handed it to me. "Knock 'em dead, tiger."

"You're the best." I gave her a quick hug before rushing for the front door. "Love you!"

"Love you, too," she called as I hurried out to meet the driver.

Ten minutes later, the car pulled up to the curb in front of the Four Seasons Hotel. I sent Mr. Calloway a text to say I was here. Before I could open the door myself, his driver had done it for me. I took a deep breath, eased my leg out—this dress was difficult to maneuver in—and stood.

Mr. Calloway was already waiting outside, dressed in the black tux I'd made sure had been cleaned and pressed for him. He looked up from his phone, and for the first time in the three years I'd worked for him, he looked right at me.

His eyes were blue, contrasting with his dark features. His hair was neatly slicked back, as usual, and his stubble trimmed to perfection. It ought to be. I made all his grooming appointments, timing them precisely so he always looked perfect.

He stared at me, but I hardly blamed him. *I'd* never seen me looking like this, so he certainly hadn't. I decided that instead of letting the weight of intimidation crush me, I'd do what I always did when it came to Shepherd Calloway: figure out what he needed and get it done.

Squaring my shoulders, I walked across the sidewalk toward him.

"Well?"

He blinked at me, his mouth slightly open. "What?"

"What am I doing here? You made it sound like an emergency. Is the dress okay? I borrowed it from a friend."

His eyes swept up and down, and if I'd thought I felt naked when I first tried on the dress, that feeling had nothing on this moment. My cheeks warmed and I was positive he could tell I wasn't wearing panties. Oh god, this was the worst thing that had ever happened to me.

Actually, that wasn't true at all. After some of the horrible dates I'd had, earning the prize for *worst thing ever* would take something much more extreme than going commando in front of my boss. That was actually comforting. Silver lining.

"The dress?" he asked.

What the hell was wrong with him? I'd never seen him act like this before.

"Yes, the dress. Mr. Calloway, are you drunk?"

"What? No." His brow furrowed, and he seemed to come back to himself. He straightened his cuffs. "The dress is fine. And it's Shepherd tonight."

He took me gently by the elbow and led me inside. We crossed the opulent lobby side-by-side, passing people in tuxes and evening gowns.

"Okay, Shepherd," I said, trying on the name. I'd never called him that before. "What am I doing here?"

He took me through a set of large double doors into the ballroom. "You're my girlfriend tonight."

I stopped dead in my tracks. "I'm sorry, what did you just say?"

His jaw hitched. Under different circumstances, that would have made me nervous. I knew that look all too well. No one questioned Shepherd Calloway. But tonight, I wasn't having it. Not when he'd called me on a Friday night, demanded I meet him at an event with no notice, and told me to *dress sexy*. He owed me an explanation.

I crossed my arms and looked him in the eye.

His nostrils flared and he pulled me to the side. "Look, I realize this is out of the ordinary. I don't have time to explain everything right now. I'm going to introduce you as my girlfriend."

"Am I also your assistant? Or am I supposed to pretend to be someone else?"

Something in his expression changed—he softened, looking me in the eyes as we spoke. "No, you're you. My assistant."

"So you're pretending to date your assistant?" This didn't make one bit of sense.

"Can you go along with this or not?"

A waiter walked by with a tray of champagne flutes. I plucked one as he passed and downed it in a few swallows.

"Jesus," Shepherd said.

I put the empty glass on a small table. "Okay, I'll do this. But you owe me."

"Fine," he said.

"Like, you owe me big."

"What do you want?"

"I don't know yet." My sister's request ran through my head, but there was no way I was bringing that up right now. "But I'll let you know."

"Deal." He offered his hand.

I placed my hand in his and he held it, his grip firm. I'd never made this much eye contact with him, but the quick infusion of champagne was helping.

He let go of my hand and placed his on the small of my back. I swallowed hard, thinking about my lack of a panty line. Trying not to think about how nice Shepherd looked in that tux.

But that was hard. He looked really, really good. It wasn't like I'd never realized how attractive my boss was. Obviously, I knew. No woman could look at Shepherd Calloway and not be a little awed at that gorgeous specimen of a man. I wasn't immune to that. But over the years I'd spent working for him, I'd tuned it out. Dwelling on how stupidly attractive he was would only distract me from doing my job, and developing a crush on my boss was a terrible idea. Even if office dating wasn't bad news in and of itself, I knew his type, and it certainly wasn't me.

So I ignored the way he steered me through the crowd. The warmth of his hand on my back. The way he walked with such confidence. It wasn't swagger. Shepherd Calloway didn't need swagger. He exuded masculinity and power. His piercing eyes, dark brow, perfect hair. His posture. His voice. It all said everything you needed to know about him. He was in charge, and he knew it.

*Ignore, ignore, ignore.*

He paused to talk to someone, so I grabbed another glass of champagne from a passing waiter. I didn't inhale this one, just held it between my fingertips and took a few sips. I noticed I was leaving red lipstick marks and wondered how soon I'd need to reapply.

The man nodded to Shepherd and moved on.

I leaned closer to him. "How's my lipstick?"

"What?"

"Does my lipstick need fixing? I got some on the glass."

His eyes went to my mouth and he licked his lips while I tried not to fidget. "Your lipstick looks fine."

I pressed my lips, rubbing them together.

"But how much are you drinking?" he asked.

"Are you serious? This is two. And if you think you can make me pose as your girlfriend, in this dress, without a few drinks you're crazy."

"Okay. I just wouldn't have guessed that you drink."

I laughed. "Then there are probably a lot of things you wouldn't have guessed about me."

He stared at me for a few seconds, like he'd never seen me before and wasn't sure who I was. Then something else caught his eye and his expression changed—he was back to the emotionless Mr. Calloway I was used to.

An older man in a black tux approached. He looked vaguely familiar, although I couldn't place him. There was a woman in a gold dress hanging on his arm and when she turned, I almost spit out my drink.

It was Svetlana.

The man smiled, his eyes crinkling at the corners. He looked a lot like—

"Son," he said to Shepherd. "It looks like your date arrived. Do I get the pleasure of an introduction?"

Oh, holy shit. This was his *dad*? What was Svetlana doing with Shepherd's father? And why was she staring at me like that? If she'd had claws, she'd have been using them on my face right about now.

"Dad, this is Everly Dalton," Shepherd said. "Everly, my father, Richard Calloway."

I swallowed, hoping I wasn't going to choke on the bubbly I'd almost spit all over him. "It's so nice to meet you, Mr. Calloway."

"Please, call me Richard. And this is my lovely date, Svetlana," he said. "I'm thrilled to meet you. It's about time Shep was serious enough about a girl to introduce her to his father."

Shep? And Svetlana was his dad's *date*? Suddenly everything became clear; I realized exactly why he'd demanded I come. I sincerely hoped his dad wasn't aware that his son had recently been dating the harpy currently perched on his arm. Because that was just creepy.

Regardless, my boss needed me to put on a little show, and I had a feeling it was more for Svetlana than for his dad. The hostility in her eyes was fierce. If looks could kill, I'd have been dead on the floor already.

This was going to be fun.

"Richard, I'm so happy to meet you, too," I said. "I've been telling Shep he needs to introduce me already. After all, has he been hiding me from you, or the other way around?"

"My thoughts exactly," Richard said with a laugh. "Although I can see why he kept you a secret. I'd want to keep a beautiful woman like you all to myself as well."

I smiled and scrunched my shoulders a little. "You are the sweetest. I can see where Shep gets it." I gave Shepherd an obvious wink.

"So, tell me, how did you meet my son?" Richard asked.

"We work together," I said, and Richard's eyes widened slightly. That surprised him. "I know, it's usually a terrible idea to date a coworker. But sometimes these things are beyond our control. You work closely with someone for a long time, and feelings start developing before you even realize it's happening. Then one day it all comes out. Once that happens, there's no going back."

"I like her," Richard said to Shepherd. "A lot. Keep this one."

Svetlana was silent, still trying to murder me with her dagger-eyes.

I ran my hand down Shepherd's arm and clasped his hand, twining our fingers together. "Don't worry. He won't be able to get rid of me so easily."

Shepherd cleared his throat and for a second, I thought maybe I'd gone too far with the hand-holding. But he squeezed my hand and turned to look me in the eyes. "But why would I want to?"

My lips parted. He held my gaze, his blue eyes freezing me in place. "Why, indeed?"

Richard smiled. "I think they need me on stage in a minute or two. Everly, so happy to meet you."

"You, too."

Richard hadn't seemed to notice Svetlana's silence. I was surprised she wasn't digging her fingernails into his arm. But he walked away with her as if nothing was amiss. As if he'd just had a pleasant interaction with his son and his girl-friend, nothing more.

Shepherd let out a breath and released my hand.

"Well, that was interesting," I said. "Any more family members lurking? Should I be prepared to meet your grandma too?"

He shot me a glare. "No. Just him."

"He was with—"

"I know," he snapped. "Believe me, I know."

He put his hand on my back again and led me to the bar. He ordered a Manhattan and glanced at me, his eyebrows raised.

"Same for me," I said.

"And she drinks whiskey? Interesting."

"It's a classic."

We waited a few minutes while the bartender mixed our drinks. Shepherd handed the first one to me, then took a long swallow of his. We wandered away from the bar to a tall table near the edge of the room.

"Are you going to tell me what that was about?" I asked. "What is *she* doing with your dad?"

Shepherd took another drink and cleared his throat. "My dad doesn't know."

"I kind of guessed that. She's obviously doing it on purpose, though, right?"

"Clearly."

"Do you know how they met?" It was so odd to be having such an in-depth conversation with him. I was having a hard time not zoning out, watching his lips move. They were very nice lips.

*Focus, Everly.*

"My dad owns the resort I sent her to. Apparently he decided to take an impromptu trip to *figure some things out*, whatever that means. He met her there."

"Why on earth didn't you pull him aside and tell him?"

He shook his head. "Not here. Not in public. My dad is... sensitive."

I laughed, and Shepherd shot me a glare. "Sensitive? Really?"

"Yes, sensitive. This is going to be hard for him to take. He's going to feel very violated and he'll need time to process it. In private. Plus, he's getting an award tonight and I didn't want to ruin that for him."

"I'm sorry, but are you sure he's your real dad?"

"What is that supposed to mean?"

"Nothing. I just didn't expect to discover you have a

father who's too sensitive to find out he's dating his son's ex-hussy-gold-digger."

Shepherd opened his mouth, but closed it again. Then he did something I'd never seen before. He smiled. Shepherd Calloway actually smiled.

Oh. My. God. Did that look good on him. He had dimples in those cheeks. For a second, I felt like I'd do just about anything to get him to smile again.

"Ex-hussy-gold-digger?"

I glanced down at my drink. Had that champagne earlier gotten to me faster than I'd thought? "Sorry, I shouldn't have said that."

"No, what do you mean?"

"I'm sorry, I just never liked her. It was so obvious she didn't care about you, she just wanted your money."

"And that bothered you?"

"Well, yeah. I know we're not... I mean, we aren't really... we're not friends or anything. But that doesn't mean I don't care. I didn't like the way she treated you. You deserve better."

He eyed me for a moment, then looked away and took another sip. I was talking too freely, and I knew I was going to regret it later. Maybe it was the dress, or sharing a drink with him in a situation that made us look like peers rather than boss and employee. But I needed to be very careful, or the floodgates would open, and I'd find myself saying a lot of things I shouldn't.

Like how fucking delicious he looked in that tux.

I held up my drink, glaring at it like it had betrayed me. Seriously, was I drunk? I could *not* think of him as *delicious*, tux or no.

*Get it together, Everly.*

While we finished our drinks, the emcee took the mic

and gave a lengthy introduction. He talked about Richard, and the impact of his generosity on the community. Richard walked up on stage, beaming. I could tell his smile came naturally; unlike his son, he seemed to do it often. He gave a heartfelt thank you speech and received a standing ovation.

"Wow," I said, when the noise had died down and people had gone back to mingling. "Your dad seems like a good man. Why have I never met him before?"

"We're both busy," Shepherd said.

We left our empty glasses on the table and Shepherd started making the rounds, talking to people. He kept up the pretense that I was his date, guiding me around the room with his hand on my lower back, or lightly gripping my elbow. He even ran his hand up and down my arm a few times, a soft touch that made my heart race and my skin tingle. I looked around, expecting to see Svetlana watching us, but I didn't see her, or Shepherd's father, again.

I went along with it, staying by his side. Leaning into him when he seemed to expect it. Smiling when he introduced me to people. He offered to get me another drink, but I declined. After the champagne and the Manhattan, I was in danger of bypassing *a little tipsy* and heading straight for *telling inappropriate stories and asking strangers for hugs*.

Not that I'd ever done *that* before.

Okay, yes I had.

Around the time my feet started to hurt, Shepherd said he'd take me home. He'd driven himself. Although he had a driver available all the time, he usually drove his own car. We went out to the parking garage, his hand still on my back. He held the passenger's side door of his Mercedes for me, and I got in.

Another first. I'd never been in his car. Scheduled it for detailing, yes. Been a passenger, no.

He was quiet on the drive to my building. I tried not to dwell on what it had felt like to have his hand on my back. Or sliding up and down my bare arm. Or twining his fingers together with mine. It had been awfully nice.

But I needed to get that out of my head right now. I was just a bit too relaxed from the drinks. I'd gone a little outside my normal assistant role, but that was all.

There was a spot on the street a block from my apartment building, so he parked. "I'll walk you to your door."

It was the first time he'd spoken since we'd left the hotel. I was about to say he didn't need to do that, but he got out and came around to open the door for me. I appreciated the hand he offered to help me out of the car. This dress was tricky.

We stopped in front of my building and I gripped my clutch tighter than necessary, feeling suddenly awkward. What were we supposed to do now? We weren't pretending anything, here. But if I said goodnight to him like I did at the end of a work day, and received no response, it was going to hurt my feelings. I didn't want the night to end like that.

"Well, I hope your dad is okay," I said. "I don't envy you the task of breaking the news to him."

"No, it's not going to be pleasant."

"Yeah. I guess... I'll see you Monday."

"Right," he said. "Monday."

I took a deep breath. "Goodnight, Mr. Calloway."

He met my eyes again. "Goodnight."

That made me smile. He'd said goodnight in return. It was all I needed.

I pulled out my key and went to the door. He turned and started back toward his car.

"Everly," he said.

I glanced over my shoulder. "Yeah?"

"Thank you."

My breath caught in my throat and I bit my lip, feeling a poignant mix of giddiness and confusion. It was the first time he'd ever thanked me for anything.

I watched him go, wondering if things would be weird between us on Monday morning. But I had a feeling they wouldn't. He'd go back to being Mr. Calloway, and this would just be a crazy story I'd tell my besties in the circle of trust.

## 7

## SHEPHERD

*I* was on my second cup of coffee and still didn't feel awake. This wasn't normal. I popped an Airborne into a glass of water and watched it fizz. Maybe I was getting sick. I hadn't slept well. I'd been haunted by visions of a blond woman in a red dress.

Where had she come from? The woman who'd posed as my girlfriend last night could not have been my assistant. Everly was just... Everly. She was punctual, efficient, hard-working, and yes, pleasant to look at. But the woman who'd answered my summons last night had been something else.

She'd been stunning. Confident and sexy. And charming as fuck. She'd had my dad in the palm of her hand after just a few words. Her performance had been utter perfection.

I liked perfection. I demanded it, but so rarely was it achieved. But Everly in that insane red dress? She'd been perfect.

In fact, she'd turned an evening that would normally have been a drudgery into a fairly enjoyable experience.

Some of that was the look on Svetlana's face when she'd seen who I was with. She'd remembered Everly, all right. I'd never bothered with revenge before—I was too busy for that nonsense—but Svetlana had crossed a line when she'd targeted my father. Waltzing around the ballroom with Everly on my arm had been worth every second of the hassle it had taken to get her there.

Now I just had to figure out how to break it to my dad that the woman he'd met in Hawaii was not who he thought.

There was a knock on my door and I glanced at the time. My brother, Ethan, was due to come over this morning. He understood our father better than I did. I figured he could help me determine the best course of action for the current dilemma.

Ethan looked like a slimmer version of me, with the same thick dark hair and blue eyes. He and his partner, Grant, liked to run marathons, and they both had a lean runner's build. Ethan and I were often mistaken for twins, although he was two years older. He was a talented architect, and Grant worked as a software engineer.

"Morning," he said with a grin when I opened the door. "Please tell me you have more coffee."

"Sure."

I stepped aside so he could come in and closed the door while he went straight for the kitchen.

"Sorry about last night." He got a mug out of the cupboard and poured himself a cup. "Grant had a work thing and I really needed to be there. How did it go? Was Dad glowing?"

"You could say that." I picked up my mug and took a sip. "His speech was good."

"Of course it was." He leaned against the counter and cradled the mug in his hands. "Did you talk to him much or was it the usual mingling?"

"Mingling." Or rather, wandering around with my

hand temptingly close to my assistant's ass. And I was pretty sure she hadn't been wearing panties. Fuck, why was I thinking about that? Ethan was eying me over his mug. "What?"

"He hasn't talked to you yet, has he?" he asked.

"Talked to me about what?"

Ethan blew out a breath. "Dad's having some... financial issues."

"What sort of financial issues?"

"I don't know all the specifics, but he had some real estate deals go bad. He lost a lot of money. And by that, I mean all his money."

My forehead tightened. "All his money? What the hell are you talking about?"

"Well, I guess he still has some. But I'm not kidding, Shep, he took a huge hit. He sold his building to absorb some of the loss, but I'm not sure if it was enough."

"His building? He lives there."

"Until the deal closes," he said. "He was hoping to work something out with the buyer, but I'm not sure if that's going to happen."

"What about his resorts? His other properties?"

"Like I said, I don't know specifics. I'm assuming at this point it's just his personal assets that are in jeopardy. Everything else is owned by the corporation. But Shep, if the board finds out about this, they could replace him."

I pinched the bridge of my nose. "Why am I just hearing about this now?"

"Come on, you aren't surprised he kept this from you."

"I'm very surprised. If he'd come to me sooner, I might have been able to prevent this."

Ethan shrugged and took a careful sip of his coffee. "You know Dad. Life's a picnic until his pride gets involved. I'm sure he didn't want to admit it. He probably hoped he could fix things and you'd never have to know."

That was probably true. But he still should have told me. "Dad has more than just financial problems."

"What's going on?"

I shook my head because I still couldn't quite believe it. "He met a woman on Maui a few weeks ago. He said he went to clear his head. Considering he's apparently broke, a trip to Hawaii is a questionable choice at best, but that's not the worst of it."

"The worst is?"

"Her name is Svetlana Genov, and I sent her to Maui because I broke up with her."

Ethan stared at me, open-mouthed. I kept my face blank, but it took some effort. Seeing it had been like something out of a horror movie, but somehow telling my brother was worse.

"You're kidding, right? You suddenly developed a sense of humor and you're trying it out on me."

"Not kidding in the least. She was with him last night."

"Does he know who she is?"

"No. And to answer your next few questions, yes, *she* knew who *he* was. Yes, I'm certain she's doing it on purpose. No, I don't know whether she's trying to get back at me, or if she's just that shameless of a gold-digger. Probably a combination of both. But she's good, Ethan. She plays the part of the sweet, caring woman masterfully. I'm not surprised she's been able to pull one on Dad."

Ethan started laughing so hard he had to put his mug down, and he still sloshed coffee onto the counter.

I scowled, grabbing a paper towel to wipe up the mess. "I fail to see the humor in this."

"Really? Because it's pretty funny."

"No, it's not funny. It's infuriating. And Jesus, Ethan, it's gross. Dad's... and I was... God, I can't even say it."

"Maybe they aren't sleeping together."

I raised an eyebrow. "If you meet her, you'll see the improbability of that statement. Even you'd be tempted."

It was his turn to raise an eyebrow at me. "Right."

"I'm not kidding. At first glance, Svetlana is exquisite. It's not until you get to know her that you realize she's a hussy."

"Hussy?"

I waved off his question, wondering where I'd picked up that word. "Never mind. The problem is, Svetlana is either after a way back to me, or she wants his money."

"Well, she's not going to get either, so what's the problem?"

"The problem is that our father is dating my ex."

"Right, I get it, and I'm with you, it's cringey as hell. But honestly, what harm can she really do? Obviously, you're not interested in her. If her plan is to get back into your life, doing it by dating Dad is just plain stupid. If you're all she wants, she's going to figure out her mistake pretty quickly and move on. And if it's Dad's money she's after... well, he doesn't have any, so she's out of luck there, too."

His logic seemed reasonable, but I still didn't like it. "True."

"And I take it she's young?"

I nodded.

"Then there's nothing to worry about. When has Dad ever had a relationship with a younger woman that lasted more than a few months? Never. He'll get bored, or he'll realize she's evil. Then he'll wallow in sorrow for a few weeks before declaring he needs a hobby. He'll probably just take up skydiving or something."

"Are you suggesting I not tell Dad that I was dating her?"

"He's going through a rough patch. Let him have a little fun. Besides, how did it make you feel to realize Dad was banging your leftovers?"

I glared at him.

"Exactly. Even you had a rush of scary *feelings*. Dad's soft on the inside. You know that. What he doesn't know won't hurt him. Trust me. I give her a few months, tops. And it's not like we're all getting together for Sunday family dinners. How often do you even see Dad? She'll be gone the next time you two cross paths."

He had a point. My schedule was always tight. I didn't see my dad often.

"I don't like lying to him, but you might be right."

"Barely a lie, and one to spare his feelings," Ethan said. "I think it's a worthy sacrifice. A year from now we'll get him drunk and tell him the truth and have a good laugh."

"All right, I won't say anything. For now."

"Good," Ethan said. "Because he'll be here any minute."

I groaned. "Did you orchestrate this?"

"It's impossible to schedule time with you, and Dad's been trying to get the three of us together. So I told him I'd be here this morning. And don't tell me you have to work. It's a Saturday."

"I do have to work."

Ethan rolled his eyes.

"What if he brings her?" I pinched the bridge of my nose again and there was another knock at the door.

"That must be him." Ethan went to answer it.

My dad came in, dressed in a casual button-down shirt and gray slacks. He smiled, although there was a tiredness in his eyes that wasn't usually there. I tried not to think about why he might be tired.

"Morning, Dad."

"Look at this, my two sons in the same room. It's been too long, we should do this more often."

I got a mug out of a cupboard. "Coffee?"

"Please. Then come sit down. I need to talk to both of you."

I brought his coffee to the table and we all took a seat. I figured he was going to confess that he'd lost money, and I wondered if it was as bad as Ethan had said.

He stared into his mug for a long moment. "Boys, I want you to know that I'm proud of both of you."

That was an odd way to begin. Ethan and I shared a glance. What was he talking about?

"You've grown into fine men," he continued. "And no matter what happens to me, I want you to know that my greatest achievement in life is the two of you."

"Dad, Ethan told me about your financial problems," I said, and Ethan glared at me. "I'm sure we can help you figure it out."

"Way to be sensitive," Ethan said.

"There's no point in beating around the bush," I said. "Let's just get this out in the open so we can start working on solutions."

"That's not what I came here to talk to you about," Dad said.

"It's not?" Ethan and I asked simultaneously.

Dad shook his head. "No. My financial situation is... not ideal, that's true, and I'll get to that. But that's not the main reason I'm here. Ethan, Shepherd... I have cancer."

I stared at him, momentarily speechless. Had he just said *cancer*?

"Oh, Dad." Ethan got up and moved around the table to sit next to him. He put his arm around Dad's shoulders.

My brain switched instantly from shock to problem-solving. "What type?"

"It's prostate cancer."

"Do you have a treatment plan?"

"I do," Dad said. "Radiation therapy."

"Where are you being treated?"

"Jesus, Shep," Ethan said. "He just said he has cancer. Can you calm down with the questions?"

"It's all right," Dad said. "He wants to make sure I'm receiving the best care, which I am. My doctor is at the forefront of current cancer research. And my prognosis is very good. The survival rate is close to one hundred percent."

Ethan let out a long breath. "So you're not dying?"

"No, it'll take more than an angry prostate to put me down. But it did get me thinking about my life, and my priorities. I've spent some time getting my affairs in order. Not because I think I'm going to keel over tomorrow. But cancer makes a man face his mortality."

"What about work?" I asked. "Are you going to tell your board?"

"Yes, I'll be frank with them. I'll take a short leave of absence while I'm undergoing treatment and return when I'm able."

That was reasonable. I rubbed my chin. "We need to talk about your finances."

Ethan leaned forward, putting his elbows on the table. "Shep—"

"It's fine, Ethan," Dad said. "He's right. We do."

"Lay it out for me. And tell me the truth."

"I took some risks and lost my shirt," Dad said. "The company is fine, but personally..."

I raised my eyebrows.

"I'm basically broke," he said with a shrug. "And I have to move."

"When?"

Dad tapped his finger on the table. He was stalling. That meant it was bad.

"Dad."

"I have to be out this week," he said.

I met Ethan's eyes again and he winced. He hadn't known either.

"This week? And you're about to start cancer treatment?" I asked. "Dad, please tell me you've found a place to go. Where are you moving?"

He took a deep breath. "That's the other thing I wanted to discuss with you. I'd planned to temporarily take up residence in one of the company's hotels in Seattle. But I'm concerned about people's perceptions."

"And by that, you mean you're trying to keep the board from finding out you pissed away your money on shit real estate deals, so you can avoid being fired from the company you founded," I said.

Ethan shook his head. "It's called tact, Shep."

Dad tilted his head in acquiescence. "Yes, essentially. So I was hoping I could come stay with one of you. Just for a few months until my health recovers. Then I'll be in a better position to find new living arrangements."

My eyes snapped to Ethan's. I knew exactly where this was going and I did *not* like it. Not one bit. But I knew what my brother was about to say. He and Grant were living in a construction zone. They'd just started a major remodel of their house on Queen Anne.

"Shep, our entire house is torn apart," Ethan said. "We don't even have a functioning kitchen. And it will be months before it's finished."

They both looked at me.

I had room. My condo was over four thousand square feet. But I had so much square footage because I liked being insulated. I did *not* share my personal space well.

And Dad was dating my ex-girlfriend. Would he expect to bring her here? I couldn't have Svetlana parading around my condo. Sleeping here with my father. God, the thought of it turned my stomach.

I widened my eyes at Ethan. His jaw tightened and he gave me a very subtle shake of his head as if to say, *don't you dare tell him right now*.

Fuck.

I knew I could buy him his own place—the money wasn't an issue—but there was his sensitivity to consider. He'd probably feel like I was blowing him off. After all, he had a serious illness. I was the least emotional man I knew, but I understood my dad was different. And if he stayed here, I could keep an eye on things. Help get his financial situation under control and make sure he was getting the best medical treatment possible.

I took a deep breath. "You'll stay here. You can have the second master suite." At least that was at the opposite end of the condo from my bedroom.

Dad's face broke into a wide smile. "Thank you, son. You don't know how much I appreciate this. It's going to make the next few months so much easier."

"Sure, Dad." I got up and took my mug to the kitchen. "Do you need me to arrange movers or do you have that covered?"

"I'll take care of it," Dad said. "Are you sure about this? Do you need to talk to your girlfriend first?"

"Girlfriend?" Ethan asked.

Dad smiled again. "I had the pleasure of meeting Shepherd's girlfriend, Everly, last night. I wish you could have been there, Ethan. She's lovely. I bet she keeps you on your toes, eh, son?"

I avoided Ethan's gaze. "Yes, she does. And I'm sure she won't mind."

"I think she'll get along well with Svetlana." Dad winked at Ethan. "I met the most extraordinary woman recently. I've been seeing a lot of her."

"That's what Shep told me," Ethan said, shooting me another *don't you dare say anything* look. "I can't wait to meet her."

"We'll all have dinner soon," Dad said. "You can bring Grant, and Shepherd will bring Everly."

Oh my god. I had to get out of here. "Now that we have things worked out, I have work to do. You two stay as long as you want."

I left them sitting at the table and went back to my office, closing the door with a soft click.

What a nightmare. I opened my laptop and did a search on prostate cancer. Spent some time getting caught up on the disease and the latest treatments. I'd find out who his doctor was to ensure he was in fact getting the best care. Maybe go with him to his next appointment so I could get more information on his specific case. I needed to be sure he didn't need a second opinion. Prostate cancer wasn't usually deadly, but I didn't want to leave anything to chance.

Leaning back in my chair, I rubbed my chin. It was disconcerting to hear my dad was ill, but at least his prognosis was good.

But there was still the problem of him moving in. Without Svetlana complicating matters, that would have been a minor inconvenience. However, she *was* complicating matters. I could simply choose to spend as much time away as possible while Dad was living here. But I didn't like the idea of Svetlana having unfettered access to my home. Which meant she and I would be here together, under the same roof.

She was going to realize rather quickly that I wasn't dating Everly.

Unless... I tipped my fingertips together beneath my chin. Unless I continued the ruse that I *was* dating Everly. Could I somehow make that work?

I ran a multi-billion-dollar corporation. I made complicated business deals every day. I was sure I could come to an arrangement with my assistant. It was only for a few months.

And Everly was perfect.

## 8

### EVERLY

*M*onday morning began as it always did. I arrived on my floor and made my way past cubicles and offices, saying hi to my coworkers. Smiling. Asking them if they'd had a good weekend or wishing them good morning. Steve had another story about his cat, which I listened to attentively.

Nothing unusual at all.

I glanced at the clock as I went about my usual Monday morning tasks. Eight twenty-two. He'd be here in five minutes.

My heart beat a little faster than it should, and a tingle of nervousness made my belly feel jumpy. I got Mr. Calloway's coffee, double-checked his schedule, made sure I had everything in order.

And tried very hard not to let my thoughts drift back to the feel of his hand on my lower back. Or on my arm. Or how his voice had sounded saying my name.

*Knock it off, Everly. That might as well have been a dream.*

Yes, a dream. He had been a dream. So dreamy in that tux.

God, I was doing it again.

The clock changed to eight twenty-seven and the elevator door opened.

Mr. Calloway walked down the hallway, dressed in his suit. He had his phone out, and he flicked his thumb across the screen as he made his way toward my desk. I grabbed his coffee and stood, ready to follow him into his office.

Nothing unusual. It was just another Monday.

He turned the corner at my desk, and just as I was about to fall in step behind him, he stopped. Looked up from his phone and met my eyes. "Good morning, Everly."

"Good morning," I managed to croak through my shock.

Steve looked like he'd just witnessed a miracle. Or maybe a murder. His eyes were wide, and his mouth hung open.

I shrugged at Steve, suddenly remembering I was holding Shepherd's—no, Mr. Calloway's—coffee. I held it away from me so I wouldn't spill it on my clothes if it sloshed out through the opening in the lid. Wincing, I hustled into Mr. Calloway's office.

He set his briefcase down and I put the coffee on his desk. I turned to take his jacket from him, but he wasn't there. He was standing next to the coat tree, hanging it up himself. What was he doing?

This wasn't a problem. He could hang up his own jacket. No big deal. I took the remote for the blinds and opened them. He took a seat at his desk.

Good. Back to normal.

"Close the door," he said.

I froze. It wasn't the first time he'd asked me to close the door so we could meet in private. As his assistant, I was often privy to confidential information. But there was something about his tone. And the way he was messing with our routine had me so off-kilter, I didn't know which way was up.

He glanced up and raised his eyebrows.

"Right." I shut the door. "Sorry."

"Have a seat."

"I'm sorry Mr. Calloway, but I'm not prepared for a meeting. I don't have a way to take notes."

"Everly," he said, a slight edge to his tone. "Just sit."

I walked around to the other side of his desk and slowly lowered myself into one of the chairs.

He sat back and pitched his fingers together. "Are you single?"

The question was so unexpected, it took me a full five seconds before I could collect myself enough to answer. "Um... single? Yes, but—"

"Hear me out," he said, cutting me off. "I find myself in a difficult situation. You met my father on Friday and saw who he was with."

"Yes..."

"It turns out my father has bigger problems than Svetlana."

"Worse than that harpy?" I asked, then clicked my mouth shut. Oh my god, why had I said that? I hadn't even been drinking.

The corner of his mouth twitched. "Yes, worse than... the harpy. He's been diagnosed with cancer."

"Oh, Shepherd, I'm so sorry." I shut my mouth again, realizing I'd just called him *Shepherd*. What the hell was wrong with me? One evening in a red dress with my boss, and suddenly I'd lost control of my mouth.

He didn't seem to notice. "His prognosis is good, although he'll need to undergo radiation therapy."

"That's good. I mean, about his prognosis."

"It is." He pressed his lips together and leaned forward, putting his elbows on his desk. "What I'm about to tell you doesn't leave this room."

"Of course."

He nodded and there we were with the eye contact again. "My father's illness isn't his only issue right now. He's also suffered a series of financial losses."

I nodded, not sure what to say.

"My brother and I will do what we can to help him, but it's important this information doesn't become public. If his board of directors gets wind of this, they'll vote him out. He'll lose the company he's spent his lifetime building."

"Okay." Had he just said *brother*? Since when did he have a brother?

"He's liquidated most of his assets, which includes the building he was living in. And given that he's undergoing cancer treatment, he's moving in with me."

"That's nice of you."

"Indeed. But I'm sure you can see how my father's relationship with Svetlana is suddenly a much larger problem than it was seventy-two hours ago."

"You didn't tell him?"

His eye twitched, the only sign of emotion I could see. "No. It's complicated."

"That's the understatement of the century. So you're moving your father in with you and... what, he's going to bring his new girlfriend over?"

"Yes. And until I can get rid of her without causing more problems for my family, I have to deal with her."

"Okay, that's... unfortunate. But why are you telling me all this? And what does it have to do with my relationship status?"

He took a deep breath. "I need a girlfriend."

"Oh, do you need me to make dinner reservations, or..."

"Not a real girlfriend." His expression softened, hinting at a bit of the personality I'd thought I'd seen on Friday night. "I'm not interested in dating anyone right now. But I also can't have Svetlana thinking I'm single."

"So you need a fake girlfriend."

"Precisely. I'm glad we're on the same page. I'll need you to move in."

"Wait," I said, holding up a finger. I felt like I'd blacked out and missed part of our conversation. Move in? What the hell was he talking about? "Not on the same page. I don't think we're reading the same book. Move in? What?"

His nostrils flared. They did that when he was frustrated or impatient. "My father already thinks we're dating. So the obvious solution is to continue with that ruse."

"Let me get this straight. You want me to pretend we're dating?"

"Yes."

"And *move in* with you?"

"Yes."

"Are you *insane*?" I asked, practically hissing out the last word.

"You did an excellent job on Friday."

I felt my filter smash to pieces, and I did not care. "Walking around with you at some event in a red dress is not the same as moving in with you and pretending we're together. I have a life. I can't just shack up with my fucking boss because he needs someone to pose as his girlfriend."

"Well, my father put me in this goddamn position, and it's not like I'm fucking happy about it. I'm going to have the woman from hell sauntering around my house like she owns the place. He brought her over yesterday and it was the longest hour of my fucking life."

We stared at each other, like we were both shocked at our own outbursts. And our copious dropping of f-bombs.

He cleared his throat and adjusted the cuffs of his sleeves. "I'll pay you."

Damn right he was going to pay me.

Wait, was I considering this? I couldn't be considering this. Going to a gala was not a big deal. In fact, it had been kind of fun. And his dad had seemed super nice. Seeing him again wouldn't be the worst. But posing as Shepherd's girl-friend? Living with him? How would that even work? It was a disaster waiting to happen.

My phone vibrated in my hand and I glanced at the screen. It was a text from Annie.

*Really, universe? Really?*

If I did this, he'd owe me big. Huge. Enormous. I could forgo whatever bonus he offered me and ask for his swim-mers instead. Be the Fairy Sperm-Mother for my sister and Miranda. Make their genetically perfect baby dreams come true. Granted, I might be dooming them to raising an emotionless robot child. But if that was what they wanted...

But Shepherd wasn't necessarily as emotionless as I'd thought. I'd seen glimmers of something in him on Friday night. Maybe it had just been the drinks, or maybe I'd imag-ined it. But I had a feeling there was a teeny-tiny, minuscule little crack in Shepherd's emotionless façade. A hairline fracture. Maybe he wasn't the only person in the world impervious to my sunshine.

And if it meant I had a good case for asking him to donate his baby batter...

I opened my mouth to reply and had a sudden out-of-body experience. It was like I was floating, looking down into Shepherd's office from above. Listening to someone else talk.

"All right. I'll do it."

## 9

## EVERLY

"You're what?" Nora asked, her drink clutched in her manicured hand. She looked at me like I'd just told her I was moving to Mars.

"I'm going to *temporarily* stay at my boss's place. Just for a few months. So not permanently. It's temporary."

"You mentioned that," Nora said, giving me the side eye. She wasn't buying my story.

I was trying to avoid telling them about the fake girlfriend thing, but I could see it wasn't going to work.

We'd gone for our usual run and were sitting in the bar at Brody's. I'd ordered a martini, but I wasn't in the mood to drink it. Ever since I'd said yes to Shepherd's offer this morning, I'd been wallowing in the *assistant who's just agreed to be her boss's fake girlfriend* version of buyer's remorse. It might mean I could get what Annie wanted, but the reality of it was starting to overwhelm me.

"Okay, circle of trust?" I held my hands out and they each clasped them, nodding.

I took a breath and told them about what had happened Friday night. And about our conversation in the office this morning. I didn't give them the details about what was happening with Shepherd's father. I simply told them that for personal reasons I couldn't disclose, he was moving in with Mr. Calloway. I knew I could trust Hazel and Nora, but confidential meant confidential. I didn't mess around with that when it came to my job.

They were properly horrified by Svetlana whoring her way into Richard's life. And I thought maybe they'd understand and be supportive about my decision to go along with this admittedly insane and probably too-elaborate plan.

"You've lost your mind," Nora said when I finished. "Why the hell did you agree to it so quickly?"

"I don't know. What would be the point of waiting?"

"To run it by us," Nora said. "We could have talked some sense into you."

"It won't be that bad."

Hazel adjusted her glasses. "Actually, the potential for this to go wrong is exceedingly high."

My shoulders slumped. "You think?"

"Everly, sweetie, you just agreed to be your boss's fake girlfriend for the next few months," Nora said. "And you're going to move in with him. You already say he's difficult to work for. What's it going to be like living with him? You'll be together twenty-four seven."

"Yeah, I know, I thought of that." I ran my finger along the rim of my glass. "And I don't know how it's all going to work."

"Is sex included?" Hazel asked.

"No." I sat up, almost knocking over my drink. "No, it is not. He's not asking me to be a prostitute. The girlfriend part is *fake*."

"Richard Gere was sleeping with Julia Roberts in *Pretty Woman*," Nora said.

"Yeah, but he picked her up on a street corner," I said. "She was an actual prostitute."

Nora shrugged. "If he wanted to go down on me on a piano, I'd do it."

"For money?" Hazel asked. "That's illegal."

"No, I just mean in general," Nora said. "Have you seen Everly's boss? God, he's exquisite. I'd let him do whatever he wanted to me."

Hazel's brow creased. "I thought you were talking about Richard Gere."

Nora shrugged. "Either way, but Shepherd Calloway is hotter."

"So why do you think I've lost my mind? If you'd do it..."

"Honey, I'd do it in a heartbeat, and I'd let him have his way with me during the off hours," Nora said. "But you, my love, are not me. And I can already see where this is going."

"Where?"

"You're going to catch feelings," Nora said.

Hazel nodded as she took another bite of salad.

"*Catch feelings*?" I asked. "What does that even mean? Feelings aren't an illness."

"In a situation like this, they are," she said. "You're going to spend all this extra time with him, get to know him better. His dad will tell you embarrassing stories from his childhood. He'll stop being Mr. Calloway and he'll start being a *man*. A man who is rich, gorgeous, and sexy as fuck. A man who is sleeping right next to you."

"What do you mean, sleeping right next to me?"

Nora rolled her eyes as she took a sip of her martini. "You have to fool his dad, right?"

"Yeah."

"And his dad is living there?"

"Yes."

She sighed, like she couldn't believe she was having to explain this to me. "Then where do you think he'll have you sleep? In a guest room? His live-in girlfriend would sleep in his bed, so that's where you'll be. Unless he decides to pull some *move in the middle of the night* thing. Or maybe he's one of those people who doesn't sleep, and he'll pretend to go to bed and then leave you there alone while he works all night or goes out and fights crime."

Hazel opened her mouth but paused before she spoke. "You didn't mean that last part literally."

"No, but I'm right about the rest of it," Nora said. "Everly is going to wind up getting hurt."

I bristled at that. I wasn't such a delicate flower that I couldn't handle this. I was Shepherd's longest-running assistant in company history. I was the woman who could handle him, when so many others had failed. My friends just didn't know how good I was at my job; what it meant that I could work for him and not let him get to me. And they didn't know what it could mean for my sister.

"There's one more aspect to this I haven't mentioned."

They raised their eyebrows.

"Annie and Miranda want me to ask him to donate his sperm so they can have a baby."

Hazel blinked at me, like she was processing what I'd said. Nora picked up her glass and gulped down the last of her drink.

"Oh, Everly," Nora said, putting her glass down.

"What?"

"Hazel, we need to start planning for the crash now," she said. "This is going to be national-disaster level, unlike anything we've been through before. Worse than the Christian Monroe incident."

"Worse than Christian Monroe?" Hazel asked, her voice awed.

"Christian Monroe?" He'd been my college boyfriend, and the man I'd expected would propose. Instead, he'd gotten another girl pregnant. The baby-mama was nice, though. I still sent little Amy a birthday card every year. "This will not be like what happened with Christian. I dated him for three years and thought we'd get married. This will be a few months living in a huge multi-million-dollar condo with a view. The worst that will happen is I'll accidentally see his dad naked and have to live with the nightmares for a while."

"Keep telling yourself that," Nora said. "But sweetie, just remember. Even though I'm going to say I told you so, we'll be there to peel you off the floor when this crashes and burns."

"Of course we will," Hazel said.

I rolled my eyes. It wasn't going to be necessary. I had this handled. A few months pretending to be my boss's girlfriend and I'd have good news for my sister. I could do this for her.

And now I *wanted* to do it, to prove to my friends that I could.

## 10

### SHEPHERD

*T*he movers would be upstairs any minute. Thankfully, Dad wasn't home. He was out to dinner with Svetlana—which made my skin crawl, but I was glad he was occupied with something else. I didn't want an audience when Everly arrived.

I'd told Dad that I'd already asked Everly to move in. He'd been predictably thrilled. Ethan and Grant didn't appear to be interested in becoming parents, and Dad had his heart set on being a grandfather. Sadly for him, he'd pinned all his hopes on me, and I'd failed to deliver. The news that I was *taking this step,* as he put it, had made him practically giddy.

That had given me a twinge of guilt. He was going to be disappointed when I ended yet another relationship without giving him a daughter-in-law. Or grandchildren.

I strummed the strings of my guitar with my calloused fingers, playing a few random chords. The one-room condo where I kept my guitar collection was three floors down from my residence. No one, save the condominium association, knew I owned this unit. Even Ethan, who knew more about me than anyone, didn't know I had this space. It was private. Intensely personal. None of it looked like the man I showed the world. The slick businessman with all the answers.

This room was dim, the only light coming from a small lamp on the counter. It wasn't a stereotypical man cave. No giant TV or well-stocked bar. No sports posters or beer signs on the walls. I kept a bottle of twenty-one-year-old Glenlivit in the kitchen, replacing as needed. Had a leather couch along one wall. Some framed posters for ambiance—Zeppelin, Deep Purple, Rush, Queen.

And my guitars. Acoustic. Electric. I had a white Fender Stratocaster. A gorgeous wood-grain Gibson Les Paul. A vintage Rickenbacker bass. Some, like the Gibson Hummingbird acoustic in my hands, I played. Others were just for display. Not to be ostentatious—I didn't show off my collection. No one knew of its existence. I had them because I loved them. Because it made this place peaceful. And mine.

Sometimes I contemplated why I kept this part of myself so separate. But the answer to that was simple. Music made me vulnerable. I'd never worn my heart on my sleeve like my father did. I was too much like my mother. Practical, logical. Cold. On the outside, at least.

I'd discovered music as an adult, and it had become my outlet. The only real way I was adept at expressing myself. And that simply wasn't something I wanted to share with the people who knew me as Shepherd Calloway.

I strummed a few more chords, the melody coming easily. I'd left the office early to give myself time to decompress before Everly arrived. The arrangements had been made quickly—by Everly, of course. It was her job, after all. She wasn't giving up her apartment. Simply moving what she'd need for the next several months. Enough to convince my father, and Svetlana, that we were a couple.

She'd be arriving soon, so I needed to get upstairs. After putting my guitar back on its stand, I slipped out and took the elevator to the penthouse.

A knock on the door heralded Everly's arrival. I opened it to find her with two movers in the hallway outside, all of them laughing hysterically.

"Yes, I'm serious," Everly said. She seemed to be in the middle of a conversation that they all found incredibly amusing. "It really happened. Cross my heart. Oh, hi, Mr. Callow—I mean, hi, Shepherd."

I glanced at the two movers and their smiles faded. "Bedroom is to the left. End of the hallway."

They nodded, readjusting their grips on the boxes they carried, and moved past me.

"Wow, way to ruin the mood," Everly said.

"Excuse me?"

She pressed her lips together, almost as if she was surprised she'd said that out loud. "Never mind. Are they..."

"My father's out for the evening."

"Oh, okay. So we don't have to..."

"No."

"Right. Good."

She was dressed in a yellow top and cropped jeans, sandals showing off her bright pink toenails. Her hair was up, just a few little wisps hanging down around her neck. Quite the contrast from the other night, when she'd owned that red dress.

The movers went back out for another load. I decided they didn't have any more need of me and went into the kitchen to pour myself a drink.

Everly followed me in. "So, are you going to show me

around or anything? Do I get the *make yourself at home* speech?"

"Do you need a speech?"

"I don't know. It might be nice."

"You've been here before."

She leaned her hip against the counter. "That's not really the same. I've been here to sign for your deliveries. I've never even used one of the bathrooms. How many are there?"

"Four."

"Wow. I guess that will come in handy, what with all the people living here now."

I definitely needed the drink. It wasn't Everly's attempt at conversation that had me reaching for the bottle of Scotch in the cupboard. Seeing her in my kitchen, dressed in comfortable clothes, was almost as disconcerting as seeing her in that red dress had been.

"Sorry, I guess you don't want to be bothered. I'll just go..." She made a vague motion over her shoulder toward the other room.

"You're not... bothering me." Why I was suddenly worried about her feelings, I had no idea. But I didn't want to hurt them. "Let me show you around."

She smiled. "Thanks."

I went to pour my drink, but paused. "Would you like one?"

"Oh my god, yes."

Her quick reply almost made me crack a smile. The corner of my mouth twitched. I poured us both a drink and handed one to her.

"Thanks."

The movers came in, dragging suitcases and another box. How much stuff had she brought? They took it past us, down the hall toward the bedroom.

"Living room," I said, gesturing. "There's a TV there. I don't use it much, but you're welcome to it. The second master suite is down that hall. My father moved in over the weekend, so he's occupying that space."

"Got it."

I pointed out the other obvious things. Guest bath. My office. Balcony. Then I walked her back to my—what was, for now, *our*—bedroom.

The movers had put her things in a corner. She stepped inside, shifting on her feet as if nervous.

"So... okay. This is nice."

My gaze strayed to the bed. I'd toyed with the notion of having her sleep in another room. But if we were going to pretend to be a couple, it was going to require bed sharing.

"We're both adults, and the bed is a king," I said, giving her the same speech I'd given myself several times. "There's another bathroom if you need more privacy. I'll respect your space; you don't have to worry about anything."

"If I was worried about you, I wouldn't have agreed to this," she said. "I trust you."

I wasn't sure why—any more than I understood why I was concerned about her feelings—but hearing her say she trusted me felt good.

"I guess I'll let you get settled."

One of the movers poked his head through the open door. "Miss Dalton?"

She gave him a warm smile. "Jason, I told you, call me Everly."

"Okay, Everly. Where should we put this?"

From where I was standing, I couldn't see what he was referring to.

Everly glanced around the room. "Hmm. Not in here. The living room, I think."

"Sure thing," he said.

She went out to the other room behind him. I took a sip of my Scotch, then headed for my office. I had work to do. But the sudden laughter from the living room made me curious. What were they laughing about now?

"Dominic, you kill me," Everly said, wiping a tear from the corner of her eye.

"We got everything," one of the movers—Dominic, apparently—said. "Is there anything else we can do to help?"

"I think that's it," Everly said. "You guys have been so great. Thank you. Bring it in."

She opened her arms and the two men both hugged her. I watched from the hallway, oddly fascinated. She walked them out and hugged them again, as if they were old friends.

"Well, that's a wrap." She shut the door behind them.

I leaned against the wall. "Friends of yours?"

"Who, Dominic and Jason? No. They were just the guys I hired to help. Not that I really needed it. I didn't bring over anything heavy. Why?"

"It just seemed like you knew them."

"No, but they were hilarious. Such fun guys." She glanced around, putting a finger to her lips. "Where did I leave my drink? Oh, there."

I followed the direction she pointed and a large yellow something—I wasn't sure what it was—in my living room caught my eye.

"What is that?"

"Hmm?" She walked over and picked up her drink. "This? Oh, it's my bean bag chair."

"You brought a bean bag chair? And you're putting it in my living room?"

She smiled. "Yes."

"Why?"

"Because it's comfortable, and a great place to read, and my favorite color."

I glanced at it again, a big yellow blob sitting among my carefully chosen furniture. "It's fuzzy. And yellow."

"That's very observant of you, Shep."

My gaze snapped to her.

"Okay, sorry. Just trying to... Never mind. Is it really going to bother you? You already said you don't use this room very much. And a real girlfriend would put her stamp on the place. I need to spread out. Mark my territory. It's part of the ruse."

It was hideous, but that did make sense. "Fair enough. But how much territory marking is going to be necessary?"

The sound of the front door opening followed by Svetlana's tinkling laugh made the muscles in my back and shoulders clench. Everly met my eyes, hers narrowing slightly. The look of determination on her face lit a fire inside me. It was on.

"Good, you're home," Dad said as he shut the door behind Svetlana. "Everly, it's lovely to see you again."

Somehow Everly was at my side, although I hadn't seen her cross the distance between us. Svetlana eyed the two of us, her expression blank. Everly slipped her hand into mine.

"It's lovely to see you too, Richard," Everly said, her voice warm as summer sunshine. "Or maybe I should just call you *roomie*."

Dad grinned at her, while Svetlana's face remained impassive.

"Roomie. I like that. Just for a short time, so no need to

be concerned. I don't want to impose, or intrude on your space."

"Of course," she said. "There's more than enough room. And you know Shep is happy to have you."

"I appreciate it very much," Dad said.

Svetlana's eyes were on me, now, and Everly tightened her grip on my hand. Just a slight pressure, but I felt it. A subtle shift of her feet, and her body angled closer to mine. There was a certain possessiveness in her stance. I could feel it, and I had no doubt Svetlana could see it.

A pleasant sense of arousal swept through me, momentarily distracting me from the conversation. My pulse quickened and blood rushed to my groin. There was something about the way Everly quietly claimed me as hers in front of another woman that I enjoyed.

"Shep?"

I blinked, disconcerted. What had Dad said? I cleared my throat, but before I could answer, Everly rubbed her hand up and down my arm.

"Thanks, but we both had a long day and I haven't even started to unpack."

"Yes, of course," Dad said. "Don't let us keep you. I have an early appointment tomorrow, so Svetlana was only joining me for a nightcap."

"Good night, Dad," I said, refusing to acknowledge the harpy. "Everly?"

She squeezed my hand again and smiled at me. God, she was good at this.

Dad led Svetlana into the living room. I noticed her eying Everly's bean bag chair. Marking territory, indeed.

Everly winked at me, then turned on her heel and walked—no, she didn't walk. It wasn't quite a skip, but there was a spring in her step that made her seem a little bit bouncy.

And bouncing made me think of her tits.

I cleared my throat, as if that could clear my head. This was proving to be more distracting than I'd anticipated. I went to my office and sat down with my Scotch. I'd give Everly some space while she unpacked.

We were both adults. This didn't have to be a big deal.

## 11

## EVERLY

*T*here had been a brief respite in the substantial tension between me and Shepherd when he'd gone to his office and I'd gone to the bedroom to unpack. There were two walk-in closets—one completely empty and outfitted with shelves, drawers, and plenty of space to hang my clothes. Half the bathroom was similarly ready for my temporary occupancy. It made me wonder if he always kept his things to the left half of the bathroom, or if he'd cleared space for me.

But as the last hour of evening ticked toward bedtime, I found myself growing increasingly nervous. I kept glancing at my phone, my desire to text Nora and Hazel at war with my desire to pretend this wasn't really starting to freak me out. In the end, the freak-out won, and I group-texted the two of them.

*Me: I'm here. I unpacked. Now what do I do?*
*Hazel: What do you feel like doing?*
*Nora: What does the bathroom look like?*
*Me: Bathroom is gorgeous. Why?*
*Nora: Does it have a tub?*

*Me: Yes, a big one.*

*Hazel: What does the bathroom have to do with anything? I think Everly is bored, not in need of improved hygiene.*

*Nora: Take a bubble bath.*

*Me: That does sound nice.*

*Hazel: Good idea.*

*Nora: Leave the door open a crack and see if he peeks.*

*Me: No!*

*Nora: Why not? It'll be fun. Bring your phone. I want live updates.*

*Me: Why would I do that?*

*Nora: Why wouldn't you do that?*

*Me: Not helping, Nora. I'm sitting on the bed I have to sleep in tonight. With my BOSS.*

*Nora: You signed up for this, E. Bubble bath.*

I sighed and put down my phone. A bath did sound nice. And his tub was enormous. My apartment only had a shower. It wasn't often that I got to take a long, hot bath.

I went to the bedroom door and leaned out, listening. I'd heard Svetlana leave well over an hour ago, and Richard seemed to have gone to bed—or at least to his room. Shepherd was still in his office, as far as I could tell. Nora's suggestion of a bath was sounding better and better. I needed to relax, or I'd never get to sleep.

The bathroom really was gorgeous. Gray and blue tile. Fluffy white towels. Everything sparkled. I turned down the lights for ambiance—they were on a dimmer, which made me wonder why all bathrooms didn't have lights on a dimmer—and turned on the water.

I set my phone on the ledge next to the bathtub. Of course I wasn't going to leave the door open and live-text Nora and Hazel. That was just silly. I just wanted my phone for something to do while I soaked.

But then again, it was getting awfully steamy with the water running. Maybe leaving the door open a tiny crack was a good idea. Just to make sure there wasn't too much moisture. It would have been a shame to create a mildew issue in this beautiful bathroom.

So I left the door open a crack, slipped out of my clothes, and got into Shepherd's glorious bathtub.

The water was perfect. I settled in, letting the heat seep into me. I hadn't seen any bubble bath—which, honestly, was a relief. If Shepherd had bubble bath, the only conclusion would be that one of his past girlfriends had left it here. There was nothing wrong with a man who liked bubble baths, but he didn't strike me as the type, so I doubted it was the sort of thing he'd keep on hand for himself. And despite the fact that this was totally fake, I didn't like the idea of finding traces of another woman here.

Call me territorial, but I was going to be the only woman in my fake boyfriend's life. While we were still faking it, of course.

My phone buzzed against the tile with a text.

*Nora: Well?*

*Me: In the bath. Nothing. I think he's working.*

*Nora: Boring.*

*Me: What do you expect me to do?*

*Nora: Did you leave the door open a little?*

*Me: Yes, but only so it wouldn't get too steamy.*

*Hazel: Mildew can be a serious health hazard.*

*Nora: Whatever makes you feel better.*

The sound of the bedroom door opening and closing almost made me drop my phone in the water. I gasped, bobbling my phone a few times. I could hear Shepherd's brisk footsteps in the other room. They stopped, then seemed to go back the direction they'd come.

*Me: He's in the bedroom, but I think he's about to leave.*

*Nora: I bet he walks by again.*

*Hazel: Curiosity is a powerful force.*

*Nora: If Hazel agrees with me, you know I'm right.*

I shifted, the water moving in a slow wave. And then I heard his footsteps again. Had he walked by the door?

*Me: Okay, heard him walk by again. I think.*

*Nora: Told you.*

I waited, scarcely daring to breathe. I was sure—positive, even—that he was doing something perfectly normal that had nothing to do with curiosity about me in his bathtub.

The footsteps stopped, but I didn't hear the bedroom door open again. He was still out there. Not going to his office.

He walked by the bathroom door again. Was I imagining things, or did he walk much slower that time?

*Me: I think he strolled past the bathroom door.*

*Nora: Strolled?*

*Me: I just mean he walked... slower.*

*Nora: It's ridiculous how much fun this is. E, move your legs so the water splashes a little.*

I shifted and the water moved, making a soft splashing sound. For a second, there was only silence. Then I heard Shepherd's quick footsteps and the bedroom door opening and closing.

*Me: He left.*

*Nora: Immediately or after a pause?*

*Me: After a pause, I guess.*

*Nora: I love this. You flustered him. I bet he went to his office to stroke the sex stick.*

*Hazel: You think? He didn't receive much stimulation.*

*Nora: He has his hot assistant naked in his bathtub. He's stimulated.*

Groaning, I leaned my head back. What was I doing? I shouldn't be making this situation more uncomfortable than it already was. That's what I got for listening to Nora.

**Me:** *I'm getting out and going to bed. I have to work in the morning.*

**Nora:** *Walk by his office and see if you hear anything.*

**Me:** *No!*

**Nora:** *Fine. You're boring. But we all know he's in there pleasuring himself to the thought of you in his tub.*

**Me:** *I'm positive he isn't.*

Neither of them replied, so I put my phone down and enjoyed the hot water for a little bit longer. I didn't hear any sign of Shepherd. I was sure he wasn't even remotely interested in what I was doing in here. He'd probably been in the bedroom to get something, or to change his clothes. Maybe he hadn't been sure I was in here, so he'd paused by the door to see if the bathroom was occupied. Nora had this all wrong. He wasn't *aroused* by the thought of me in his bathtub. The guy was practically a robot. Sometimes I figured he dated just to project the illusion that he was human.

Then again, when he'd taken me home from the gala, he'd seemed remarkably human.

I got out, took a quick shower to rinse off and wash my hair, and got ready for bed. Shepherd was apparently still in his office—did he ever *not* work?—when I stood facing the bed, my hands on my hips, dressed in my *good morning sunshine* t-shirt and shorts pajama set.

This was where things got real. I was standing here, staring at my boss's bed, and somehow, I had to talk myself into getting in it.

A noise from the hallway made me gasp. He was coming. As quickly as I could, I turned off the lamp and jumped into bed, whipping the covers up over my shoulder. I'd pretend to be asleep. Then he could do what he needed to do, get in bed, and we'd both be spared the worst of the awkwardness.

I scarcely dared to breathe as the door whispered open. He clicked it shut almost silently. Was he trying to be quiet for me? That was nice of him. He went into the bathroom and closed the door.

The tension of the day was finally wearing on me. I'd tried to keep things light and friendly with Shepherd, but he was so serious. It was hard to know what he was thinking. At work, I'd learned not to worry about it. But this was different. I needed to figure out how to navigate this new dynamic, and I needed to do it fast.

My eyes were just starting to get heavy when Shepherd came out of the bathroom. My back was toward his side of the bed, but I swore I could feel his movements. Usually, he was brusque and exacting. I could envision him getting into his bed at night with authority, the way he did everything else.

But the man on the other side of the bed seemed to be moving with quietness and care. Was he as nervous about this as I was? Or was he simply hoping to keep from waking me so I wouldn't bother him as he was trying to fall asleep?

The covers moved and I felt his weight slide onto the mattress. Oh my god, I was in bed with my boss.

Okay, this was fine. I'd thought about this ever since Nora had brought it up over martinis. It was part of the deal. Like Shepherd had said earlier, we were both adults, and it was a king-sized bed.

Neither of us moved and tiredness started to get the best of me. I was warm from the bath and exhausted from moving. His bed was amazingly comfortable, and I sank deeper into the mattress as my body relaxed. My eyes drifted closed.

And then he moved.

He rolled over, the silky sheets rustling against his body. Oh my god, what was he wearing? I hadn't looked. Did he wear pajamas to bed? Was he in his underwear? Did he usually sleep naked and he'd have to get used to sleeping with something on since I was here? I wanted to turn over and peek, but I couldn't move. It was like I'd been paralyzed.

In the silence of the dark room, I heard him take a slow, deep breath. I could imagine the air filling his lungs, his broad chest expanding. I wondered if he had chest hair. The hair on his head was dark and thick—chest hair seemed likely. And, oh god, did he have a happy trail on his lower...

*Stop it, Everly. Stop it, now.*

This wasn't helping me sleep, and I had to work tomorrow. What was I supposed to say to him? *Sorry I dozed off during the meeting, I was up late contemplating your body hair.*

No. Not good.

My back was getting stiff from lying in the same position for too long. I needed to move, but I was afraid to try. What if I accidentally touched him? What if my toes brushed his leg?

I kept still for a while longer, but eventually I had to risk it. I'd never fall asleep like this. Lifting the covers slightly, so I wouldn't pull them off Shepherd when I moved, I rolled over to my other side.

This put me facing him, so I kept my eyes squeezed shut. I hadn't accidentally touched him, so that was good. Realistically, there were probably three feet of space between us. I was as close to the edge of the bed as I could get without falling off. He'd probably done the same thing.

Risking a quick peek, I opened my eyes just a crack. His back was to me, the covers pulled up to his shoulder. In the darkness, I couldn't tell what he was wearing.

I'd never given it a lot of thought, but sharing a bed was awfully intimate. There was a certain vulnerability to it. Shepherd was an exceedingly private person, and he never made decisions without careful consideration. The fact that he trusted me enough for this was oddly touching.

It made me want to be the best fake girlfriend ever.

## 12

## SHEPHERD

*I*t took me a few seconds to realize I hadn't pressed the button to my floor after I'd stepped into the elevator. That would explain why the doors had slid closed, but I wasn't moving. I hit twenty-seven and felt the elevator begin to rise.

For the second time in less than a week, I hadn't slept well. Except that last night, instead of being haunted by visions of a woman in a red dress, I'd had a woman who smelled like fucking heaven lying next to me.

How the hell did she smell *that* good? I'd never noticed it before. Although I'd never been in such close quarters with her for a long period of time. Her scent was subtle, nothing overpowering. She smelled like strawberries, which I would never have considered an appealing way for a woman to smell before Everly. But she did, and it was delicious... and distracting as hell.

Her scent must have been from something she'd used in the bath. I was certain she hadn't been trying to tempt me with anything by taking a bath—and leaving the door open a crack—but the effect had been dramatic. The thought of her lying in my bathtub, naked, had been overwhelmingly arousing. I'd gone back to my office to calm down and wound up rubbing one out in a futile attempt to relax. I'd come fast, and hard, but I'd still been plagued with yet another uncooperative erection as soon as I'd smelled her in my bed.

I was a man, I had needs. But I was accustomed to being in control of those needs. Everly had me feeling out-of-control, and it was enormously uncomfortable. I didn't know what was wrong with me.

I hadn't counted on any of this when I'd asked her to pose as my girlfriend.

The elevator dinged and the doors opened. Clearing my throat, I straightened the collar of my coat and walked to my office.

She was already here—she was always here before I arrived, wasn't she?—and she stood, my coffee in her hand, as soon as she saw me.

I couldn't look her in the eyes. My body was already reacting to the memory of that little splash of water—the sound I'd heard when I'd paused by the bathroom door. I'd been overcome with the image of her bare legs tipping apart, revealing a shimmery view of her pussy.

God, I was doing it again.

"Good morning, Mr. Calloway."

Her voice was hesitant, and I didn't answer. Just walked into my office, knowing she'd follow. Wondering if she still smelled like summer.

I heard the click of her heels behind me. Why did she have me so disconcerted? It must have been the sleep deprivation. I took sleep—as well as exercise and proper diet—very seriously. The lack of sleep was clearly getting to me.

Regardless of what was going on, I needed her out of my office as quickly as possible.

"So... okay," she said as I hung my coat. "I guess... your schedule. Sorry. It's... this is... should we talk about things, or..."

No, I didn't want to talk. I wanted to have my coffee and focus on contract negotiations and cash flow reports. Anything to get my head back in the game where it needed to be.

I moved past her and sat at my desk. "Just my schedule."

Her face fell and I instantly regretted what I'd said.

"Of course." She swallowed, the emotion disappearing from her expression, and brought out her phone. "You have a ten o'clock with—"

"Everly."

She stopped, pressing her lips together.

"Close the door."

Without looking at me, she walked over and closed the door, then took a seat on the other side of my desk.

"What do you want to talk about?" I asked.

"I'm just not sure how to act when we're here. Are we pretending? Are we pretending we're trying to hide it? Are we pretending that we're not pretending?"

She did have a point. We needed our stories to be consistent. I didn't want this to become more of a distraction at work than it already was. "When we're here, we're all business. Keeping it strictly professional."

"What if word gets out that I'm living with you? Am I supposed to deny we're together?"

"Your personal life is personal. You don't have to deny anything, but you're not obligated to share details, either."

"Okay. That seems reasonable. So, we can act normal

when we're here. The pretending is mostly for your dad and the harpy anyway."

"Precisely."

She nodded, appearing to relax, and that smile she always wore returned. "Okay, then."

I tried to focus as she launched into a rundown of my schedule. She had things well in hand, as she always did. Her calm voice was soothing, and by the time she finished debriefing, my mind was clear. I was still tired, but the coffee would help. And I was back to seeing Everly as my practical and efficient assistant.

Mostly.

She went out to her desk and I forced my eyes to my laptop screen. I had work to do. But her questions about our ruse had me thinking.

It wasn't going to be enough for Everly to simply sleep in my bedroom at night. If that was the extent of our fabricated relationship, it was going to become apparent rather quickly that something was missing. My dad would notice—and start asking questions.

That was something I wanted to avoid. I couldn't have my father doubting the veracity of this relationship. And the answer was quite simple.

I needed to date her.

Taking Everly out regularly would make it clear that we were indeed a couple. Dad wouldn't have reason to question things, regardless of anything Svetlana might put into his ear. Taking her out on evenings or weekends would keep office gossip to a minimum. And we'd be home less, therefore less likely to be around Svetlana if she was visiting my father.

Besides, dinners with Everly wouldn't be a bad way to spend some evenings. She was pleasant company.

I was about to message her, asking her to make a reservation, when I stopped. She always made my dinner reservations when I had a date. That was part of her job. But asking her, as my assistant, to make a dinner reservation for the two of us felt... odd, and somehow wrong.

Instead, I looked up the number to El Gaucho and called them myself. Made a reservation for Friday evening for two.

## 13

# EVERLY

*A* message from Shepherd popped up on the bottom of my screen. My eyes darted around, as if I needed to be careful of who was watching. Which was ridiculous. No one was paying attention to my computer screen. And he sent me messages all the time. I was his assistant. That was how this worked.

But for some reason, that little notification, less than five minutes before I was scheduled to leave for the day, felt ominous. And not in the sense that I was afraid he was about to dump a bunch of work on me and I'd have to stay late, or work on Saturday. In the sense that I had a feeling it wasn't about work.

It was Friday, and we'd managed to navigate our first week as boss and assistant by day, fake boyfriend and girlfriend by night. Things at work had been more or less normal. Of course, there was the part where he said good morning when he walked by my desk, and thanked me for things sometimes. But other than that, normal.

With the exception of the sleeping in the same bed thing —which was getting easier every night—faking the relationship was a breeze. Shepherd worked late a lot, and when he was home, he spent time in his office. I'd decided the best thing to do to ensure that his dad—and Svetlana—believed our little game was to make myself at home. So I helped myself to his beautiful gourmet kitchen and cooked a few meals. I laid in my bean bag chair to read. Did yoga in the living room. I added my collection of coffee mugs to the cupboard, and even sat out on the balcony with a glass of wine after dinner last night.

Richard was nice, and seemed to be trying his best to be unobtrusive. He was friendly, but he tended to keep to himself when Shepherd was home. Svetlana was not nice— she glared daggers at me whenever she saw me—but she hadn't been around enough to make things terribly uncomfortable. Yet.

With another quick glance at Steve to make sure he didn't seem suspicious—I really didn't want him to find out about this—I clicked on the notification from Shepherd.

**Shepherd:** Dinner tonight at seven.

I checked his calendar, but I didn't see anything. I didn't remember him mentioning a dinner. That was odd. What was he talking about?

**Me:** You don't have anything on your calendar tonight. Do you need me to add it?

**Shepherd:** No, I made reservations for seven.

Oh my god, had he asked me to make dinner reservations and I'd forgotten? I never forgot things, not even the tiniest detail. It was one of the reasons I was so good at my job.

**Me:** Did you ask me to and I forgot? You could have just reminded me.

**Me:** But I don't remember you asking.

**Me:** Am I going crazy?

**Shepherd:** Come here.

I minimized our conversation and went into his office. His brow furrowed as he looked at me.

"I'm sorry if I missed something. I guess I've been a little off this week—"

"Everly."

I closed my mouth and pressed my lips together.

"I made dinner reservations for us."

"Dinner?"

"Yes, dinner. The meal that usually takes place after work. And sometimes people have dinner together. At a restaurant."

Oh my god, was he teasing me? My mouth turned up in a small smile. "Shepherd, are you making a joke?"

He sighed and glanced away, as if annoyed, but I could see the hint of a smile on his face. "I figured we should have dinner together."

"Oh," I said, feeling like a dork. "Right, like a date. Because we're... I get it."

"Yes."

I crossed my arms. "Aren't you supposed to ask me?"

"Ask you what?"

"Out on a date."

His jaw hitched. "You want me to ask you? We're supposed to be—"

"Dating."

"And living together."

"Well, I know, but how'd you know I'd be free for dinner?"

"Because you're dating *me*."

Why was his emphasis on the word *me* so freaking sexy?

"Fake-dating you. I could have had plans." I could practically hear his teeth grinding. Riling him up was fun, but I didn't want to take it too far. "I meant with my girl-friends."

He appeared to relax. At least he no longer looked like he was in danger of popping a blood vessel. "Fine. Everly, would you like to have dinner with me tonight?"

"Why, yes, Shepherd, I'd love to."

"Seven," he said, turning back to his laptop.

"Lovely," I said, and went back to my desk.

Wait, this was not lovely. I had to go on a date with him? A real, actual date?

I had terrible luck when it came to dating. I was basically the queen of first date disasters. But maybe this didn't count as a *first* date. We'd gone to the gala together. Of course, that had been fake. But so was this.

I needed help, so I texted Nora.

*Me: 911. Shepherd is taking me on a date.*

*Nora: What's the emergency? Do you need an outfit?*

*Me: No. Maybe. But that's not the emergency.*

*Nora: ...*

*Me: Did you read my text? A date, Nora. DATE.*

*Nora: A fake date or a real date?*

*Me: Real. I mean, it's all fake, but we're actually going on a date.*

*Nora: Again, what's the emergency? Do you need shoes?*

*Me: No. Maybe. That's not the point. Is this a first date? Or was the gala our first date?*

*Nora: Does it matter?*

*Me: Yes. It matters. You know how first dates are for me.*

*Nora: Oh god, you're right. Let's count the gala as your first date. Better?*

*Me: Much.*

*Nora: Shoes? How about the mint heels?*

*Me: You're the best. I'll stop by on my way home.*

Letting out a relieved breath, I put down my phone. Tonight was our second date. Good. I could handle a second date. And I loved Nora's mint heels. Sharing a shoe size with Nora Lakes was one of my life's greatest blessings.

THE MINT HEELS WERE PERFECT. I paired them with a black mini-dress. A little sexy, maybe—it did show a lot of leg— but I was only trying to play the part.

Plus, this dress did look pretty great on me.

Shepherd was waiting for me near the front door. He'd changed into a different suit—this one deep blue with a coordinating tie. The color made his eyes pop.

His eyebrows lifted ever so slightly as I approached with my coat draped over my arm. "You look... very nice."

"Thank you," I said with a smile.

I heard voices in the other room—Richard and Svetlana —and it sounded like they were heading our direction. Shepherd and I locked eyes and gave each other the subtlest of nods.

Shepherd took my coat and stepped in close to help me put it on. He was so imposing when he stood near me like this. So tall and undeniably masculine. Moving slowly, he guided each sleeve over my arms, drawing out the process while Richard and Svetlana came into view.

With gentle hands, Shepherd swept my hair out of the collar of my coat, his eyes on my face. I couldn't stop staring at him. At his fierce eyes and square jaw. This close, his scent was almost intoxicating. How could a man smell so good all the time? Honestly, did he have a single flaw?

There was the part where he was a robot with no feelings. At least, that was what I tried to tell myself as I fell prey to his hypnotic gaze and man-heaven scent.

He traced a thumb down the side of my face, his touch sending a zap of electricity through my veins. Why was he... Did he just... Where was I?

Richard cleared his throat, snapping me out of my stupor. Right. They were watching. This was part of the act.

"Sorry to interrupt such a tender moment," Richard said.

Svetlana's features were carefully neutral, her jaw relaxed. But her eyes were once again shooting daggers at me. Swords, even. Or maybe laser beams. I had to stifle a giggle at the momentary image of Svetlana with glowing red eyes.

"It's fine, Dad," Shepherd said. "We were just leaving."

"Date night?" Richard asked, his eyes crinkling with a smile.

"Indeed," Shepherd said, draping a possessive arm around my shoulders. "You?"

"Casual night in," Richard said.

I wondered if Svetlana had known they weren't going out before she'd come over. She wasn't dressed for a night in —at least not by my standards. She wore a form-fitting blouse with a plunging neckline with a pair of flowy pants and gold stilettos.

I decided to pretend she'd expected an expensive dinner —likely what I was getting—and gave them both a sweet smile. "That sounds fun. Have a good night, you two. Don't wait up." I winked at Richard.

He grinned back at me. "Have a great time."

With his arm still around my shoulders, Shepherd steered me out into the hallway. As soon as the door closed behind us, he let go and shifted so there were several inches of space between us.

Right. Faking it. Our audience was gone.

I took a deep breath to center myself as we walked to the elevator. Maybe it was catty of me, but the fact that Shepherd was taking me out to a nice dinner—treating me to something Svetlana likely wanted—gave me warm fuzzies.

Shepherd was quiet on the ride down the elevator to the parking garage. He didn't say much on the way to the restaurant, either. I was used to that. And being with Shepherd like this—outside of work—had grown increasingly comfortable. I didn't feel the need to fidget, or try to make conversation as we drove. I sat with my legs crossed, admired my cute heels once or twice, and watched the bright lights of the city twinkle in the evening darkness.

We pulled up to the curb and a valet opened my door and helped me out of the car. Shepherd was there a second later, offering me his arm. That was interesting. This date was only to maintain the charade that we were indeed dating, but there wasn't anyone out here who knew us. We didn't have to act too couple-ish. But maybe he figured we were better safe than sorry.

I took his arm and we walked into the dimly lit restaurant. El Gaucho was beautiful, with glamorous retro decor and live piano music in the background. Shepherd helped me out of my coat, then pulled out my chair for me before taking his own.

We got menus and ordered drinks. A martini for me—gin, with a twist—and a Manhattan for him.

"Do you know what you'd like?" he asked.

I pursed my lips as I perused the menu. "Probably the fish. Definitely not steak."

"Do you not eat red meat?"

"No, I do. It's just…" I hesitated, not sure if I wanted to share the details of one of my worst bad first dates. But I guess it didn't matter. It wasn't like I was here to impress him. "The one time I had dinner here, I choked on a piece of steak. My date just kind of watched in horror while a lady from a nearby table did the Heimlich maneuver on me. Then in the aftermath, he ditched me and stuck me with the bill."

Shepherd blinked once. "Is that a joke?"

"Unfortunately, no. It actually happened."

"You were choking and he left you here?"

I nodded. "Yeah. I don't exactly have great luck in the dating department. Especially when it comes to first dates. That's probably the worst one, though." I paused, the menu loose between my fingertips. "Well, maybe not the worst."

"What could be worse than that?"

"Well, let's see. There was the guy who was trying to find women who looked like his ex-girlfriend," I said. "He asked me to take a selfie with him, even though we'd only just met for coffee. And then he sent it to his ex, who also happened to be working right next door. She marched over and they got in an argument. It was really awkward."

Shepherd's brow furrowed. "I don't know what to say to that."

"I know," I said with a sigh. "The guy who took me to a wedding on the first date was pretty bad, too. It was two hours away and I didn't have my own car. Everyone got really drunk and got in a cake food-fight. He left me there because I didn't want to go to a hotel for a threesome with him and a drunk bridesmaid."

"I can't tell if you're kidding," he said.

"Nope. And then there was the guy who kind of muscled me into playing a no-hands balloon-popping game at a bar.

He got stabbed in the... well, you know." I pointed downward. "With the pin that had been holding the balloon to my clothes. Served him right, though. This was after he grabbed my hips and started thrusting his crotch against me to pop the balloon."

I pressed my lips closed to stop myself from making this worse. Why was I telling him all these stories?

But instead of continuing to eye me like I was crazy, he smiled, laughing softly. "That's... awful."

"Yeah, it was. Needless to say, there weren't second dates in any of those cases."

"I should hope not."

"Like I said, I don't have great luck. Obviously, I'm here with you, aren't I?" I closed my eyes again. "That came out wrong. I just meant—"

"Everly, stop," he said. "It's okay, I know what you meant. And I have to agree with you on the bad luck. That's an impressive list of horror stories."

I stopped myself from telling him that those weren't the only ones. But at a certain point, it was going to start making me look pathetic. "Yeah, it's pretty bad."

"You're not the only one who's had bad dates."

"Well, I know that. Most people have a bad date story or two. But you can't mean *you*."

He raised his eyebrows. "I once went on a date with a woman who drank an entire bottle of champagne while we were waiting for our dinner. By the end of the meal, she'd hit on the man next to us, cried twice, called an ex-boyfriend, had a lengthy debate with the bartender about someone on a reality show, and taken off her bra by doing that thing women do when they slip it out the sleeve of their top."

I covered my mouth, trying not to laugh. "You're kidding."

He shook his head. "I wish I was."

"I'm sorry, I'm not laughing *at* you. I guess it's nice to know I'm not alone in the terrible date department."

He lifted his glass and raised an eyebrow. "To no more bad dates."

I clicked my glass against his. "Cheers to that."

After dinner—during which there was absolutely zero choking—Shepherd drove us home. The food had been delicious, the conversation interesting and fun. I'd had a great time. If it had been a real date, I would have gone home giddy, floating on a cloud of endorphins, and texted my girlfriends to gush about what an amazing time I'd had.

But I didn't. It had been a great evening, but instead of making me feel light and happy, it made me a little bit sad. Because none of it had been real.

## 14

### SHEPHERD

*T*he waiting room at the oncologist's office was surprisingly comfortable. Light gray walls. Soft lighting. A large saltwater fish tank took up almost an entire wall.

I'd spoken with my dad's doctor when we'd first arrived. I wanted to make sure there wasn't anything Dad had been keeping from us regarding his illness or treatment plan. He hadn't been. His prognosis was good, his course of treatment what I expected.

I flipped through my messages on my phone while I waited. I'd left the office early so I could come to his appointment, but it looked like I hadn't missed much. Everly had things well in hand. In fact, she'd probably gone home for the evening.

Everly. My gaze slipped from my phone screen, my eyes losing focus. She was so perplexing. At work she was as competent as ever. Smart, punctual, efficient. But she wasn't just my assistant anymore, and the change was seriously fucking with my head.

She padded around my condo barefoot, in tank tops and

shorts that showed all kinds of skin. Hair up off her neck, tempting me. She happily wished me good morning, or good night, always in that bright, cheery voice. Always with a smile. She sat in her hideous yellow bean bag chair with a book or drank wine with my dad, their laughter carrying to every corner of my home.

Moving her in with me had been my idea, but I hadn't counted on her presence being such a mindfuck. She was everywhere, a constant distraction. Flitting through my thoughts in those tantalizing pajamas. Sleeping next to me, making my sheets smell like strawberries.

"Shepherd?"

I blinked, glancing up at my father. He raised his eyebrows and I had a feeling he'd been trying to get my attention.

"Finished?" I asked.

"Yes, finally. Sorry, son, I didn't think we'd be here this long."

I stood and pocketed my phone. "It's fine."

We went out to the parking garage and got in my car. I glanced at my dad a few times as we headed home. He'd been uncharacteristically quiet this afternoon. The appointment with his doctor had gone fine. Perhaps things were already cooling off with Svetlana—that could account for his solemn mood.

What if he was about to end things with her? Or she with him? That would mean an end to the charade with Everly. That thought was oddly alarming.

"Are you all right?" I asked. "You seem quiet."

"Yes, I'm fine," he said, in a voice that indicated he was anything but.

"Dad."

"All right. I'm concerned about my financial situation.

I'm not getting any younger, and I lost a lot of money. I can't keep living with you indefinitely."

So it wasn't Svetlana that was bothering him. I didn't know whether to be frustrated or relieved.

"Look, we'll figure it out," I said. "We have a plan to get you back on your feet."

"I just wish I hadn't put you in this position."

"There's no need for you to feel guilty. You took some risks and they didn't pay off. The timing could have been better, all things considered, but you'll be fine. You always bounce back."

A slow smile spread across his face. "Thank you, son. I appreciate that."

By the time we got back to my building, he was his usual cheerful self. We rode the elevator up to my penthouse. Dad thanked me again for taking him to his appointment before disappearing down the hallway toward his room.

I was already distracted by Everly.

She was here. I'd seen her car in the parking garage—in the spot next to mine—but that wasn't why I knew. My skin buzzed with electricity, the hairs on my arms standing on end. Where was she? Curled up on the couch, texting her friends? Flitting around the kitchen making a mess? Maybe soaking in the bath again?

I paused just inside the door, imagining Everly naked in my bathtub. Her tits floating in soapy water. Her knees gently tipping open, the water lapping against the sides of the tub.

A voice in the other room jolted me out of my momentary fantasy. A voice I did not want to hear. Svetlana. "How nice."

Who was she talking to? I couldn't see her from where I

was standing. It sounded like she was in the hallway near my office.

"I thought so."

Oh no. That was Everly. Why were they together? They must not have heard us come in.

"There's something I need to say, woman to woman," Svetlana said. "Whatever it is you think you have with Shepherd, it isn't real. He's not capable of a real relationship. At least not long-term. I should have seen it sooner, but that was my mistake. I don't want you to wind up like me."

"Like you?" Everly asked. "Do you mean dating his father?"

"No. My meeting Richard was fate. The fact that he's Shepherd's father is a... strange coincidence."

"I don't really buy that," Everly said. There was nothing antagonistic or confrontational in her voice. Just a simple statement of fact.

"Believe what you will," Svetlana said. "I don't blame you for being suspicious. That's why I wanted to talk to you. Richard is a wonderful man. But Shepherd..."

Everly's voice was hard. "What about Shepherd?"

My feet moved me closer to the hall, almost as if they were operating outside my control.

"He's not one of those cold businessmen who's soft on the inside. If that type even exists. He's calculating and ruthless. I'm concerned you don't understand what you've gotten yourself into by dating him."

"I've known Shepherd for a long time," Everly said. "I know exactly what I've gotten myself into."

"I don't think you do. Shepherd doesn't care about you, and he's certainly not going to change for you. He's not in love with you, Everly. That man doesn't love anyone, except himself. I wouldn't get comfortable here. You won't be staying."

"I suppose you would think that," Everly said.

"I'm trying to help you. Shepherd is going to use you and cast you aside without a second thought."

"Shepherd is not the sort of man to use people and spit them out like chewed-up gum," Everly said, the heat in her tone rising with every word. "He's a good man who cares about the people in his life. And maybe he hasn't been in a long-term relationship, but he just hadn't found the right woman."

"Everly, don't be silly."

"I'm not being silly. Not in the least. He's in love with me, and we're very committed to each other."

"Perhaps it seems that way now, but it won't last."

"No? Then why did he propose?"

I stopped, my body freezing in place. Did she just say propose? As in marriage?

"He... what?" Svetlana asked.

"He proposed," Everly said. "We're getting married."

"You're getting married?" Dad asked.

His voice made me jump and I whipped around. I hadn't heard him approach.

"What?" I asked, as if I hadn't just heard what she said.

"Why didn't you tell me?" Dad smiled and I swear to god, his eyes were sparkling.

"Richard, you're home," Svetlana said. She and Everly both stepped out of the hall.

"Wonderful, we're all here." Dad smiled at Svetlana, then wrapped Everly in a hug. "Congratulations. This is such great news."

I stared at Everly, my jaw clenched. Why the hell had she

said we were *engaged*? She looked back at me, her eyes wide while Dad hugged her.

"Dad, you can let go of her now." I grabbed his arm and nudged him back.

He chuckled. "Don't worry, son, she's all yours. I'm thrilled. When's the wedding?"

Everly gestured with her hands. "Oh, well, we haven't exactly talked about—"

"No, we haven't." I stepped forward and took her arm. "Honey, I thought we agreed to keep it quiet for now?"

"Well, sweetie, you know how it is," Everly said. "A girl gets excited about these things."

"Of course you're excited," Dad said. "Oh, Shep, we need to throw you an engagement party. Svetlana loves parties. She can help me plan. Don't worry, we'll take care of everything."

Svetlana's expression was uncharacteristically shocked. Her mouth moved like she was trying to speak but couldn't find the right words.

"That does sound fun," Everly said.

Oh my god. Grinding my teeth together, I tightened my grip on Everly's arm and pulled her toward the bedroom. "Our schedule is already very full, Dad, but thank you. Everly, can I see you in the other room?"

I didn't wait for either of them to reply. Just led Everly down the hall and shut the bedroom door behind us.

She held her hands up. "Okay, before you get mad—"

"What were you thinking?" I hissed. "Engaged? Why did you tell her I proposed?"

Her lips parted and those blue eyes of hers seemed to get bigger. "If you'd heard what she said—"

"I *did* hear what she said. Who cares what she thinks?"

Squaring her shoulders, she crossed her arms. "I care. I

know that you don't use people. I mean, sure, the women you date always fit the same mold, so it's no wonder your relationships don't last. But I couldn't let her get away with saying those things about you. Not when she's the one who uses people. She's using your dad, and he's one of the nicest men I've ever met."

I almost asked her to clarify what she meant by *no wonder your relationships don't last*. But we had a more pressing issue to deal with. "Did you hear my dad? He wants to throw an engagement party."

"So?"

Groaning, I turned away. I'd simply have to tell my dad we didn't have time in our schedules for a party. "I'll deal with my dad. But you just made this much more complicated."

"I know. I'm sorry. It just sort of came out."

"Fine. I'm going to the office."

"Now?" she asked. "You don't have to leave. Shep—"

"I have things to do." It wasn't exactly a lie. "I'll be back late."

Her shoulders slumped and she sighed. "Okay. I'll see you later."

A very odd desire poked at the edges of my mind. I thought about gathering her in my arms. Comforting her. Rubbing her back while I smelled her hair.

I walked out, leaving her alone, before I did something stupid.

## 15

### EVERLY

$\mathcal{I}$ hadn't been this anxious at work since my first day. Then, I'd been worried about normal new job stuff, like whether I'd get along with my coworkers, spill coffee on my boss, or walk out of the bathroom with the back of my skirt tucked into the waist.

Not that those last two things had ever happened.

Okay, yes they had.

Today, I was worried about how mad my boss was after I'd accidentally elevated our relationship from fake-dating to fake-engaged.

Shepherd hadn't come home last night until late. I'd been half asleep when he'd finally come to bed. He'd silently slipped beneath the sheets like he always did. And maybe I'd been imagining things, but it had seemed like he'd stayed even closer to the edge of the bed on his side than usual.

I hadn't meant to blurt out that we were engaged. It wasn't like that had been part of our plan, so I understood why Shepherd was frustrated. But Svetlana made me so angry. I was usually something of a conflict avoider—or conflict smoother-overer, really—but I just couldn't deal with her. She had the nerve to say Shepherd was just using me? As if *he'd* been the problem in their relationship? Shepherd was many things, but at his core, he was a good man.

Maybe I should have just called her a gold-digging harpy and outed her to Richard. As far as I knew, he still didn't know she'd dated Shepherd first. But Shepherd had asked me not to tell, and I wanted to respect that.

Although saying we were engaged probably hadn't been a better tactic.

He came into the office and we went through our morning routine—minus the pleasantries and *good morning*s I'd grown accustomed to recently. I did my best to put it all out of my mind and simply do my job.

Besides, I already knew what I was going to do. I was going to tell Richard that I'd gotten ahead of myself. That I'd jumped to the conclusion that Shepherd was proposing based on something he'd said, but that we weren't officially engaged. I'd tell him I cared about his son very much and apologize for putting everyone in an awkward position last night.

It felt like layering lies on top of lies. I hadn't thought about that part when I'd agreed to the ruse. But sharp points of guilt pricked at me every time I looked at Richard. He was so nice and friendly—and so excited to see his son in what appeared to be a serious relationship. And I'd gone and made it worse, getting his hopes up that his son would finally get married.

But it was okay. I'd fix it.

I didn't want to think about how we were going to tell him that our entire relationship was only for show. Maybe we'd have to fake a break-up. That wouldn't be too hard, especially with the way Shepherd was currently ignoring me.

With a heavy sigh, I turned back to my computer.

"Everything okay over there?" Steve asked. He was wearing a navy sweater vest over a blue plaid short-sleeved shirt and he gave me a friendly smile.

"Yeah, I'm fine. Just some personal stuff."

"You know what I do when I'm stressed?"

"What?"

"Spend some time at the cat cafe."

I blinked at him. "What's a cat cafe?"

"It's called Neko, over on Capitol Hill. They serve drinks and snacks, and you can hang out with their cats. Some are permanent residents, and some are still looking for their forever homes. It's very relaxing."

"Wow, I had no idea that sort of thing existed."

He nodded. "I was there just last week. I've been thinking about adopting a brother or sister for Millie, but I'm not sure how well she'd get along with another feline."

"That is an issue."

"It's important to consider the needs of your current pet when deciding whether to introduce a new animal into your home."

"Of course." My phone rang so I gave Steve an apologetic smile. "I should take this."

He waved his hand, as if to shoo me away. "Of course, of course. Back to work."

I picked up my phone, but it wasn't a work call. It was Annie. "Hey, sis."

"Hey, how's your day going?"

I could practically feel Shepherd's silent presence in his office behind me, the weight of his displeasure sitting heavily on my shoulders. "Um, it's fine. How about you?"

"I'm good. Are you free for lunch? I'm downtown and I thought we could get together."

"Yeah, I'm free."

"Great. Should I come up to your office, or…"

For some reason, I didn't like the idea of Annie being near Shepherd right now. It wasn't like she wanted *him;* she wasn't even attracted to men. But the idea of her trying to sneak a peek into his office or eying him like he was an interesting genetic specimen made my back clench tight.

"That's okay, I'll just meet you at that sandwich place or something. Does that sound good?"

"Sure, that's perfect. Noon?"

"Yep. I'll see you then."

Shepherd didn't leave his office all morning. He had a lunch meeting, but I'd already sent him his schedule for the day. He didn't message me with any requests. I wasn't sure what I wanted from him. An excuse to go into his office so we could talk, maybe. I just didn't like the feeling of this problem between us simmering in the background.

I had to leave to meet Annie before his meeting, but he didn't need anything from me, so I just left. The restaurant wasn't far from my building. The fresh air felt good as I walked, as did the sun on my face. The sidewalk was busy with pedestrians—lots of people dressed in business casual attire, heading to lunch meetings or taking a break with friends or coworkers. Music spilled out of a bar on the corner and I wistfully imagined that I was meeting Nora and Hazel for lunch mimosas, rather than my sister for sensible salads.

Annie was waiting at the restaurant and the host took us to our table. I followed her lead, ordering water to drink and a salad with grilled chicken.

"So, what's new?" she asked.

I hadn't said a word to her about my current living situation. For all she knew, my life was still the same. Living in my cute, if small, apartment in the same building as Nora and Hazel. Going to work, like everything was normal. Three-mile runs and girls' nights with martinis.

She had no idea I was living in a palatial penthouse with my wealthy, and very private, boss. Trading banter with his father over morning coffee. Doing yoga in his living room and sipping wine in the evenings on a balcony that overlooked the city. Sleeping next to him in his bed, on the softest, most luxurious sheets I'd ever felt. Trying very hard to ignore the way my body responded to his scent.

"Oh, you know, not much. What about you?"

She took a bite of her salad and shrugged. "Not much. Work has been crazy the last few weeks. I feel like I could be there twelve hours a day, seven days a week and still not catch up."

"That's tough. I hope you're taking some me-time to recharge."

"Yeah, Miranda has been making me. She can always tell when I need a break. You know how she is with self-care and all that."

"Good."

"Oh, before I forget." She brought out her soft leather briefcase and pulled out a manila folder. "This is the paperwork for Mr. Calloway. We had a contract drawn up by a lawyer with experience in both genetic material donations, and more traditional adoptions. He's welcome to have his lawyer look at it and we're open to any changes he might want to make."

I swallowed hard and tried to keep my hand from trembling as I took the folder. "Thanks, but I haven't had a chance to bring it up. And honestly, Annie, I'm still not sure this is the best idea."

She smiled. "I have complete faith in you."

It was suddenly difficult to look my sister in the eyes. I tucked the folder beneath my purse on the chair next to me, focusing on my lunch. "Thanks."

The stack of paperwork seemed to whisper at me all through lunch. Annie didn't bring it up again, but I couldn't stop thinking about it. The whole thing was making me slightly nauseated, but I couldn't understand why. Annie and Miranda didn't have malicious motives. They weren't after his money, and I was sure the contract spelled that out in exacting detail. They simply wanted the best match for their hoped-for child. They liked his physical and intellectual traits—and who could blame them. Shepherd was basically perfect.

Other than being a robot, of course.

But damn it, he wasn't a robot. Not at all. He seemed like one at work—and he'd certainly been back to his old robotic self this morning. But underneath it all, there was a lot more to Shepherd Calloway than met the eye.

Which, when I thought about it, made him an even better candidate to be their sperm donor.

It was probably a good thing this hadn't been a mimosa or martini lunch. I managed to get through the meal without blurting out anything about living with Shepherd, pretending to be his girlfriend, or the fake-fiancée mess I'd gotten myself into.

After saying goodbye to Annie, I took my time walking back to my office, the folder with the donor contract tucked beneath my arm. I still had no idea how I was going to ask Shepherd. Or if I really could. When he'd asked me to pose as his girlfriend, it had seemed like the perfect lead-in. I'd do him this very large favor. He could at least *consider* doing me this favor in return. Even if he ultimately said no, at least I'd have tried. I wasn't going to insist or guilt him into it. It was a business deal. He dealt with those every day. He could determine if the terms were favorable and make his decision from there.

But I still hated the idea of even asking. Now more than ever.

I shuffled back to my desk, absent the usual spring in my step. Steve gave me a sympathetic smile, but didn't have any more cat-themed suggestions for dealing with stress. I put the folder away in my desk drawer and sat down, telling myself I needed to focus on work. Not on the fact that Shepherd was mad at me, or how I was ever going to broach the subject of him donating his sperm to make my sister's baby dreams come true.

Shepherd's office door opened behind me and I almost jumped out of my chair. My back clenched as his footsteps approached. He was going to walk right by and not even look at me. I just knew it.

Although, what would be wrong with that? For three years, he'd walked by this desk numerous times a day without glancing at me. He'd never been friendly, and I hadn't expected him to be. Our working relationship had been simple and routine, and there had been nothing wrong with it.

But nothing was the same anymore. I was a big, swirling mess of feelings, and I had no idea what to do about it.

To my enormous shock, he didn't walk by. He stopped, the smooth lines of his expensive suit in my peripheral vision. I froze, my palms planted on my desk, my heart racing. I couldn't make myself look up.

"Everly?" His voice was deceptively soft, lacking the edge that usually told me he was frustrated or impatient.

I slowly lifted my gaze to meet his. That was a terrible idea. Those eyes. That jaw. That spot in his cheek where a dimple puckered if he smiled. I could almost see the little indent now, as if at any moment, his serious mask would melt away and he'd smile at me.

"Yes?" I managed to choke out.

"Come with me."

I cast a nervous glance at Steve. He looked stricken, his eyes wide, his mouth hanging open. He watched me get up, staring as if I were being led to my execution.

Unsure as to where we were going, or why, I snatched up my purse and followed Shepherd to the elevator. It felt as if all eyes were on me as we walked down the hallway. I held my purse close to my body, trying to keep my face neutral. Office gossip spread like wildfire, but I was pretty sure the worst anyone would say was that it looked like I was in trouble. Which, to be fair, I was—just not in the way they'd think.

Plus, Shepherd's robotic stoicism scared everyone. Any apparent fear on my face wouldn't be too surprising.

I didn't ask him where we were going as we rode down the elevator. He didn't offer any information, either. Just stood next to me, looking deliciously perfect in his suit and tie. That neatly trimmed stubble that would probably feel amazing against my—

God, why was I thinking like that? This fake relationship thing was messing with my head.

He led me to his car and I got in. Silence. We drove to another building and went in the parking garage. It hadn't registered where we were—what street or what building this was. Were we here for lunch? Should I have told him I'd already eaten? Hadn't he had a lunch meeting?

I was so absorbed in my thoughts, I blinked in surprise, realizing I was standing at street level in front of a glass door. Shepherd opened it and gestured for me to go inside.

I stepped into a world of soft beige and precisely positioned lighting. The room was lined with dark wood cabinets topped by glass display cases. Well-lit niches in the walls displayed sparkling necklaces, rings, and bracelets. The glass cases glittered with diamonds, gold, and platinum.

Oh my god. We were in Turgeon Raine, one of the best high-end jewelers in Seattle.

"What are we doing here?" I whispered. Which was a silly question. It was obvious what we were doing here. But I couldn't quite believe it.

Shepherd gently grabbed my elbow and leaned closer, speaking low into my ear. "If we're engaged, we need to play the part."

"Shepherd, you don't have to do this." I turned so I could meet his eyes. "I was going to talk to your dad tonight and tell him I misspoke. That we aren't officially engaged and there's definitely no need for a party."

His expression was soft as he gazed down at me. "It's all right. I think this way is better."

I smiled, relief filling me. We were okay.

And then Shepherd did a terrible thing. He smiled. That genuine, beautiful smile that showed his perfect teeth and puckered his adorable dimples. It squeezed my heart—hard. Made my traitorous body light up with little sparks and tingles. It was like a window into the real Shepherd, the man he kept hidden on the inside.

I liked that man. A lot. Far too much for my own good.

A woman with curly dark hair wearing a stylish pinstripe pantsuit and deep burgundy lipstick walked over, holding out her hand. "You must be Mr. Calloway. Welcome."

Her presence broke me from my trance. He'd made an appointment? He'd actually planned this.

"This is Everly." Shepherd's hand moved from my elbow across my back, to slide around my waist.

"Lovely to meet you, Everly, and congratulations on your engagement. I'm Shauna. If you'll follow me, please?"

Shepherd's hand on the small of my back was oddly reassuring as we followed Shauna past the glittering display cases and through a door. I glanced back, wondering why we weren't going to look through their selection. We'd passed dozens of engagement rings, if not more.

The room was the same soft beige, but the niches in the walls had some of the most opulent—and no doubt expensive—jewels I'd ever seen. A dark wood desk sat near the back wall, the shelves behind it decorated with exotic sculptures and a few pieces of jewelry in glass cases.

Shepherd pulled out a chair for me and we both sat on one side of the desk while Shauna took the other.

"I have some beautiful options for you." Shauna lifted a black cloth, revealing a variety of diamond rings held in a velvet tray. "We have many more to choose from, so if none of these speak to you, I'll be happy to show you more. But this should get you started."

Of course—a private showing. That's exactly how Shepherd would do this. I could feel his eyes on me, rather than the rings, as I gazed at the selection. One on the end instantly caught my eye. The band was rose gold, and it was much smaller than the rest, with a center stone surrounded by a halo of little diamonds.

"It looks like you're drawn to this one." Shauna plucked the ring off the tray and held it up. "Would you like to try it on?"

"Please." I held up my hand and she slipped the ring on my finger.

For a heartbeat, it felt like the stars all aligned, triumphant music played in the distance, and a beam of sunlight cut straight through the building to shine on my outstretched hand. It was perfect. The engagement ring of my dreams.

My heart squeezed again. I would have loved a ring like this. It was exactly what I'd always envisioned.

But I couldn't use it. I'd ruin it forever if I got fake-engaged with this ring. Not that I thought my someday-fiancé would buy this exact ring. But I was afraid I'd never be able to wear one like it if I wore one now, when this was all just for show.

"Hmm, I don't know." I took it off and handed it back to Shauna. "Maybe I should try a few more."

"How about I let you two peruse in private." She rose from her seat. "I'll come check on you in a little while. In the meantime, if you have any questions, or would like to see something else, please don't hesitate to ask."

"Thank you," I said, and Shepherd nodded to her.

Shauna left and I let out a long exhale. "This is so over-whelming."

"It seemed as if you liked that one." Shepherd gestured to the ring I'd tried on.

"I don't just like it. I love it."

"Then what's the problem?"

I lowered my voice, almost to a whisper, although no one was here. "I can't use my dream ring for a fake engagement."

Shepherd regarded me through narrowed eyes for a long

moment before speaking. "All right. Do you want to know which one I think we should choose?"

"I do, actually."

The ring he picked up from the tray was a simple solitaire—a platinum band with a single setting. But the simplicity ended there. The diamond was enormous. I didn't think I'd ever seen a diamond so large in person before.

"That?"

"Here." He motioned for me to give him my hand, so I let him slide the ring on my finger.

I held out my hand, fingers splayed, the giant rock glittering. I was surprised it didn't bend the light and cast rainbows all over the room. "This one?"

"We'll choose the diamond separately," he said. "So if you think it should be larger, that's not a problem."

"Larger? Are you joking?" I moved my hand closer to his face. "I can hardly lift this thing."

He laughed softly and there went another heart-squeeze. "It's not that big."

"Yes, it is. How do people function with rings this size? It'll get caught on everything."

"It's what Shepherd Calloway would buy his fiancée," he said, his voice nonchalant. "And it'll make Svetlana insane."

"You evil man." I couldn't help but grin at him. "You're right, this would make her crazy with jealousy. It's exactly what she'd want."

"She'll probably hope it'll give my dad ideas." He winced.

I held out my hand, looking at the monstrosity that was going to be my fake-engagement ring. "No, regardless of your dad's perceived wealth, that's not her goal. She wants you."

"I can't fathom how she thinks sleeping with my father is going to get her what she wants."

"Are you sure they're sleeping together, though?" I asked. It was something I'd wondered, but it wasn't the kind of thing you brought up to your boss slash fake boyfriend out of the blue. "He's receiving treatment for prostate cancer. He might not even be able to... you know. Plus, I've never seen her spend the night, and I'm almost positive he's never slept at her place. Not that you have to sleep over if you're having sex, but still. It does raise the question."

"Hm."

Since Shepherd didn't say anything else, I let the subject drop. After all, the whole situation was terribly awkward. I wished Shepherd would have just told his dad the truth right away. But since I'd gotten to know Richard, I'd caught some glimpses as to why. He was a sensitive man and he was already going through so much, what with his illness and financial crisis. And according to Shepherd, his relationships were always very short-lived, especially when the woman was considerably younger. He was clearly going through something and if Shepherd—and his brother, who had apparently encouraged Shepherd to keep quiet—thought this was best, maybe they were right.

One thing I was sure of: If and when Richard found out the truth, even if he was hurt, he'd understand that his sons did it to protect him. I just hoped he'd be able to forgive me for my part in it, too.

I held up my hand again. This was turning out to be so much more complicated than I'd ever thought. And the feelings simmering in my tummy weren't helping. I kept trying to tamp them down, keep them from flaring into an inferno of emotions. But it was a struggle.

Oh god, had Nora been right? Had I *caught feelings*?

No. Absolutely not, and this ring was proof. It was ostentatious and flashy, and nothing like the real me. A ring as fake as the engagement it represented.

I could still do this. It would be fine.

"All right, then. I think this is the one."

## 16

## SHEPHERD

*I* came home from the gym on Saturday to an empty house. My dad had gone somewhere with Ethan and Grant for the day. Everly had said she was going for a run, but she wasn't back yet.

It was so quiet. And empty.

I downed a glass of water in the kitchen. I liked it quiet. I'd lived alone for years, and never once thought of this place as feeling empty. But I found myself mildly disappointed that Everly wasn't here.

Why? I had work to do, anyway.

I needed a shower, so I went to my bedroom. Our bedroom? Evidence of Everly was everywhere. She kept her things neat, but I could see her yellow slippers next to the bed. A book on her nightstand. A pink tank top tossed on a chair. Her clothes peeked out from the partially open closet. So many colors. Pinks, yellows, and blues.

She was going out with her friends tonight. Glancing at her clothes made me wonder what she'd wear. That little black dress she'd worn when I'd taken her to dinner? My hands clenched into fists. She looked sexy as fuck in that dress, and I didn't like the idea of her wearing it to some random bar with her girlfriends.

Of course, she'd have a ring on her finger. A big one, at that. It had only taken a week to get her ring and she'd been wearing it for the last several days. My lips twitched in a half-smile. Her ring would certainly be a deterrent. No man would hit on her when she was wearing that thing.

Unexpected benefit of Everly now posing as my fiancée: She had my ring to mark her as mine.

It was something of a mindfuck to realize how much I liked that idea. She wasn't mine. In fact, I'd never thought of a woman that way before, even women I'd actually dated. So why did I enjoy the thought of her delicate fingers lifting her martini glass, an enormous diamond glittering on her left hand, declaring to the world that she was unavailable?

She was right about the ring. It was hideous. I knew it wasn't something she'd wear under normal circumstances. But nothing about this was normal, and the ostentation of the ring signified that.

And Svetlana eyed it with open envy, which meant it had been the right choice.

I stripped off my clothes and tossed them in the hamper while I waited for the shower to get hot. The bathroom was filled with Everly as well. Her toothbrush was on the counter, along with a few cosmetics, a hair brush, and a bottle of pink nail polish. The little pops of color looked so foreign and strange among my blue and gray decor.

Steam filled the air and I got into the shower. It felt good after a hard workout. I washed up and let the hot water stream over me. Closed my eyes and felt it run down my face.

When I opened my eyes, Everly's pink shampoo bottle caught my eye. I'd sniffed it before, so I knew it was why she smelled so fucking good. This, and something else that seemed to be just *her*. I couldn't explain it. I'd held this bottle to my nose more than once, trying to decipher what it was that made it so captivating. It smelled great, but on her? It was intensely arousing.

I grabbed it and flipped the top open. Took a deep breath. Strawberry. Why did this botanical something-or-other strawberry-scented shampoo do it for me? I had no idea, but my dick was waking up.

The scent reminded me of the way my bed smelled after she'd slept in it. The sound of the shower running and the times I'd pictured what she looked like standing here, beneath the streaming water. Or lying in my bathtub, her nipples glistening wet.

This train of thought, and the scent of strawberry shampoo in my nose, was making my hard-on worse. How had I gone three years with Everly as my assistant without ever thinking about her sexually, to living with her for a few weeks and practically losing control of my dick? I couldn't have counted the number of times I'd dealt with an unexpected erection since she'd moved in.

The pressure was frustratingly intense, but I couldn't stop thinking about her tits. What they'd look like dripping wet. Her hands slowly running over her body as she washed herself.

I smelled the shampoo again. Fuck it.

Squeezing a glob of pink into my hand, I inhaled as the scent of strawberries filled the air. Bracing myself with one hand against the tile, I grabbed my solid erection and started to stroke.

There was no point in fighting it now. I let the images of a naked Everly flit through my mind. All that smooth skin. Those curves. Her perky tits and tapered waist.

I liked imagining her in the bath, but my mind moved her to the bed. My hand gripped my dick tighter as I stroked up and down the length of my cock, still slow and deliberate. Thinking about Everly on her back, her hair fanned out over my sheets. Her hands on her tits, teasing her nipples. I'd climb on top of her and sink my cock in deep. Get lost in her pussy.

Stroking faster, I imagined her in my office. On her knees, my cock in her mouth, a wicked gleam in her eyes. Bent over my desk with her skirt hiked up to her waist, her luscious ass in the air. I'd pound her from behind while she whimpered my name, trying to stay quiet.

Fuck, this was good. The entire shower smelled like her and my dick was stiff in my hand. Grunting as my muscles tensed, I stroked it out hard. Faster. I was immersed in hot water, steam, and strawberry shampoo, riding the edge of climax. My dick pulsed as I started to come, the sweet release making my eyes roll back. I grunted again.

It wasn't sex, and it wasn't her, but it was pretty fucking good.

Leaning against the tile, I let my dick drop and caught my breath. What was I going to do about her? Fuck her and get it over with?

No. That wasn't really my style, but even if it had been, I knew it was a bad idea to get too close to her. Dad's fling would end, and there'd be no more reason for Everly to stay. We'd have to go back to what we'd been before—boss and assistant.

That ring didn't really make her mine.

I finished washing up, then got out of the shower and toweled off. No sound came from the bedroom to indicate Everly might be there, and when I peeked through the door, I found it empty. I dressed, putting on a white t-shirt and sweats. Everly had teased me the first time she'd seen me wearing sweats, saying she hadn't thought *casual Shepherd* existed. As if I walked around in a suit and tie even on weekends.

If she only knew. Casual Shepherd did exist, and not just the guy wearing sweats at home. I just didn't let people see him. Not anyone I knew personally, at least.

Relaxed from my shower, I wandered out to the kitchen to find something to eat, my mind already switching to work. I had proposals to review and a contract to go over. I'd get some food and spend the evening in my office tonight. Everly wouldn't be home, anyway.

Not that it mattered what she was doing. We'd gone on several dates-for-show recently, so why did I keep thinking about her plans for tonight? She didn't have to spend every evening with me.

I needed to get her out of my head.

Coming around the corner into the kitchen, I almost ran right into her. She yelped, clutching a silver water bottle to her chest.

"Oh my god, you scared me," she said. "I didn't hear you coming."

"Sorry. I didn't know you were home."

She was dressed in a blue tank top with a pair of skin-tight leggings that showed every curve. With her hair up in a ponytail and her skin glistening from her run, it made me want to lick her to see if she tasted salty.

Her full, pink lips parted in a bright smile. "That's okay, no harm done. Did you have a good workout?"

It took me two tries to get a word out. "Yeah."

"You okay?"

*No, I'm fucking distracted because I just gave myself an Everly-scented orgasm.*

Oh shit, what if she smelled me? I ran a hand through my hair, although that certainly wasn't what I'd used her shampoo for. "Fine. Just a lot on my mind."

She took a drink of her water. "Okay. I'll let you do your thing. Are you done with the shower? I need to take one."

Damn it, just the mention of her in the shower was getting me hard again. "Yeah, go ahead."

Her eyes narrowed and she tilted her head. "Are you sure you're feeling okay?"

"Yes."

She shrugged. "All right."

Just as she was about to walk away, her hands caught my attention. Her left hand, specifically. It was bare.

"Where's your ring?"

She held her hand out and glanced down at it. "Oh, I took it off to go running."

It was the oddest thing. We'd already decided that she wouldn't wear it in the office; she was concerned about the gossip and I agreed it was best to keep things quiet at work. But there was a deeply primal part of me that wanted to insist—no, command—that she wear my ring at all other times. Running, shopping, out with her friends drinking martinis—I wanted that ring on her finger.

But I stopped myself from insisting. Clenched my teeth and looked at her hand for a few seconds. She stood frozen, her arm outstretched, her eyes on my face.

I cleared my throat and moved past her into the kitchen. It didn't matter if she took it off to go running. It wasn't real. She wasn't my girlfriend, or my fiancée. She was just Everly, my assistant.

Except she wasn't. She was a hell of a lot more, and I didn't know what the fuck I was going to do about that.

## 17

## EVERLY

*T*he bar was crowded, with a playful energy filling the air. People milled around in small groups while an endless stream of anti-love songs played in the background. Crossed-out hearts hung from the ceiling and papered the side of the bar, an ode to tonight's theme—Stupid Cupid Saturday.

I sat at a tall table, already sipping a martini—dirty tonight—and tapped my high-heeled foot to a cover of "Love Stinks." Nora and Hazel had arrived after me and were at the bar, ordering their drinks. I was so glad we were having a girls' night. I hadn't seen them in a couple of weeks and with everything that had been going on, I wanted some normalcy. Saturday night out with the girls was perfect.

They made their way through the crowd to our table. Nora's hair was down, the thick waves framing her face. She wore a short black dress and the cutest red heels—the ensemble looked magnificent on her. Hazel was dressed in a cardigan over a blouse and pencil skirt. Adorable, in a Hazel sort of way. She adjusted her glasses as she and Nora each took a seat, setting their martinis on the table.

"What in the hell is that?" Nora asked, pointing at my ring.

I sighed. I'd considered leaving the ring at home, but the look Shepherd had given me when I'd told him I'd taken it off for my run had been so odd. He'd looked mad—sort of. Or maybe confused. It was hard to tell with him, and he hadn't said anything else. But I'd slipped it back on before I'd left, feeling like I should probably wear it when I went out. Even though it would mean fessing up to my friends about my fake-engagement debacle.

"It's an engagement ring," I said. "A *fake* engagement ring."

Nora visibly relaxed. "Oh, I see. It's not real. I was going to say, holy shit that rock is enormous."

"Oh, no—the diamond is real."

Her eyes widened and she stared at the monstrosity on my hand. "What?"

"I mean the engagement is fake. Obviously I'm not marrying Shepherd. But it's a real diamond."

"We're coming back to the part where you're pretending to be engaged now, because obviously you need to tell us what the fuck that's about," Nora said. "But look at that thing. He bought that? It's not on loan or something?"

"No, he bought it."

Hazel lifted my hand to inspect the ring up close. "That's quite the investment in an engagement that isn't real."

"It's ridiculous," I said. "I don't know how people wear things like this all the time. It keeps catching on everything."

"A worthy sacrifice," Nora said, her voice awed. "It's gorgeous."

I pulled it off my finger and held it out to her. "Want to try it on?"

"Do I ever." Nora smiled as she slipped the ring on. She held out her hand, manicured fingers splayed. "Oh yes."

"Should you start dropping hints to Max?" I asked, grinning at her. "An engagement ring looks good on you."

Nora glared at me and switched the ring to her right hand. "No thanks. We broke up anyway."

"Oh, I'm sorry."

"Don't be," she said, tilting her head to admire the ring. "He was pretty, and his dick wasn't bad, but I just wasn't that into him."

"But Everly," Hazel said, "why did he buy you an engagement ring? Was the ruse not convincing enough?"

"No, it was. But I kind of blurted out to Svetlana that Shepherd proposed."

"Why?"

I sighed again. "She came over while Shepherd was taking Richard to an appointment. I invited her in to wait and we ended up talking. She said she wanted to warn me about Shepherd. That I didn't know what I was getting into by dating him."

Nora rolled her eyes. "I'm sure she only had your best interests at heart."

"Hardly. That woman hates me. Anyway, she said Shepherd doesn't *do commitment*." I made air quotes. "And that he just uses people. She said he's cold and ruthless, and he'll cast me aside when he's done with me. It made me so mad. Shepherd isn't like that. It's true he doesn't usually date women for long, but look at the women he dates. They're like her. He's the one constantly being used, not them."

"So you tried to counter her argument by claiming to be engaged," Hazel said.

"Obviously I had to prove her wrong."

"Well, this must certainly have shut her up," Nora said,

pulling the ring from her finger. She handed it back to me and I put it on.

"I didn't want to get one this large, but Shepherd pointed out that it's what she would want. She saw me with it the other night and I have to admit, the look on her face was hilarious."

Nora sipped her drink, then set it back on the table. "I'd have paid good money to see that."

"Agreed," Hazel said.

As I sat with Nora and Hazel, chatting while we had a few drinks, I noticed something odd. No men approached our table. It wasn't like we got hit on every time we went out. But to be fair, it was rare to go a night in a place like this without someone showing an interest in at least one of us.

Tonight, it was as if the giant diamond on my finger acted as a man-repellent. Granted, the theme was anti-love —a celebration of being single. But I could tell that wasn't it. More than once I noticed a man eying our table, only to turn away as soon as his gaze found my left hand. No one approached Nora or Hazel, either, as if my ring created an invisible barrier that extended all the way around our little table.

I didn't mind, of course. I was here to spend time with my girlfriends, not meet someone. The relationship was fake, but I still wasn't going to cheat on Shepherd. When this was over, I could think about venturing back into the murky waters of the dating pool.

That thought made my shoulders slump and a sad feeling curl its way through my tummy. Svetlana was sure to lose interest in her game sooner rather than later, if Richard didn't decide to end it first. How long did we have? A few more weeks? A month? Glancing at the ring on my finger, I thought about going back to my apartment. Sleeping in my own bed again—alone. Only seeing Shepherd at work. Everything going back to normal.

Why did that make me so sad?

Pushing those thoughts from my mind—although they still simmered in the background—I focused on enjoying the night with my girls.

THE BED WAS empty when I woke up. Like I did every morning, I glanced around to see if Shepherd was here. Sleeping next to him had become much more comfortable —I wasn't going to think about how much I enjoyed the sound of his soft breathing—but I still felt awkward in the morning. I didn't want to roll out of bed with one of my boobs hanging out of my tank top or look up to find him naked after a shower.

Okay, that second one wouldn't have been so bad. But the boob thing was a real issue. Tank tops had a way of playing peek-a-boob on me while I slept.

He wasn't in the bedroom, and the bathroom door was ajar, the light off. It was safe to get up.

I used the bathroom, then changed into a t-shirt and my weekend shorts—they were too worn and faded to wear in public, but they were so comfortable, I couldn't get rid of them. I put my hair in a bun just to get it off my neck, slid my feet into my fuzzy yellow slippers, and went in search of coffee and breakfast.

Shepherd was in his office, absorbed in something on his laptop. I hesitated in front of his half-open door, debating whether to ask if he wanted breakfast. But he looked so busy, I didn't want to interrupt.

The kitchen in this place was magnificent. I wasn't a

gourmet cook by any stretch, but I did enjoy cooking a nice meal. And in this expanse of maple, stainless steel, and granite, cooking was a pleasure. The long countertops gave me plenty of space, and everything was top of the line.

I'd anticipated my Sunday-morning-after-girls'-night need for bacon and eggs—I was nothing if not a planner—so I had everything I needed. I made myself a cup of coffee and got to work.

Just as I was heating the pan for the bacon, Richard wandered in, already dressed for the day in a casual shirt and pants. He leaned against the counter, a mug of coffee in his hand.

"Morning." His eyes crinkled with his smile. Shepherd looked so much like him, but the physical resemblance seemed to be where their similarities ended. It made me wonder why Shepherd was so serious all the time.

"Good morning. Sleep well?"

"Yes, for the most part," he said.

It didn't escape my attention that Richard was alone. No Svetlana. Had he spent less time with her this last week? She hadn't been here in a few days, and she never spent the night. I'd be so relieved when Richard was finally free of her talons, even though I knew what it would mean for me.

I laid a strip of bacon in the pan and it sizzled. "What are you up to today?"

"I'm supposed to take it easy, but I think I'll get out for a walk. The weather's nice."

"That sounds like a good idea. Can I make you some breakfast first?"

"Tempting, but no." He patted his trim waist. "I have to be more careful about what I eat these days."

"Fair enough." I put more bacon in the pan and poked it with tongs to spread it out.

Richard took a sip of his coffee. "You should see if you can get Shep outside. He works too much."

"He really does, doesn't he?"

"That's probably my fault. I didn't set a very good example. His mother and I both spent most of our energy on our careers when the boys were young."

I perked up at the mention of both a young Shepherd and his mother as I stepped to the sink to wash my hands. Shepherd rarely mentioned his mom. Of course, before the night of the gala, I hadn't known anything about his family. He kept so many things to himself.

"What was he like when he was little?"

Richard tilted his head, a wistful expression crossing his features. "He was a good kid. Got good grades, didn't cause a lot of trouble. He was... focused. He's a lot like his mother."

"He must be. You two seem like night and day."

"I suppose we are. I think he worries about turning out too much like her. I don't want to badmouth my sons' mom, but... Actually, she's a cold-hearted bitch. I don't have anything nice to say about her." He grinned and took another drink.

I couldn't help but laugh. "Ouch. Tell me how you really feel."

"You'll see when you meet her. What about you? What's your family like?"

"My parents are... well, they're busy people. They retired and moved to Florida, but they also love to travel. They road trip around the country in their RV in the summer and go on cruises in the winter. And they always have some sort of project going on at their house. Remodeling, landscaping, gardening. I don't think either of them knows how to sit still."

"What about your sister? Just the one sibling?"

"Yep. Annie's younger and basically perfect. She's a successful CPA, married, settled. She's very good at this whole adulting thing in ways that I'm not."

"You seem like you're doing just fine."

I shrugged and started flipping the bacon. "I guess so. I like my life, but..." I trailed off because I was skirting too close to the truth, and the lie of my relationship with Shepherd. Because the truth was, I felt inadequate next to my younger sister. She'd found her person, gotten married, and was ready for a family. All things I wanted. All things I appeared to now have, but didn't.

"Anyway," I continued, trying to change the subject. "I think you're right about Shepherd needing to get out. I'll see what I can do."

"That's my girl." He winked at me and rinsed his mug in the sink.

I sighed as he walked away, turning the bacon over again. The front door opened and shut—Richard leaving for his walk. My life was so weird right now.

Before I could get too lost in my feelings, I felt Shepherd's presence behind me. I hadn't even heard him approach, but he electrified the air, making the hair on my arms stand on end.

I glanced over my shoulder. "Hi."

"Morning."

His expression was disarmingly open. It was so subtle, if I hadn't known him so well, I probably would have missed it. But there was a softness in his eyes, the hint of a smile on his lips. I could see emotion in his face, which was so rare it left me feeling a little jumpy and off-balance.

"Do you want some breakfast?" I asked, turning to face him.

That hint of a smile grew the tiniest bit. "Thanks. It smells good."

"Ah, so it's bacon that'll get you to come out of your cave."

"Bacon is very tempting."

The way his eyes swept up and down when he said *tempting* sent a tingle down my spine. Great, now I was imagining things. Shepherd was not looking at me with lust in his gaze. He was here for the bacon, and it did smell good.

I quickly turned back to the pan and took the slices out, setting them on a paper towel to drain. My back prickled. Had he just stepped closer to me? Sure I was imagining things, I busied myself with laying more bacon in the pan, then washed my hands. I was almost afraid to look behind me. My heart beat faster and I had an almost uncontrollable urge to turn around and kiss him.

*Focus, Everly. Breakfast.*

But standing in the kitchen together with the smell of coffee and bacon in the air felt so intimate. Not in a sexual way. In a relationshippy way. Which was almost worse. This felt so natural. Like I could turn around and lean against the counter while we chatted about our upcoming week. Maybe he'd get close to me and nuzzle my neck or plant little kisses on my bare shoulder. I'd giggle and push him away, telling him I was going to burn breakfast.

My hands were still wet, but Shepherd was between me and the towel on the counter. This was so stupid. My feelings were spinning out of control and I needed to get a handle on them. Now.

I spun around, coming face to face with Shepherd. He was so close, as if he'd been inching toward me this whole time. His eyes went to my face—my mouth, to be specific. He didn't move. Just stared at my lips.

Oh my god, this was happening. The world seemed to move in slow motion, the hiss and pop of the food on the stove fading from notice. I licked my lips—an involuntary movement—and Shepherd's brow furrowed. I was already feeling melty inside and he hadn't even touched me.

My lips tingled with anticipation. I lifted my chin, my heart beating fast. All the many reasons this was a terrible idea started running through my mind. But the intensity in Shepherd's gaze silenced my thoughts.

*Kiss me, Shepherd. Do it. I want you to.*

His eyes widened. "Oh shit."

He grabbed me around the waist, lifted me up and spun me around, setting me down behind him. Dizzy from the sudden movement—what had just happened?—I put a hand to my forehead and blinked.

Flames shot up from the pan. Shepherd quickly pulled a large baking sheet out of the cupboard. He put it on the pan, smothering the fire, and turned off the burner.

He whipped around. "Are you okay? Did you get burned?"

I touched the back of my hair and neck. "No, I don't think so."

"Let me see."

Still disoriented, I turned so he could look at my back. "I really think I'm fine."

"I don't see anything."

My back tingled with the desire for his touch. I wanted him to run a hand down my back, smoothing my shirt, making sure I was okay. But he didn't.

"Oh no." I turned back to the stove and waved a hand in front of my nose. The fire was out but a haze filled the air. "It smells like smoke in here. We should open a window."

He turned on the vent fan and when he lowered his

hand, I could have acted—salvaged the moment that had almost happened. I was standing so close, I could have reached out and put my hand on his chest. Slid it around to the back of his neck and whispered a thank you for saving me from being burned. Popped up on my tiptoes and kissed him.

But I didn't. A million thoughts raced through my mind, leaving me frozen in place. I couldn't kiss Shepherd. He was my boss. This was only for show. Just a way to keep his ex at a distance. If we kissed, it would change everything.

The openness in his expression was gone. He helped me clean up in silence. I tried to tell myself I was just glad it hadn't set off the fire alarm or the sprinkler system. Now that would have been a real disaster. That little almost-kiss wasn't even worth worrying about, considering I'd almost caught his condo on fire.

But that was a big fat lie. The little kitchen fire had been startling, but it hadn't done any damage. I wasn't so sure about that almost-kiss.

## 18

## SHEPHERD

$I$'d been out of the office since early this morning —busy with off-site meetings and a trip to the doctor with my dad. What should have been running through my mind while I walked to my office were the hundred things I needed to do today. For work. For my company. Not the fact that I'd been inches away from kissing Everly in my kitchen yesterday.

The fire hadn't caused any damage. But I hadn't missed the look on Everly's face when I'd gone back to my office. She hadn't said anything about what had almost happened. Neither had I, but I probably should have.

I'd spent the rest of the day avoiding her. Stayed in my office and went to bed late. Which made me feel like an idiot.

I had serious issues when it came to feelings. Every time I started to experience a deep emotion, I clammed up. Shut down. I'd seen my mother do the very same thing. I didn't know why I did it. My dad had always been free and open with his emotions. Ethan was too. They talked about how they felt with what appeared to be ease and comfort.

But me? Strong emotions made me retreat into myself.

Maybe that was why I'd always chosen shallow women to date. They were safe. They wouldn't stir things up that would make me uncomfortable.

That was a disturbing revelation to have, especially since I was having it right as I walked by Everly's desk.

I gave her a curt nod and went into my office. Shutting the door, I pushed her—and the confusing knot of feelings —out of my mind. I rolled up the sleeves of my button-down shirt, sat at my desk, and got to work. I had another meeting this afternoon and I needed to be sharp.

Losing myself in financial reports helped. But she was still there, a constant presence on the edge of my consciousness.

I glanced at the clock. Nolan Carter, my CFO, would be calling in for our meeting in a few minutes. His wife had just had a baby, so he was working from home several days a week. I opened the meeting app and waited for him to connect.

There was a soft knock on my door and Everly peeked her head in. "Hi. Sorry, I know you're about to get on a call, but can I see you afterward?"

"Sure."

She wasn't quite looking me in the eye. "Thanks."

Maybe I should have said something. After all, it had been me who'd almost kissed her. I'd been the one stalking her like a predator while she cooked. Who'd stared at her mouth so long there was no way she hadn't noticed.

But there was that barrier again. I couldn't articulate what I wanted to say. Hell, I wasn't even sure *what* I wanted to say. So I didn't say anything.

She slipped back out and quietly shut the door.

Fuck.

Nolan connected to the app, so I tore my focus away from the door—and the image of a forlorn Everly—and answered.

Not ten minutes into my meeting, my phone lit up with a call. Normally I wouldn't answer, but it was my dad. An instinct flared to life. Something was wrong.

"Nolan, can you give me a second. I have to take this call."

"Sure, no problem."

I muted him and answered my phone. "Dad? Is everything okay?"

"Thank god you answered. No. Something happened to Ethan at work. They had to call 911."

"What happened? Where is he?"

"I'm not sure, but we think anaphylaxis. They're taking him to the ER at Virginia Mason. Grant's trying to get over there, but he's stuck in traffic. So am I."

Ethan had a severe peanut allergy. One of my sharpest childhood memories was when Ethan had unknowingly eaten something contaminated with peanuts. It had almost been fatal.

"I'll be right there."

"Thanks, son."

I hung up and quickly told Nolan I had to go for a family emergency. Making sure I had my phone and keys, I rushed out of my office. It barely registered that Everly wasn't at her desk—she was probably in the restroom. I headed straight for my car and drove to the hospital.

My mind raced. Ethan's allergy was life-threatening, but he carried an EpiPen. His co-workers were all aware. How had this happened? How bad must it have been if he was being rushed to the hospital? The thought of Ethan going into anaphylactic shock—or worse—left me with a sick feeling in the pit of my stomach. Fear turned my blood to ice and I gripped the steering wheel, clenching my teeth.

He had to be okay.

I wasn't what you'd call close to my brother. But I wasn't close to anyone. That was my fault, not his. Even so, there were very few people in this world I cared about more than him.

Traffic on the surface streets wasn't bad. I made it to the hospital, parked in the garage, and hurried to the ER.

The woman at the front desk couldn't tell me anything. I texted Dad and Grant to let them know I was here. They were both still fighting traffic on the freeway. I paced around the waiting room, consumed with worry. Why didn't they know anything yet? Where was he?

I was about to go back to the front desk and bark at the receptionist to let me the fuck back to see Ethan, when I felt a gentle hand on my arm.

Everly stood next to me, her eyes soft with concern. "Are you okay?"

I stared at her. "What are you doing here?"

"I saw you leave and I could tell something was wrong. You didn't answer your phone, so I called your dad. Do you know anything yet?"

Her hand on my arm was so soothing, her simple touch enough to keep me calm. "No, not yet."

"I'm sure he's okay." She rubbed my forearm. "He's getting the medical attention he needs."

I nodded, desperately hoping she was right.

She led me to a chair and we both sat. I stared at the floor, tense with worry. I hated feeling so helpless. I was usually good in a crisis—always calm and controlled. But this was different. There was nothing I could do but wait.

It occurred to me suddenly that Everly was holding my

hand, our fingers twined together. She leaned her head against my shoulder and rubbed my arm.

Turning my head slightly, I inhaled her strawberry scent and squeezed her hand. She squeezed back, her gentle touch reassuring.

"Excuse me, Mr. Calloway?" A nurse with a clipboard in her hand approached.

Keeping Everly's hand gripped tightly in mine, I stood. "Yes."

"We're treating your brother for anaphylaxis, but I wanted to let you know he's conscious and breathing on his own. It was severe, but the worst is over and we're doing everything we can for him."

"Can we see him?"

"Soon," she said and Everly squeezed my hand again. "We'll come get you as soon as he can have visitors."

"Thank you."

The nurse left and we went back to our seats. I dropped Everly's hand and slid my arm around her shoulders, hugging her against me. I didn't worry about whether or not I should. Didn't care that no one was here to see it. This wasn't for show. I was scared for Ethan—I was man enough to admit that—and holding her felt good. It felt right.

Grant came in, followed closely by Dad. I gave them what little information I had. Grant was visibly relieved, but he didn't sit. He paced around the waiting room like I had when I'd first arrived. Dad sat with his hands in his lap, his expression uncharacteristically serious.

No one mentioned my mother. She lived in Portland, so it wasn't as if she could rush over here. Neither of us had much of a relationship with her, but she'd want to know. I decided to let Grant and Ethan handle that when it was over and we were sure Ethan would be fine.

It took a while before we were given another update. We all stood as soon as the doctor came out. Ethan was doing better and so far showing no sign of a secondary reaction. He'd been at a restaurant and had been served something contaminated with peanuts. It made me furious. I wanted to burn that fucking restaurant to the ground.

But Everly slipped her arms around my waist and rested her head on my chest. I held her close, ignoring the line I was crossing. My dad was here now, so it stood to reason I could do this—hold her and stroke her arm with so much familiarity. But I wasn't doing it for him, any more than I'd held her hand for show. This had nothing to do with our ruse, and I didn't give a fuck.

I wanted this. Needed it. Needed her.

Eventually, we were all taken back to see Ethan. He'd been admitted overnight as a precaution, so the nurse led us to his room on another floor. Everly, Dad, and I waited outside while Grant went in first. Gave them some privacy.

When we went in to see my brother, he looked pale, but smiled. He was hooked up to an IV and there were still traces of redness and swelling around his mouth.

I stood at the foot of the bed, my hand once again clasped with Everly's. "It's good to see you're okay."

"Thanks." His voice sounded hoarse. "I still feel like I got hit by a bus, but the worst is over." His gaze flicked to Everly and he raised an eyebrow at me.

"Sorry, I know this is private and not the best way to meet, but I'm Everly." She wiggled her fingers at Ethan and Grant. "I'm really glad you're all right."

"It's still nice to meet you," Ethan said.

She squeezed my hand. "I'll wait outside. Take your time."

I spoke quietly with Ethan, Grant, and Dad for a few

more minutes before excusing myself. Ethan was okay, and he needed rest after his ordeal. He had Grant to support him and Dad said he'd stay a bit longer.

"Are you ready to go?" Everly asked.

"Yeah."

She slipped her hand in mine as we walked down the long hallway. It felt good to touch her like this. Natural, like she really was my fiancée. Like that ring on her finger wasn't just for show.

We stopped in front of the elevator and I pushed the button to the parking garage.

I glanced at her. "Thank you for coming."

She looked up and smiled. "Of course. I'm glad he's okay."

"Me too."

I didn't look away, losing myself in her eyes—those sparkling pools of blue. Neither did she. Her expression changed, her smile fading into a look of resolve. She grabbed my shirt, right in the center of my chest, popped up on her tip toes, and kissed me.

Her soft lips pressed against mine for a few seconds before she pulled back. Her eyes widened and she took a breath as if to say something. I didn't wait to find out what it was.

Surging in, I cupped her face and kissed her back. For a beat, we were both stiff. But like ice on a hot day, she melted into me, her body going languid. She slid her hands up my chest and around my neck, leaning into me.

I traced the seam of her lips with my tongue. She opened for me, tilting her head, sliding her tongue against mine. God, this felt good. A deep sense of satisfaction filled me. I'd wanted to do this for longer than I'd let myself admit. And now that I was, it felt better than I'd imagined.

Our mouths tangled, tongues mingling. A long, deep kiss, pushing all my thoughts aside. Vaguely, I was aware that we were blocking someone's access to the elevator. I didn't give a shit. I was going to kiss the hell out of this woman, right here and now.

Gradually, I pulled away. We stood together in silence for a long moment, foreheads touching.

"Wow," she breathed. "That was... I don't... where are we?"

I laughed softly and brushed her hair back from her face. "That wasn't in the plan, was it?"

"No."

"Thank you again for being here."

Her tongue darted out over her lips. "That was a really nice way to say thank you."

The elevator dinged and the doors opened. I ushered her inside and hit the button for the parking garage.

She tucked her hair behind her ear. "So, are you going home now?"

I opened my mouth to answer, but paused. I had some-where to be tonight, and tempting as it was to take Everly home and see where that kiss led, it was an obligation I didn't want to miss. But maybe...

"I actually have to go somewhere tonight," I said.

Her face fell. "Oh, sure. That's fine. We drove separately anyway."

"But I'd like you to meet me there later."

The glimmer of hope in her eyes made it hard not to scoop her up and kiss her again. "Sure. Where?"

"The Office."

"You have to go back to work?"

"No, it's a bar called the Office." I got out my phone. "I'll text you the address. I have to get over there early, but be there around eight. I'll find you."

Her expression was bewildered, but I decided not to explain. It would be easier to show her, anyway.

"Okay, I'll be there."

The elevator doors opened and I walked her to her car. I stood aside and watched her leave, wondering if I'd just made a big mistake. Kissing her had changed everything. I felt it, deep in my chest.

She didn't know it yet, but I was about to trust her with one of my biggest secrets. The thought left me feeling raw, like an open wound. I wasn't used to this. But instead of shying away—burying myself in work—I let it happen. Felt the uncertainty, acknowledged it, and decided I was doing it anyway.

## 19

## EVERLY

*M*y ride pulled up to the curb on a side street downtown. Shepherd had said he'd meet me, so I'd taken an Uber rather than drive my own car.

I glanced out the window again. Dim light illuminated a sign that read *The Office* over a nondescript door. A couple came out, the guy's arm slung over the girl's shoulders.

"I guess this is it," I said, but there wasn't any confidence in my voice. This place looked like a dive bar. Why would Shepherd ask me to meet him here?

I got out and tucked my phone back in my little handbag. He hadn't told me what we were doing, so I'd been at a loss as to what to wear. I'd opted for a teal shirt and black skirt with heels. My hair was down and I fluffed it a little before going inside.

Live rock music filled the bar. It was definitely a dive. Concrete walls were papered with newspaper clippings and band posters. Exposed bulbs in the ceiling cast a dim light and the floor was sticky.

My tummy did a little flip. I was so nervous to see Shepherd. That kiss. I'd surprised myself when I'd grabbed his shirt and kissed him. But nothing could have prepared me for the way he'd reacted. He'd kissed me back, leaving me breathless.

And now? I wasn't sure what it meant. Everything at the hospital had been so intense. We were supposed to be pretending, but things were getting all too real. I assumed he'd asked me to meet him because he wanted to talk. But here? It was crowded and loud and not the kind of place I'd have thought Shepherd would go.

I didn't see him anywhere—which was odd because he'd stick out like a sore thumb in this place. It was crowded— surprising on a Monday night—and it was clear people were here for the music. A few sat at the bar or the small tables, but the rest packed in around the stage.

It was an eclectic mix of people. Guys with tattoos and piercings. Girls with brightly dyed hair and badass red lipstick. Rockers with long hair and leather. A group of guys in button-down shirts, the sleeves cuffed. They looked more like Shepherd, but even they seemed too casual. There were older people, young couples, and everything in between. Although it was different than most of the places my girlfriends and I hung out, I liked it.

I texted Shepherd to let him know I was here, then wandered through the crowd toward the stage, keeping my eye out for him. The music was good. Really good. I found myself a little bit mesmerized by the melody. The singer had a great voice, but it was more than that. The band had an energy to them that drew me in. No wonder this place was so packed on a weeknight.

The bass drum had the band name on it—*Incognito*. The drummer beat the drums, sweat gleaming on his forehead. A guitar player sang backup into a mic next to the lead singer. The bass player stood toward the back of the stage where the light was dim. My eyes almost passed over him—where the heck was Shepherd?—when I did a double take.

Oh my god. The bass player looked exactly like Shepherd.

Holy shit. It *was* Shepherd.

I barely recognized him, with his disheveled hair and plain black t-shirt and jeans. He played a dark red bass guitar, his fingers busy strumming, his head bobbing slightly to the beat of the music. He seemed lost in the song, hardly paying attention to the crowd.

I'd seen Shepherd Calloway looking every bit the hot, wealthy businessman in a designer tux or a perfectly-tailored suit. I'd seen him at the end of a long day with the sleeves of his button-down shirt cuffed to his elbows. I'd even seen him in gym clothes after a workout and rubbing sleep from his eyes in the kitchen early in the morning while he waited for his coffee.

But this? I'd never dreamed I'd see Shepherd like this. Messy and a little sweaty, playing bass in a band at a dive bar?

He was so sexy I thought I might die.

I stared at him, open-mouthed, while he played. The bass line thumped, reverberating through my body. He didn't look up. Just stood back there, almost in shadow, rocking out on his bass.

The crowd cheered while the band moved into a new song. I watched him, transfixed. Although he wasn't working the audience the way the other guys were, he seemed at home up there. Relaxed in a way I'd never seen before.

The final song ended, and the singer thanked everyone for being here tonight. Shepherd finally looked up. He brushed the hair off his forehead, his eyes scanning the crowd.

Our gazes met and his lips turned up in a slow smile. He gave me a slight shrug, looking hesitant—almost shy. Before this moment, I never would have used that word to describe him. But there he was, with a boyish grin, glancing around at his surroundings as if to say, *Yeah, I know this is weird.*

He motioned for me to wait, then disappeared backstage with the rest of the band. Someone came on stage to introduce the next act—a woman named Dahlia Marlow. She was older—probably in her late fifties—with wildly curly hair and an acoustic guitar. The crowd gave her just as much love as they had the band, and when she started singing, I could see why. Her voice was hypnotically beautiful.

It took a while before Shepherd came out, still dressed in a t-shirt and jeans. He ran a hand through his hair and gave me that little smile again.

"Hey."

I blinked at him a few times, realizing too late that I was staring, open-mouthed. "Hey. Sorry. I'm just... I didn't know you played. Or owned jeans."

"Yeah, well, I'd get hot up there in a suit."

*You're hot right now, Shepherd. Oh my god are you hot.*

My eyes swept up and down, taking him in. Trying to reconcile this with the Shepherd Calloway I knew. Or thought I'd known. "How long have you been playing bass? Do you do this a lot? Is that your band? I have so many questions."

He reached out and slid his hand to the small of my back, steering me toward the bar. "Yeah, I knew you would. Let's get a drink."

We got two whiskeys and found a small table near the

outskirts of the bar. It was quieter here, a little corner shrouded in shadow.

"How is this possible?" I asked, gesturing at him, then behind me at the stage. "You're in a band?"

"Yeah, it's just a hobby for all of us. A side thing we like to do."

"So you're not about to give up the suits and corner office for a record deal," I said and nudged his leg under the table.

"No, nothing like that. They even have another bassist who plays with them since I can't get over here all that often."

The significance of the bar's name was finally dawning on me. "Is this where you go when you say you have to go to *the office* at night?"

He nodded, looking adorably guilty, like a kid caught with his hand in the cookie jar. "Yeah, sometimes. But, listen, no one knows about this. I mean that literally. No one."

"Your dad doesn't know?"

"No, he has no idea. Ethan doesn't either, although he knows I learned to play."

"Why haven't you told them? Your dad would love to see you play. He'd lose his mind."

Rubbing his chin, he looked away. "I don't know. I've always kept this part of my life separate. It wasn't something I wanted people to know about."

My heart fluttered, my breath catching in my throat. He never told anyone? Not even his family? And he'd invited me here to see him play?

Nora had been wrong about catching feelings. There was no catching involved. They smashed into me, shattering into my soul with a million tiny sparks, filling me with a warm tingly sensation.

He turned back, meeting my gaze, a disarming openness in his eyes. Right there, in that exact moment, I did a terrible, terrible thing.

I fell in love with my boss.

"I won't tell anyone," I said.

"I know. I trust you."

Biting my lower lip, I glanced down at my drink. My heart raced and my cheeks felt warm. He was so sexy and charming and nothing like the stoic robot I'd thought he was. He wore his Mr. Calloway persona like armor. But he'd let me in. Let me see a part of him he'd never shown anyone.

I looked up, meeting his eyes. Before I even started speaking, I could tell my filter was gone—smashed to pieces by Shepherd's vulnerability. "Thank you for inviting me. Your band is amazing and you're really good and I'm having a very hard time staying over here on my side of the table. Because you're so sexy all I want to do right now is launch myself at you."

Without a second's hesitation, he stood and yanked me off my stool. His strong hands held me tight against him as he leaned down and took my mouth in a hard kiss.

I flung my arms around his shoulders and had to stop myself from jumping up to wrap my legs around his waist. My fingers tangled in his messy hair as his tongue delved into my mouth. He tasted like whiskey and sex and potent masculinity. Under normal circumstances, I would have held back a little. After all, we were in a public place.

But there was no holding back now. His arms were hot steel around me, his delicious mouth tangling with mine. My heart beat furiously as he sucked on my lower lip, one hand moving beneath my shirt to splay across my ribs. I wanted to rip his clothes off—rip my clothes off—but a tiny part of me, way back in the recesses of my hormone-soaked brain, was still rational. We were in a bar, surrounded by people.

I pulled back, almost gasping for breath. "Where's your car?"

"I'm parked out back."

"Let's go."

He nodded, grabbing my hand, and led me through the crowd to a side door. My vision was hazy, my lips sensitive and swollen, every nerve ending attuned to him.

We burst out the door into a small parking lot behind the bar. A single bulb cast a dingy light over the cars. After the noise inside, it was almost silent. Just the hum of traffic a few blocks away.

His car unlocked automatically as soon as he got next to it. He grabbed the driver's side door handle, but I put a hand on his chest.

"Back seat."

A low growl rumbled in his throat. He opened the back door and practically shoved me inside.

As soon as he sat down, I climbed into his lap. My skirt hiked up my legs as our mouths crashed together, messy and wet. His hands slid up my thighs and I ran my fingers through his hair.

He eagerly licked into my mouth, his tongue sliding along mine. I already knew Shepherd was a fantastic kisser, but this was melting my brain. His lips were soft, but insistent, his hands grabbing me with demanding authority.

Pressing myself closer, I felt his hard-on through his jeans. Oh dear god, that felt good. His hands moved up my thighs and slipped beneath my panties to cup my ass. I rubbed myself against him, tilting my hips, indulging in a little friction against my clit.

"Fuck," he growled into my mouth.

I'd never felt like this before. So frantic. I was on fire for him, my worries about what this meant burning away to ash.

His stubble on my face was deliciously rough. I couldn't get enough of him. His tongue, his lips, his hands all over me. He pressed me against his erection and grunted as I nipped his bottom lip with my teeth.

My panties were soaked, the insistent pressure between my legs begging to be sated. His jeans looked sexy as hell, but right now, they were really in my way. Maybe if I just...

Still kissing him, I reached between us to unfasten his pants.

"Everly," he mumbled. "I'm not—"

The button popped open. He grunted again.

"We're not—"

I lowered the zipper.

His grip on my ass tightened and he pulled back slightly. "I'm not fucking you for the first time in the back seat of my car."

*First time*... first time implied a second time which implied multiple times. I wasn't just crossing a line out here. I was getting a running start and leaping over it, leaving the line far behind.

"I know," I said and returned to kissing him while my fingers worked his zipper the rest of the way down. "I just want these out of my way."

I hadn't meant to expose him fully. The loose plan in my lust-filled brain was simply to remove the denim barrier between my desperately aroused lady parts and his very tempting cock. I just wanted to rub on him a little more while we made out. But he was so hard—and so big—he stuck out the top of his underwear. And the sight of that magnificent dick, glistening with a drop of precum on the tip, was too much to resist.

Ignoring the fact that we were in a car in a dingy parking lot outside a dive bar, I pulled his underwear down, revealing the length of his glorious cock.

I was so glad I'd worn a skirt. I shifted my hips closer so I could rub myself along his length and his fingers dug into my skin as he guided me, moving me up and down. My panties were still between us, but the friction was intense.

I was dry-humping my boss's exposed cock in the back of his car and it was fucking amazing.

Shepherd's hand moved over the top of my thigh, reaching between my legs. His fingertips hooked beneath my panties. "I need to feel your pussy."

"Do you have a condom?" I panted.

"I won't... just want a little more."

He pulled my panties to the side, bringing my wet folds in direct contact with his shaft. I moaned and he grunted as I slowly slid along his length.

"Fuck, you're so wet."

"We can't, can we?"

He groaned as I slid back down. "No. I won't go in. Not here. But... fuck, you feel so good."

It did feel good. It felt incredible. Somewhere in the back of my mind, I made a mental note to ask Nora whether it counted as sex if you didn't achieve actual penetration.

For now, I rubbed myself along his cock as we frantically kissed. Pressure built between my legs, the breathtaking ache of an impending orgasm. I moved faster, grinding my clit against his erection while he gripped my thighs with his strong hands.

"That's it," he murmured. "Fuck yes, baby."

I was too far gone to stop. He thrust against me, guiding

me with his hands. Our mouths separated and we both looked down, watching as I rubbed my slit up and down the outside of his glistening cock. It would have been so easy for him to reach in and pick up his dick so I could slide on. Forget the condom situation and fuck me right here.

But he didn't. He watched with parted lips as I drew my clit against him, over and over, moving faster.

"Yes, baby," he said. "Don't stop. Don't fucking stop."

I wasn't about to unless he made me. I chased my orgasm all the way to the brink, whimpering as the intensity built.

Just...

A little...

More...

One last long drag up his cock and I burst apart, throwing my head back. He held me while I rode out the waves of pleasure, my wetness soaking him.

I slowed down as I finished, breathing hard. Oh my god, what had I done? I'd just dry-humped—was it dry-humping if there weren't any clothes between you?—my boss until I came all over him.

Before I could worry about what was supposed to happen next—he was still hard as steel beneath me—he wrapped his hand around the back of my neck. His jaw hitched and his brow furrowed.

"We're going home and I'm going to fuck the shit out of you when we get there."

## 20

---

## SHEPHERD

*T*he drive to my condo went by in a haze of explosive sexual tension. My entire groin ached, the pressure radiating outward, making my back tense and my shoulders tight. Her scent and the feel of her silky wetness sliding over me lingered, tortuous and tempting.

I'd wanted to fuck her right then, in the back of my car. The primal urge to take her—to thrust my cock inside her and claim her as mine—had been almost overpowering. But enough of my rational brain had been functional to stop me.

Plus, watching her make herself come like that had been fucking incredible. The sight of her straddling me with her skirt hiked up her thighs, her panties pulled to the side, had been hot as fuck. A few more minutes of that, and I probably would have come too.

She sat next to me, her hands in her lap, her cheeks still flushed an adorable shade of pink. It was hard to keep my attention on the road. We were both silent, but I couldn't have held a normal conversation even if I'd tried. There wasn't enough blood in my brain. Luckily, it was late, the roads were fairly empty, and we made it back to my building without any delays.

I parked and we got out, my heart still thumping, my dick aching. With my hand on the small of her back, I led her to the elevator. When we got in, I didn't press the button for the penthouse. Instead, I selected the floor of my other condo. My escape. The place I never showed anyone.

Showing her was a risk. I was crossing lines with Everly that I'd never crossed with a woman. A part of me realized I'd have to deal with that later.

But she'd seen me play, and I never shared that with people, either. And the way I felt now, I didn't want to take a chance that my dad—or worse, Dad *and* Svetlana—would be home. The last thing I needed was my father wanting to chat when we walked in the door.

I was a man with a singular purpose. And that was to fuck the hell out of this woman. Now.

"Um..." Everly's voice was hesitant. "Where are we going?"

"I'll show you."

She nestled closer to me and I tightened my grip on her waist. The temptation to push her against the wall and kiss her was strong. But I knew once I started, I wouldn't be able to stop. My self-control was at a breaking point.

The elevator doors opened, and I led her to my studio unit. Inside was dark—the blackout curtains blocking the light from the city outside—so I turned on the lamp on the side table.

Everly stood just inside the door, looking around wide-eyed, her full lips parted. As she took in our surroundings—my collection of guitars, the band posters—a strange feeling hit me in the chest. The same one I'd felt onstage when our eyes had met and I'd realized she was seeing me. Truly seeing me. But the intense vulnerability only increased my desire. I wanted to fuck her a hundred different ways in here.

"Come here."

She moved toward me, stepping out of her heels, and pulled her shirt over her head, letting it drop to the floor.

*Good girl.*

We frantically tore off our clothes and I made sure to grab the condom out of my wallet. Her body was a fucking sight, but I wasn't in any state to appreciate the beauty of those curves. Grabbing her at the waist, I hauled her against me. Leaned down and captured her mouth.

Kissing Everly felt different. Her lips were soft and sweet, but it was more than that. She was reaching inside me, unlocking places I kept hidden. I felt a connection I'd never experienced before.

I trusted her.

It was why we were here. Why I was laying her down on the couch in a room no one else had set foot in since the day I moved in. Wasting no time, I put on the condom while she watched, licking her lips.

"Are you ready for this?" I asked, running my hands down the smooth skin of her thighs. She offered no resistance as I pushed her legs open.

"Oh my god, yes."

Lowering myself on top of her, I aligned the tip of my cock with her entrance and groaned as I thrust inside.

There was no hesitation. No pausing to appreciate the exquisiteness of her pussy wrapped around my dick. I needed to fuck her, and I needed to fuck her hard.

Driving in deep, I slid easily through her wetness. Out, then in. She hooked her legs around the backs of my thighs and gripped my back, tilting her hips to meet my thrusts. I pounded her into the couch, unleashing all my pent-up tension. All the unbridled lust I'd been holding inside.

Her fingernails scratched my back and the infusion of pain fueled my passion. I grunted, my body stiffening, and the pressure in my groin skyrocketed.

"You feel so fucking good," I growled into her ear.

She started to reply but a hard thrust transformed her words into a breathy moan.

My dick was still achingly hard. I couldn't get enough of her. I drove in deep, fucking her with everything I had. She was hot and wet and perfect, her pussy tight around me, her nipples dragging across my chest.

I kissed her mouth, tasting the hint of whiskey still on her tongue. Kissed down her neck to her collarbone. Still thrusting, I picked myself up so I could see her. Fuck, she had beautiful tits. She lay beneath me, skin flushed, arms overhead, her tits bouncing as I fucked her.

Leaning down, I palmed one of her tits and lapped my tongue over her nipple. I groaned, enjoying their softness. They were real. Of course they were. This was Everly. Everything about her was real.

As much as I wanted to explode inside her, these fantastic tits needed my attention. I sucked her nipple into my mouth, running the rough pad of my tongue over her hard peak. Her body reacted with a shiver, her pussy clenching tight around me.

I released her nipple with a pop and moved to the other side. She tasted so fucking good. I loved the feel of her soft tits in my mouth, her nipples against my tongue.

"Oh my god, yes," she breathed.

I pulled out and rolled us over so I was lying on the couch, my back propped up against the side. Sitting upright, her legs straddling me, she slid back onto my cock. I held her hips, guiding her as she started to ride me.

Her luscious hips rolled and her thighs clenched as she slid up and down my hard length. I thrust up into her, burying myself deep. Reaching up, I grabbed her tits, feeling her hard pink nipples pressing into my palms. She raked her hands through my chest hair as she rode my cock hard and fast.

"Yes, Shepherd," she said, her voice a whimper, eyes fluttering. "You feel so good."

The pressure was agonizing but I didn't want this to end. She leaned into my hands, lifting her hips and slamming down again while I kneaded her tits. I grunted with every movement, losing myself in the heat of her pussy. In the sight of her riding up and down my dick.

Her fingernails pinched as they dug into my chest. The heat in her pussy grew and she moved faster, grinding her clit against me every time she sank down.

I watched in awe as she started to come again. Her pussy was tight, pulsing around me, and she threw her head back, moaning.

It was one of the sexiest things I'd ever seen.

Somehow, watching her come all over my dick didn't set me off. I rode the edge, holding back just enough. She was so fucking beautiful. Her movements slowed as her orgasm subsided and she paused, breathing hard.

I held her hips, groaning at the feel of her. Her glassy eyes fluttered open, her full lips parted.

"Knees," I growled.

A wicked smile crossed her lips and she climbed off me. She got on her knees, facing the back of the couch, and arched her back. With her ass lifted, she looked over her shoulder and bit her lip.

My chest and back stung from her nails, but I fucking loved it. I smacked one of her ass cheeks, just hard enough to make her gasp.

"Again," she said.

Who the hell was she? I smacked her again with a satisfying slap.

She gasped and giggled. "Have I been a bad girl?"

"So bad."

"Spank me again."

Growling, I spanked her on the other side. I was so keyed up, just a few strokes and I'd probably come all over her delicious ass. But I wanted more of that wet pussy.

I grabbed her hips and thrust inside. She arched her back, moaning as I drove into her. I fucked her hard and fast, slamming into her, my hips colliding with her ass.

We were both unfettered. Thrusting and groaning, heedless of the noise we were making. We existed in a haze of sex-fueled energy, feeding off each other.

She tossed her hair over her shoulder and looked back at me. "Spank me while you fuck me."

Holy shit. I smacked her ass, amazed I didn't come right then. My dick pulsed, but I was still on the edge.

"Harder, Shepherd. Fuck me harder."

With my fingers digging into her hips, I growled, pounding her from behind. She giggled with bliss, holding onto the back of the couch, arching her ass in the air for me.

I reached forward and grabbed her hair, pulling her head back. "You dirty girl. You like it when I fuck you hard, don't you?"

"So good," she breathed.

I was on the brink of losing my mind. Driving into Everly from behind, pulling her hair, her ass cheeks pink from where I'd spanked her. Who knew this sweet girl was a dirty fucking sex goddess?

She clenched tight around me. I dropped her hair and reached between her legs to brush her clit with my fingertips. I was ready to explode, but I wasn't finishing until I teased another orgasm out of her.

"Oh fuck," she whimpered.

"That's it, my dirty girl," I murmured. "Fucking come again, baby."

I rubbed her clit while I fucked her, my hips driving hard. The pressure intensified. She braced herself against the back of the couch, moaning with each thrust, her pussy so hot I could barely hold back.

"Yes, Everly," I growled. "Come all over me, baby."

Her whole body shuddered and her pussy clenched hard. I unleashed inside her, groaning as I finally hit sweet release. My cock pulsed, an overwhelming eruption, drowning all my senses. The orgasm reverberated through my whole body, like shockwaves after a blast.

By the time it was over, I was practically panting. I pulled out and ran my hands gently over the red marks on her ass. She glanced over her shoulder, her cheeks flushed, and bit her lip.

I caressed her ass again, then leaned down to kiss the red spots. She sighed, almost a purr, and I moved to the other side. Kissed her skin where I'd spanked her.

She rolled over and leaned her head back. "I have no idea what you just did to me."

Still breathing hard, I took off the condom and tied it off, setting it aside. I'd clean up later. I sank down next to her. Gathered her in my arms. She tucked her legs up and leaned her head against my chest.

"I don't know what you just did to *me*."

I kissed the top of her head. Fuck, this was going to be complicated. Fake engagement but real sex? Very real sex. The realest sex I'd ever had.

But I couldn't think about that now. I was too sex-drunk to think about much of anything.

She traced her fingers through my chest hair, then suddenly sat up. "Oh no. I'm sorry."

"Sorry for what?"

"I scratched you." She leaned in and kissed a red mark on my chest.

I'd barely noticed. "It's fine."

"Did I hurt you?" She kissed my chest again.

"Baby, you can't hurt me."

She kissed me a few more times, then settled back against me. I felt her take a deep breath. "No one knows about this place, do they?"

"Nope."

"Like the band?"

"Yeah. Like the band."

She nuzzled her face against me and tilted her chin up to kiss my neck. "Thank you for sharing it with me."

"Mm hmm."

I let my eyes drift closed, enjoying the feel of her in my arms. Her breathing was smooth and even, her body warm against mine. I hadn't planned for any of this, which was decidedly unlike me.

But in this moment, basking in the glow of the best sex I'd ever had, I didn't worry about that. It felt good to let go a little. And maybe that wasn't such a bad thing after all.

## 21

## EVERLY

$\mathcal{M}$y mind was not where it needed to be. I had a to-do list a mile long, but I sat at my desk, eyes unfocused. Head in the clouds.

Or, more specifically, on the couch in Shepherd's secret hideaway.

I couldn't stop thinking about him. What he'd looked like up on stage, his nimble fingers strumming his bass. What he'd felt like in the back seat of his car. The heat between us had been scorching. And it had only been the beginning.

Then he'd treated me to the best sex I'd ever had in my entire life.

In.

My.

Life.

I'd never had so many orgasms so close together. Despite Nora's insistence that they were real, I'd always thought multiples were a myth.

But it wasn't just the three orgasms in one night that made it amazing. It was... all of it. The bar. The band. The condo. The secrets he'd shared. The things I'd done, and the things I'd let him do to me. I'd felt a deep and undeniable connection to him—something I'd never experienced before.

Which meant I was a total mess today.

He'd been up for a conference call with someone in New York when I'd left this morning. When he'd come into the office, he'd said good morning as he walked by my desk. To anyone looking, nothing would have seemed different. But I'd noticed. He'd paused, just the slightest hesitation, and met my eyes. The corner of his mouth had turned up and one of his dimples had puckered.

Quick as it was, that look had made me blush furiously. I'd gathered up my notepad and a few files and followed him into his office, hoping no one had seen my crimson face.

By the way Steve kept looking at me across the aisle, I had a feeling he had.

The other thing on my mind was Annie. Regardless of whether Shepherd and I were just faking it with a side of hot sex, or something more, I couldn't ask him to be her sperm donor. There was just no way. But I hated the idea of disappointing her.

I turned back to my computer, trying to put Shepherd—and sperm donations—out of my mind. But there he was, at the edge of my consciousness. That mouth. Those hands. That di—

"Everly," Steve whispered.

I gasped, realizing he was standing next to my desk. "God, Steve, you scared me. Why are you whispering?"

He looked around cautiously, then leaned a little closer. "I just want you to know, your secret is safe with me."

Oh no. "Um, what secret?"

"Your crush on Mr. Calloway." His eyes flicked to Shepherd's door. "You're doing a pretty good job hiding it, but we've worked together long enough, I can tell."

My crush? Well, he wasn't wrong. I'd fallen head over heels for the man. But at least he didn't seem to know the rest—especially that I was living with him, and that he'd fucked me senseless last night.

I figured the best thing to do was agree—fess up to crushing on my boss. Maybe that would satisfy Steve's curiosity and keep him from asking too many awkward questions.

Putting a finger to my lips, I shushed him. "Quiet. It's... complicated. And who could blame me? He's spectacular." *Especially the way he gets all growly when he comes...*

*Focus, Everly.*

Steve patted my shoulder. "It's okay. It happens to most women here at some point. Frankly, I'm surprised you held out this long. Just don't get yourself into trouble. I like you. I'd hate to see you go anywhere."

"You don't have to worry about me. It's not a big deal at all." *Liar, liar, pants on fire.*

He smiled and went back to his desk.

I took a deep breath. That had been the opposite of helpful. Now I really couldn't concentrate. What had made Steve think I had a crush? Was I mooning over Shepherd when he walked by? Had it been the way I'd blushed earlier? Had he noticed me staring off into space, reliving the strange and wonderful evening I'd had last night?

Probably all of the above.

Thankfully I was meeting Nora and Hazel for lunch today. They'd help me get my head on straight.

After another mostly unproductive hour, Nora and Hazel came walking down the hallway toward my desk.

Heads turned, my co-workers watching as they passed. Hazel, looking like a sexy librarian with her dark-rimmed glasses, blouse and pencil skirt. And Nora in a low-cut V-neck and high-waisted jeans that made her look like a vintage pinup model.

"You ready?" Nora asked when she got to my desk.

"Yes. Very." I grabbed my purse. "What sounds good?"

Hazel opened her mouth to answer but stopped as Shepherd came out of his office.

He paused outside his door, his hand still on the handle. His gaze fell on me first, lingering there for a second longer than was strictly appropriate, given the intense heat in his eyes. Then he seemed to notice Nora and Hazel. His eyes swept over them before coming back to rest on me.

"Leaving for lunch?" he asked.

I cleared my throat and fumbled my purse, almost dropping it. "Um, yes. Lunch. With them. My friends."

He nodded but didn't walk by. He kept standing there, his eyebrows raised, as if he expected me to say something else.

Finally, he reached his hand out to Nora. "Shepherd Calloway."

Nora shook his hand with a smile. "Nora Lakes. And this is Hazel Kiegen."

I started sputtering as he shook Hazel's hand. "Sorry. Right. Introductions. My girlfriends Nora and Hazel. But she said that already. So, yes, going to lunch with my friends. Who are these two, right here."

"Nice to meet you both." His gaze moved back to me, making my heart beat wildly in my chest. "Have a good time."

"Thanks," I managed to squeak out.

The corner of his mouth did that thing—the almost

smile with the hint of dimple. With a brief nod to Nora and Hazel, he walked away.

It wasn't until Nora cleared her throat that I realized I was watching his ass as he left.

"What?"

Nora crossed her arms. "Mm hmm."

I glanced around, wondering who else had just witnessed me making a total fool of myself. Thankfully the only person nearby was Steve. He gave me an exaggerated wink.

Oh, lord. "Can we just go to lunch, please?"

Nora and Hazel shared a look. I knew that look. It meant I was about to face the inquisition.

We chose a restaurant a block from my building and went in. The hostess seated us and I hid behind my menu, hoping the fire in my cheeks would simmer down before the waitress came to take our orders.

No such luck. I was positive I was still a bright pink disaster by the time I had to order lunch and hand her my menu.

Nora's eyes were practically glittering with excitement. "So how long have you been fucking him?"

"You say that as if it's a foregone conclusion," Hazel said.

"Because it is," Nora said. "You were standing right there. Don't you study this stuff for a living?"

"Not exactly," Hazel said. "My specialty is in the area of—"

"Since last night," I blurted out. "We slept together last night and oh my god, it was the most amazing night of my life."

"Details." Nora did a *gimme* gesture with her hand.

There was so much I couldn't tell them. Shepherd had asked me to keep his secrets, and I wasn't about to betray that trust. But the fact that we'd had sex was not something I could keep to myself. Not from them.

"This is going to sound crazy, but his brother had to be rushed to the hospital yesterday. I went down there to wait with him and—"

"Did you guys bang in a supply closet?" Nora asked.

"No, we didn't bang at the hospital. But we did kiss, and it was really amazing. And later... well, we spent some time together and he shared some things with me, and it felt like we really connected. And then came the sex."

"I told you this would happen," Nora said.

"Actually, I think you predicted that Everly would develop feelings for him," Hazel said. "Not that they would wind up sleeping together."

"That's what I'm talking about. Look at her." Nora gestured toward me. "She's smitten."

"I'm not smitten." Liar again.

"You are," Nora said. "But tell me more. Where were you? How many orgasms did you have?"

"Three," I said with a heavy sigh, then lowered my voice. "We weren't really having sex for the first one. At least I don't think we were. We were making out in the backseat of his car. Is it still dry-humping if there aren't clothes between you?"

"Meaning?" Hazel asked.

"Like he had his peen out and you had your panties off, but there was no penetration?" Nora asked.

I opened my mouth to answer, but clamped it shut again as the waitress brought our lunch.

"Thank you," Nora said, smiling at her as if we weren't sitting here having a conversation about dry-humping exposed penises.

I waited until our plates were on the table and the waitress was halfway back to the kitchen before replying. "His underwear were... well, down. My panties were on, but moved to the side. And no penetration."

"Why not?" Nora asked.

"He said he wasn't going to fuck me for the first time in the back seat of his car."

"First time?" Hazel asked. "That seems to imply he intends for there to be repeat performances."

I nodded and poked at my salad. "Yeah, I picked up on that too."

"Dry-humping isn't quite the right term, is it?" Nora asked, more to herself than to us. She tapped a finger against her lips, her fork dangling from her other hand. "Wet-humping, maybe? I don't know, but that should be a thing. He really gave you a big O with just the surface of his lady dagger?"

I wanted to duck under the table. "Nora, shush. And yes, he did."

"Did he come too, or was it just you?"

"In the car it was just me."

"And then?"

"We went back to his place and did it on the couch and I came two more times," I said in a rush.

Nora took a casual bite of her salad. "I have to say, I'm impressed."

"With what?" I asked.

"With you, for getting a threebie last night. You deserve it. And with him. A guy who lets you get off on his peen and waits to get you home to fuck you? If it were anyone else telling me this story—except you, Hazel—I'd think you were lying. I didn't think a unicorn like that existed. I might have to write an article about this. No names, of course."

"He was very exceptional."

"But Everly," Hazel said, her voice soft. "Are you sure this is wise? You're pretending to be engaged, but now you're not pretending to be having sex?"

"Believe me, I know. I have no idea what this means. Maybe it was just inevitable. How long was I supposed to hold out? I'm sleeping right next to him and you guys, he smells like man heaven."

"He likes the way you smell, too," Nora said.

"What? How do you know?"

"Didn't you see the way he leaned closer to you?" she asked. "He was totally indulging in a whiff."

"Studies show scent is a powerful force in attraction," Hazel said. "In fact, there's evidence to suggest that a percentage of failed marriages have, at their root, an insurmountable scent incompatibility."

"You mean people get divorced because they don't like the way their partner smells?" Nora asked.

"It's not usually a conscious thing, and more study is needed to draw solid conclusions, but yes. That's how strongly humans react to scent."

"So Everly and Shepherd have scent compatibility on their side," Nora said brightly. "I amend my previous warning about catching feelings. You've clearly caught them, but I don't think that's a bad thing."

I eyed my friend. Who was this, and what had she done with Nora? "You don't?"

"Not at all."

Hazel appeared similarly perplexed. "You realize this has the potential to go badly for at least a dozen reasons."

"I know it does." Nora waved her hand like those things didn't matter. "You're supposed to be faking Ms. Right, and what happens when you don't have to fake it anymore? And he's your boss, so there's the added complication of your career. But I'm on Team Shepherd. I think this is it, Everly."

My heart sang with hope at the suggestion. But there were so many unknowns. So many potential problems. Just because I'd slept with Shepherd didn't mean he intended to take our relationship from fake to real. Maybe we were just indulging in pure physical attraction.

But if he'd just wanted in my pants, he wouldn't have had to show me his band. Or his secret hideaway. Was there really something happening between us? Something deeper than the raw power of sexual attraction?

Could Shepherd have feelings for me too?

I was afraid to hope Nora was right.

## 22

# SHEPHERD

*L*eaning my hip against the kitchen counter, I took a sip of my whiskey while I eyed Everly. She was curled up in that ugly yellow bean bag chair, reading a book, an almost-empty glass of wine perched on her knee. Dressed in a pink shirt and a pair of light blue shorts that showed a hell of a lot of leg, she was a bright pop of color in my living room.

Not just in the room. In my life.

I wasn't playing at the bar tonight, so normally I would have poured my whiskey and gone straight to my office. Instead, I lingered, watching her, my eyes roving over her skin. Her silky hair. Thinking of all the ways I wanted to fuck her tonight.

As if she could feel my eyes on her, she glanced up.

The hint of shyness in her face drove me crazy. She smiled, nibbling her bottom lip, and uncurled herself to stand.

"Hi," she said as she came into the kitchen. She finished the last of her wine and set the glass by the sink.

I looked her up and down, not bothering to hide the heat in my gaze. "Hi."

She was magnetic, her pull irresistible. I closed the distance between us, slipping a hand around her waist. Leaned in to brush my lips against hers.

"Shep—oh, sorry. I didn't mean to interrupt."

I stepped back and turned to my dad. "Do you need something?"

"Yes, as a matter of fact. I'm glad you're both here. We need to talk details about your engagement party."

"We don't need an engagement party."

"Of course you do," he said, as if the very notion shocked him. "Don't worry, we'll keep it very private. No public announcements. No press. In fact, keeping it secretive will increase the appeal. Maybe we can work that into the theme."

"Theme?" Everly asked, her voice amused.

"I'm thinking Roaring Twenties. Something very *Great Gatsby*, with glitz and glamour. Live jazz. What do you think?"

"Dad, *The Great Gatsby* is a tragedy."

"True, but I'm going for style over substance. And I know all things Gatsby were very trendy a while back, but really, the style is timeless."

I absolutely did not want my dad—or anyone— throwing us an engagement party. It had nothing to do with the engagement being fake. Even if Everly and I were planning an actual wedding, I would have vetoed a party.

"That sounds amazing," Everly said.

My eyes darted to her. She couldn't be taking his side.

She looked right at me, a playful smile on her lips. "Come on, Shep. It's just a little party."

"Exactly," Dad said. "This is a big deal. We need to celebrate. Just an intimate gathering, nothing too extravagant. I already talked to your brother. He and Grant are looking forward to it."

Everly winked. "See? Ethan and Grant are excited."

The little vixen was fucking with me. I'd just have to fuck with her right back. "Well, we'll have to invite your parents and sister, Everly."

Her smile faded and she started fidgeting with her hair. "Right. Well, my parents live in Florida. And they're busy, and they travel a lot. I'm not sure if they'd be able to make it."

"Your sister, though," I said, enjoying the way she was trying not to squirm. "She lives in the area, doesn't she?"

The color drained from her face.

"I can't wait to meet her," Dad said. "Just think, both families, together in one place."

"I'll, um..." She fumbled over her words. "I'll have to check the calendar."

"Great," Dad said. "I'm taking Svetlana to a benefit luncheon tomorrow. We'll start working on the details. You won't have to lift a finger."

I had to stop myself from groaning at the mention of Svetlana.

"And just to let you know, things are looking up," Dad said. "The market's been turning in my favor, and I have some big deals going through that are going to put me back in the black. Well in the black, if all goes according to plan."

"Dad—"

He put up a hand. "Nothing too risky. I learned that lesson. But you won't have dear old dad as a roommate much longer."

The reminder that this—all of this—was temporary poked at something in my chest. "Right. Glad to hear it."

"How's your treatment going?" Everly asked.

"Uncomfortable and inconvenient. But if that's the worst of it, I'll consider myself a very lucky man. Things are looking good there too. Thanks for asking." He smiled at her. "Well, I won't keep you. Goodnight, you two."

"Night, Richard."

I nodded. "Night, Dad."

As soon as he left, Everly grabbed my arm. "Can I talk to you for a minute?"

I let her lead me to the bedroom and she shut the door behind us.

"Invite my parents and my sister?" she asked.

"The party *sounds amazing*?" I shot back.

She put her hands on her hips. "Your dad was so excited. I don't know how you say no to him when he has that adorable little gleam in his eyes."

I pinched the bridge of my nose. "Gleam in his eyes?"

"Shepherd, I can't invite my family. What am I supposed to say? Oh hey, Mom and Dad, can you fly out to Seattle for my engagement party? No, I'm not actually making all your dreams come true by getting married. I'm pretending to be marrying my boss, but everyone else there is going to think it's real. You can go along with that, right?"

"Can they?"

She groaned. "No, it would be a disaster. My sister totally would, but that's beside the point."

"Then don't invite anyone. They don't have to know."

"Yeah, but your dad was so excited about meeting my family."

"Because he thinks this is real," I said.

Her expression fell and she leaned away. "Right. There isn't actually anything between us."

Damn it. "That's not what I meant."

"No, it's fine. I get it." She gestured toward the bathroom. "I think I'm going to take a bath and read. I'll be sure to put the party on your calendar when your dad sets a date."

She grabbed a book from her nightstand and went into the bathroom without looking back.

I stared at the closed door for a long moment. Fuck. I hadn't meant to hurt her feelings.

My phone rang, so I pulled it out of my pocket. As if to add insult to injury, it was my mother. Why was she calling? I hadn't talked to her in months.

I answered on the way to my office. "Hi, Mom."

"Shepherd. What's this about you getting married?"

Oh, for fuck's sake. "Did you talk to Dad?"

"He called to find out my availability for your engagement party. I pretended that wasn't the first I'd heard of this. Of course you wouldn't get engaged without calling your mother to tell her the news."

*I would if the engagement was fake and there wasn't any reason for you to know.* "It was sudden."

"Indeed. Is she pregnant?"

I sank down into my chair, grinding my teeth together. "No, she's not pregnant."

"Blackmail?"

"Mom, what the hell? No, she's not blackmailing me."

She paused for a beat. "Then why on earth are you getting married?"

*Because I fell in love with her.* Jesus, where had that thought come from? "Is it really that hard to believe?"

"Shepherd, marriage is an archaic institution. A legally binding contract between two people to stay together for life? It's completely unrealistic. Move her in with you. Let her play house if that's what she wants. But for god's sake, don't get married."

"You've made your thoughts on marriage abundantly clear."

"And don't get her pregnant," she said. "That's almost as bad as getting married."

"That's an interesting thing to say to your son."

"Oh god, don't start. You sound like your brother. You've worked too hard for everything you have to risk it all for some woman."

"Look, you don't have to come to the party. It's Dad's idea anyway. But Everly's not..." I trailed off, not sure what I wanted to say. Or rather, not sure I should say it.

"She's not what?"

"She's not like you. I'm not marrying her because I'm being coerced." *You're not marrying her at all, Shepherd.* "She wouldn't know how to blackmail someone even if she wanted to. She doesn't think like that. People aren't assets or liabilities to her."

"So she's naive. Sounds like your father."

"Jesus, Mom. At least Dad's a decent human being."

"I don't want to talk about your father. It sounds like you're intent on marrying this girl who is—" she cleared her throat "—not like me, but I'm afraid I won't be able to make it to your party."

"That's fine."

She huffed, like she was insulted. If she wanted me to beg her to come, she was going to be disappointed. I wasn't playing that game with her.

"Fine. Congratulations."

We said goodbye and I tossed my phone on my desk. This was turning into a shit show.

I took a deep breath, pinching the bridge of my nose again. When had my mom gotten so bitter? She'd never been warm and nurturing—not even when Ethan and I were kids—but she'd seemed to reject her life as a wife and mother more vehemently as the years went by.

And I was so much like her.

Ethan had gotten our father's warmth. I'd been born of ice. The stoic coldness that had made me so successful had come from her. I wanted to think it had been tempered by my dad's compassion. That perhaps I'd learned to be less of a cold-hearted bastard because of his influence.

Not that I had the track record to prove it. I was well aware of my reputation in my company. Cold. Ruthless. I had colleagues and contacts rather than friends. I wasn't close to my family—or I hadn't been, before Dad had moved in. I'd seen him—and Ethan—more lately than I had in years.

My past with women painted the same picture. Short, shallow relationships. I'd thought it was bad luck. But deep down, I knew the truth. I'd gone after the same type of woman, over and over. Women who were more interested in my money than me. Women I'd never connect with.

Because I didn't know how to connect. I was too much like my mother.

Leaving my phone where it sat—I needed to check out for a while—I went downstairs to my other condo. I sat on the couch with my Gibson Les Paul and played. Felt the pressure of the strings against my fingertips. Focused on the quiet melody in my headphones.

I didn't know what I was going to do about this party. Or about Everly. Maybe I shouldn't have slept with her. Or invited her to see me play.

But despite the knot of confusion sitting in the pit of my stomach, I still didn't regret it.

## 23

## EVERLY

*C*rawling into bed, my skin warm from a very long bath, I pulled the sheets up. I didn't know where Shepherd was—if he was in his office, or downstairs with his guitar collection. Or maybe at the bar again.

It didn't matter. I wasn't his fiancée, or even his girl-friend, as he'd so helpfully reminded me. He could do what he wanted.

But man, that comment had stung.

What had I expected? That Shepherd inviting me to see him play at a dive bar, giving me an orgasm in the back of his car, then fucking me senseless in his secret guitar lair meant this wasn't fake anymore? That something was actually happening between us?

Okay, yes, that's kind of what I'd thought.

Shifting, I tried to get comfortable. Soaking in the bath hadn't done much to help me relax. I'd tried to read, but mostly I'd sat in the water replaying our conversation. I was hurt and frustrated, making it very difficult to enjoy Shepherd's fantastic bathtub.

The door whispered open and my back stiffened. I barely heard his footsteps as he went into the bathroom and quietly shut the door. Was he trying to keep from waking me to be polite, or because he didn't want to face me right now?

A few minutes later, he came out, still moving almost silently through the room. My skin prickled as he slipped into bed next to me. I felt every shift in the mattress, every tiny movement of the sheets.

Great. Now that he was here, I really wasn't going to be able to sleep.

The minutes ticked by with agonizing slowness. His breathing was even and he hardly moved. He must have gone to sleep already.

How could he just fall asleep like nothing was wrong? Didn't it bother him that we were basically fighting? What was I supposed to do tomorrow? Pretend like nothing had happened?

"Everly."

His soft voice startled me from my thoughts. "Yeah?"

"You're mad at me."

*Oh, you think?* "I'm fine."

He sighed. "That's a lie."

"Like our relationship?"

He made a growly noise in his throat and I clenched my teeth, trying to deny the way my body reacted to that sound. I did not need heat rushing to my core right now.

"I didn't mean it that way," he said.

"You don't have to explain yourself. You're right. We're pretending. That was the deal."

He moved. I couldn't see him, but it felt like he'd turned on his side to face me. "I wasn't pretending when I kissed you at the hospital."

"You'd just been through a really stressful experience."

"Or at the bar."

"That was intense. No one you know has ever seen you play before."

"Did it seem like I was pretending in the car?" he asked, his voice low.

I hesitated, the insistent tingling between my legs getting harder to ignore. "We were... it was just... any man would respond to a woman straddling him in the back seat of his car."

"Everly—"

"Fine, I'm sure your hard-ons last night were very real. But an erection doesn't mean anything. Guys can get erections for all kinds of reasons. They don't even have to like a woman to have a physical response to her."

"That's not my point."

I flipped over to face him. In the darkness, I could just make out his features. "Then what is your point?"

"That I'm sorry. I only meant my dad thinks the engagement is real. Regardless of what happened last night, I think we can both agree we're not actually engaged."

Okay, he did have a point. Even though I was positively drowning in feelings for him, the engagement was most certainly not real.

"Yeah, that's true." I rubbed my bare finger with my thumb. I kept the golf ball on a band that was my fake-engagement ring in a little dish on the bathroom counter at night. "I guess I can kind of see your point."

He took another deep breath. I could practically feel his chest expand with his slow inhale. "Last night was..."

I bit my lip, waiting for him to continue. It was what? Amazing? Mind-blowing? A night that would alter the course of his life forever?

"It was hard for me," he said. "You're right, it was intense."

Oh god, vulnerable Shepherd was showing himself again. That was worse than if he'd said it was the best sex he'd ever had. I wanted to grab him and cradle his head against my chest.

"Yeah, it was," I said.

"But I'm glad I shared it with you."

My heart did a little pirouette in my chest. "Me too."

We lay together in silence for a moment. My toes brushed his leg and I almost gasped. I hadn't realized I'd been stretching my foot toward him. Judging by how close his leg was, he'd been doing the same.

Reaching. Inching toward each other.

"Everly?"

"Yeah?"

He hooked his arm around my waist and pulled me toward him. I found myself on his side of the bed for the first time, crossing yet another invisible line. He was shirtless, dressed in nothing but a pair of boxer briefs. I could feel the warmth of his body through the thin fabric of my nightie.

He propped himself up to look down at me and skimmed his hand over my ribs. "I like you."

"Okay, fine, I like you too."

God, that smile. One corner of his mouth pulled up, puckering his dimple. The fact that he so rarely smiled made each one feel like gold.

He leaned down and brought his mouth to mine. His lips were firm, brushing across mine in a soft caress. I ran my hands across his dusting of chest hair. It felt so indulgent to touch him, here in his bed. Like I could finally have what I'd been secretly craving. Him.

His hand slid beneath my nightie and palmed my breast. The feel of him touching me like this made me want to purr like a cat. I ran my hands up his chest and around his back, feeling the hard planes of muscle. His body was positively glorious. Fit and strong, with bulges and ridges in all the right places.

The tension between my legs grew as he kissed and touched me. Why was he hesitating? Why didn't he yank my clothes off, climb on top of me, and make it all better with that magnificent cock?

I wasn't mad anymore, but my earlier pout-fest had left me with a lot of pent-up frustration. I wanted some of the fire from last night.

Tilting his head, he slanted his mouth over mine. He tasted so good, I wanted to bite him. I nipped at his bottom lip, and he groaned, pressing his erection against me.

That was interesting.

His tongue slid against mine and when he pulled back, I caught his lip between my teeth and held it. He growled, low in his throat. I bit harder, pulling on his lip with my teeth before letting go.

Grunting, he hooked his thumb beneath my panties and yanked them down. I kicked them off and pulled my nightie over my head while he took off his underwear and quickly got a condom.

Wasting no more time, he climbed on top of me, pressing the head of his cock against my opening. Despite the way my lady parts wanted me to beg him to fuck the hell out of me, another thought flitted through my mind.

Did Shepherd like pain?

He kissed down my neck as he slid inside. My eyes rolled back, the pressure of his thickness filling me. God, yes. He thrust in and out, his cock dragging through my wetness.

I ran my hands along his back. I didn't want to hurt him, but he'd definitely reacted when I'd bitten his lip. I'd accidentally scratched him last night—and who could blame me? I'd been in the throes of the best sexual experience of my life. He'd said I couldn't hurt him. But had he liked it?

He thrust again—hard—and I clutched at him, letting my fingernails dig into his back.

He growled into my neck, long and low, and his body melted against me. I did it again with his next thrust, scratching my nails down his back.

It drove him crazy.

I'd never felt a man react like this. He grunted, driving into me harder. The more I clawed at him, the more he let go. He was savage—muscles flexing, hips hammering. And I loved every bit of it.

He pulled out and turned me onto my tummy, smacking my ass as I rolled over. Giggling, I arched my back and he draped himself over me, thrusting in from behind.

His hand slid under my shoulder to my neck. With his face close to my ear, he wrapped his hand around my throat. I was pinned down, totally in his control. It was exhilarating. He grunted with every thrust, driving his cock in deep. This angle was amazing, giving me friction in all the right places.

"Don't stop fucking me," I said.

He growled in my ear. His grip on my throat was firm, without cutting off my air, and his cock drove into me in a steady rhythm. The heat in my core grew, the tantalizing pressure building.

"Your pussy feels so good," he murmured. "I'm going to come in you so fucking hard."

I gasped as he pulled out again, but I loved the way he manhandled me into the positions he wanted. He rolled onto his back and hauled me on top of him. I sank down onto his cock, reveling in the feeling of his thickness filling me.

He reached up and threaded his fingers through my hair, pulling my mouth to his. I rolled my hips to slide up and down his cock while he kissed me deeply. My tits dragged across his chest, his coarse hair tingling against my smooth skin.

Grinding him like this felt so good, I was teetering on the edge of climax in no time. I nipped his lip with my teeth and he let go of my hair to grab my hips. He thrust up, hard, as I rode him faster.

We were both lost in the moment, saturated with pure lust. His brow furrowed and he grunted, his cock thickening. I chased my orgasm to the brink, letting the tension overtake me.

Still grinding on him, I burst apart, my breathless moans filling the air. His cock throbbed, deep inside me, as we came together. It was magic, our bodies moving in sync, the waves of pleasure rolling through us both.

He pulled me down again, kissing me while my body trembled with the last pulses of my orgasm.

I slid off him and lay on the sheets, catching my breath. My eyes fluttered closed. I couldn't move. He got up to deal with the condom, then I peeled myself out of bed to take care of basic necessities in the bathroom.

When I came back, he pulled me against him in the center of the bed, wrapping his arms around me. I rested my head against his shoulder, letting my arm drape across his chest. His skin on mine and the warmth of his body felt so good, I resolved to stop wearing pajamas to bed.

We lay together in silence for a few minutes. The rush of orgasm was gone, but it left a warm glow in its wake. I breathed him in and slid my fingers through his chest hair, completely relaxed.

"You know, maybe we should stop your dad from throwing this party," I said, breaking the silence. "He's going to spend all this time and effort for an engagement that isn't real."

Shepherd rested his cheek against my head. "True."

"But the thing is, and maybe I'm imagining it, he seems so excited. Like this is fun for him."

"It is. He was the one who planned all our birthday parties when Ethan and I were kids. He loves this stuff."

"God, your dad is the cutest. What do you think we should do?"

He took a deep breath, his arms tightening around me. "I think we play along. He's spending my money, not his. And it's giving him something else to focus on besides having cancer and trying to dig himself out of a financial hole."

"That's kind of what I was thinking, too."

"I am going to get him to tone it down, though," he said. "Dad has a tendency to go overboard. If we're not careful, we might wind up with a two-hour fireworks show over Lake Union or a private concert by some old boy band."

I laughed. "No, he wouldn't."

"He did. The fireworks were for my eleventh. I still don't know how he got the city to issue the permits. The boy band was for Ethan's thirteenth."

"He got a boy band to play at Ethan's thirteenth birthday party?"

"Yeah."

"So you're saying I shouldn't have encouraged him."

"Probably not."

"Sorry."

He kissed my head. "Don't be. We'll get through it."

I nestled into him, enjoying the warmth of his body. His arms around me. I was floating on a cloud of sex-induced endorphins, wrapped up in bed with the sexiest man I'd ever known. We would get through it. It was going to be fine.

We were going to be fine. I hoped.

## 24

### EVERLY

*S*hepherd had been right. Richard was really into this party planning stuff.

He sat at the dining table with his laptop, plus a mess of magazine clippings, post-it notes, lists, and menus spread out in front of him. He'd spent the last couple of weeks immersed in this party, happy as could be. Today, he hummed to himself, jotted down notes, held up samples, and seemed to come up with one new idea after another.

Svetlana sat across from him, resting bitch face out in full force. He'd invited her over for dinner, and I wondered if she'd known he meant *dinner while planning Shepherd and Everly's engagement party*. Her plate of food sat mostly untouched in front of her. I was pretty sure her meal consisted primarily of vodka tonight.

I stood in the kitchen, pretending to be busy with something, stealing glances at them. It was hard not to laugh out loud. Richard looking happy as could be, asking for her opinion on invitations or declaring *I have the best idea* for the tenth time. Svetlana, arms crossed, legs crossed, glaring down at Richard's jumble of party preparations.

How he was oblivious to her pouting was beyond me. But Richard did tend to see mostly what he wanted to see. Shepherd thought his sensitivity was his weakness, but I disagreed. It was his unbridled optimism that seemed to get him into the most trouble. He saw the absolute best in everyone and everything—even when it wasn't really there.

Maybe I recognized it because I shared the tendency. It was probably why I'd been on so many bad dates. I always tried to see the best in people, and sometimes it got me into trouble too. That was part of why I liked Richard so much. I understood him.

I'd decided I needed some representation at this party if it was going to seem authentic. And Richard asked me every day whether I'd invited my family yet. My parents weren't an option. They were *color inside the lines* people. *Do things by the book* people. Not *go along with their daughter's fake engagement* people.

And trying to convince them I was actually engaged to Shepherd was an even worse idea. I took flack about being single every time I talked to my parents. I'd committed the cardinal sin of turning thirty without a wedding ring on my finger. If I told them I was engaged—to my boss, no less— and then had to break the news that the engagement was off? I'd be the ultimate failure. On the brink of landing the much-coveted *Mrs.* designation, only to have lost it before I could seal the deal.

No, my parents could stay happily in Florida, judging my singlehood from afar.

I tried to ignore the voice in my head that whispered soft suggestions about the engagement never ending. About this sham turning into a real engagement someday.

*Slow down, Everly. The weight of this ring is messing with your brain.*

I needed to call Annie and ask her if she'd come. I knew she'd have my back, but this was going to be hard to explain. And I needed to tell her I couldn't ask Shepherd to be their donor.

As far as I was concerned, me sleeping with Shepherd was the final deal-breaker when it came to donating his swimmers. There was an unwritten rule, I was sure of it. You couldn't ask a man who'd had his peen in your sister to be your sperm donor. It felt wrong to me.

But I didn't want to tell her I was sleeping with him. It would just make her worry about me, and I didn't need the lecture about the potential consequences of engaging in a sexual relationship with my boss. I loved my sister, but she was intensely practical. It was going to be hard enough to explain that I'd spent the last month pretending to be his fiancée.

But the girls? They were easy. I knew Nora and Hazel would show up for me. They always did. I sent a group text.

**Me:** *I need you two to come to my fake-engagement party and pretend it's real. Two weeks from Saturday. You'll get an invitation in the mail, but save the date, k?*

**Hazel:** *I'm so glad you asked. This is going to be a fascinating social experiment.*

**Hazel:** *Do you mind if I conduct some informal interviews with guests? Not for official research, just for my own analysis.*

**Nora:** *Aw, look at you, making Hazel's science-loving heart happy.*

**Me:** *Sure, Hazel. Just don't blow my cover.*

**Hazel:** *Of course not. I'll behave as if it's a double-blind experiment.*

**Nora:** *What are you wearing? And how many single men will be there?*

**Me:** *I don't know yet. And I'm not sure.*

**Nora:** *I'll come regardless, but add more single men to the guest list if you can. Hot ones.*

**Nora:** *Do you need me to dress you?*

**Nora:** *Oh! I already have some ideas. How do you feel about blush versus white? Or maybe mixing it up with an animal print?*

**Me:** *Blush, yes. Animal print, no.*

**Nora:** *Maybe I'll wear an animal print.*

**Me:** *The party has a theme. Everything is going to be in the style of the Roaring Twenties. Richard's idea.*

**Nora:** *Oh my god.*

**Nora:** *Are you serious?*

**Hazel:** *Does this mean our clothes have to reflect the theme?*

**Me:** *They don't have to, but they can if you want.*

**Nora:** *Oh my god.*

**Me:** *You said that already.*

**Hazel:** *Nora, I'm going to need your help, too.*

My phone went silent for a long moment. Did Nora hate the theme? Was that why she'd gone suddenly silent?

**Nora:** *Sorry. I'm just really overwhelmed right now.*

**Me:** *Why?*

**Nora:** *Do you know how long I've wanted to style someone for a Roaring Twenties party?*

**Me:** *No, how long?*

**Nora:** *BASICALLY FOREVER*

**Nora:** *But no one's doing them anymore.*

**Nora:** *Everly, you just made my day. No! My week. My month.*

**Nora:** *Block out Saturday, girls. All day. We have work to do.*

**Hazel:** *Do we need to bring dates to the party?*

**Nora:** *Why wouldn't we bring dates?*

**Me:** *You just asked me to invite more single men and you plan to bring a date too?*

**Nora:** *I like having options.*

*Hazel: I'm not dating anyone. And I don't want to date anyone.*

*Nora: You don't have to be dating someone to bring a date. Tell you what, I'll get you a dress and a date. Deal?*

*Hazel: That sounds like a terrible idea.*

*Nora: Don't you trust me to find you a good date?*

*Hazel: No. Can't we just be each other's dates?*

I covered my mouth to stifle a giggle. Hazel was still on her anti-dating kick, something Nora couldn't fathom.

*Nora: Fine, I'll be your date. But if there's a hot man at Everly's party, I'm ditching you.*

*Hazel: That's fine. I can always Uber home.*

*Nora: Thank you, my love!*

*Me: So you're both good to go? You'll be there?*

*Hazel: I'm looking forward to it.*

*Nora: Wouldn't miss it.*

And that was why I loved my friends.

I PUT off calling my sister for another hour, but finally I decided to get it over with. I went into the bedroom and sat on the bed, then brought up her number and hit send.

"Hey, Everly," Annie said when she answered.

"Hi, how are you and Miranda?"

"We're doing well. What's up?

"This is going to sound complicated, and also strange, but hear me out, okay?"

"Um, sure?"

I took a breath. "I've been pretending to be my boss's girlfriend."

"You what?"

"I know, I know. Like I said, hear me out. His dad started

dating his ex, who's a gold-digging harpy. But his dad doesn't know she's Shepherd's ex, and Shepherd is pretty sure he'll break up with her soon, because his dad has flings with younger women sometimes. But this woman, the gold-digging harpy, is actually trying to get to Shepherd. He didn't want her to think he's single, so he moved me in, and I sort of made things more complicated by telling her that Shepherd and I are getting married. So now I'm fake-engaged to my boss. And his dad is throwing us an engagement party and it would help us both so much if you and Miranda would come."

"I…" She trailed off. "I have no idea how to reply to that. Are you joking?"

"No, I'm serious. I'm pretending to be marrying my boss, and now there's an engagement party, and it would be odd if all the guests were Shepherd's. The thing is, Shepherd's dad, Richard? He's such a nice man. He has terrible taste in women, but he's like a big teddy bear. And he's so excited about this. Shepherd has done a lot for him recently, and I think this is Richard's way of thanking him. He keeps asking me if my family is coming, and I don't want to disappoint him."

"Everly, what were you thinking? Do you realize how crazy this is?"

*Oh Annie, you have no idea.* "It's fine. Really. It's not that big of a deal."

She took a deep breath. "So, you need me and Miranda to come to an engagement party and pretend that we think you're marrying Shepherd Calloway?"

"Exactly."

"This is probably the weirdest thing you've ever asked me to do. But sure, we'll come."

"Really? Oh my god, thank you so much. But don't tell Mom and Dad."

"Oh god no, I wouldn't dream of it."

I smiled. "Thanks, Annie."

"You're—" She stopped talking and I heard the faint sound of Miranda's voice in the background. "It's what? Oh no. Everly, I'm sorry, I have to go. The toilet in the bathroom we just finished is flooding."

"That's not good."

"Hang on, Miranda, I'll be right there. Oh god, I can smell it from down here. I have to go. Love you, sis."

"Love you, too."

I could hear her calling up to Miranda again just before she hung up. Flooding toilet. Yikes.

She'd had to go before I could talk to her about Shepherd, but maybe that was a good thing. If they met Shepherd in person—in a non-work setting, where he was less likely to act like a robot—maybe they'd see him as more than just a potential source of DNA. He was a person. A man.

A man I happened to be crushing on, hard, but that was beside the point.

For now, I texted Richard to update him on my guest list. Then I decided I was going to treat myself to a nice hot bath.

Shepherd came into the bedroom and paused, looking me up and down. "There you are."

"Hey. I was just talking to my sister. She and Miranda will come to the party. And, you know, go along with everything."

"Good." His eyes were intense—predatory. I loved it when he looked at me like that. "What are you doing now?"

"I was thinking about taking a bath, but I could do something else."

"No, take the bath." He started cuffing the sleeves of his button-down shirt. "I want to watch."

Nibbling my lip, I got up and darted into the bathroom, already thinking about ways to make this fun. Lying in the water did make my boobs look amazing. He came in and dimmed the lights while I started the bathwater.

I slowly peeled off my clothes while he watched.

Oh yes. This was fun.

Was this still fake? Was it just sex? I really didn't know. And, for the moment at least, I was okay with that.

## 25

# SHEPHERD

$\mathcal{M}$y focus shifted as soon as I got to the conference room—from work, to Everly. I'd been reading an email from my CFO, but as soon as I heard her voice, I stopped outside the door.

That sweet voice made me feel like I was unraveling. Suddenly all I could think about was the taste of her lips. The feel of her skin. The sting of her nails on my back. No one would suspect what the girl with the sunshine smile was capable of in the bedroom. I still had her bite marks on my chest.

I was an addict, and she was my secret dealer.

I'd never indulged with a woman the way I did with her. She bit and clawed at me and I fucking loved it. I couldn't get enough. My body craved the powerful sensory stimulation. It wasn't pain to me, so much as raw intensity. Every bite and scratch cut through my emotional paralysis and made me *feel*.

I worked hard to keep my personal life out of the public eye. The fact that the elusive business mogul Shepherd Calloway had a thing for pain in the bedroom would spread like wildfire in the gossip columns if it ever got out. Until Everly, I'd never trusted a woman with that. I didn't like trusting people too far—it made me vulnerable.

But I'd trusted her with everything.

Her tone brought my attention back to reality. There was a sharpness to her voice. We had a meeting in about ten minutes, but she was talking to someone in the conference room. It sounded like Damian Fillsburg, head of sales.

"Mr. Calloway needs those figures by Monday."

"By when?" Damian sounded distracted, like he was only half-listening to her.

"I'm standing right here, Damian," she said. "So I'm sure you heard me say Monday. Just as it said in the email I sent."

I peeked around the partially open door. Damian stood in front of her, eyes on his phone. She had her arms crossed around a stack of blue folders. I could practically feel the irritation coming off her. Not that I blamed her. Damian was fairly new and his arrogance was already grating on me.

He looked up as if only just now noticing she was there. "You can just fudge something for me, right? Make me look good for the boss-man?"

Everly pressed her lips together as she shook her head. "No, I can't fudge something for you."

"Everly, help a guy out here," he said, tilting his head. He took a step closer. "How about this. Come to dinner with me on Friday and we can work on it together."

A bolt of anger flashed through me. How dare he hit on my woman. I was about to step in and fire the fucker, but Everly didn't miss a beat.

She clicked her tongue. "I'm sorry to hear that, Damian."

"Sorry to hear what?"

"That Autumn broke up with you. Autumn was your girlfriend's name, right? The one with pretty blond hair, wore a sundress to the company picnic? In fact, didn't you propose to her a few months ago? It's too bad it ended."

"Wait, what? No. I mean, Autumn is her name, but we didn't... What are you talking about?"

"Well, you just rather inappropriately asked me to dinner, which I assume means you and Autumn broke up. Or did I misunderstand what you were asking?"

"No, I didn't mean..." Damian fumbled for words. "We didn't break up."

"Oh, I see," Everly said. "So you weren't asking me to dinner, because of course you wouldn't cheat on your lovely fiancée."

"No, of course not."

"So you also didn't just ask me to falsify data in the sales reports. I must have misunderstood that too."

He stared at her, open-mouthed, for a few seconds. "Right, no. I wouldn't ask you to do that."

"I didn't think so," she said with a friendly smile. "So how about you have those reports to me by Friday instead of Monday, just so I can make sure everything is accurate and ready on time."

"Uh, yeah, Friday." He straightened, flashing a fake smile, as if he could possibly recover his dignity. "Sales reports will be in your inbox."

"Excellent. Thanks, Damian," she said.

I stepped into the conference room. Damian didn't make eye contact with me as he left.

Everly started placing a blue folder in front of each chair. "You're early."

She was right. I was. But she hadn't been at her desk. Her pull was like gravity to me. I'd come down to the conference room early because I figured she'd be here.

"I know." I looked her up and down, enjoying the way

her yellow dress showed off her curves. But it wasn't her gorgeous body that was impressing me right now. "You really put Damian in his place."

Glancing at me from the corner of her eye, she set another folder down. "You heard that?"

"Some of it."

She gave me a little shrug. "He thinks he can push people's boundaries and get away with it. I'm happy to disabuse him of that notion."

"You're something else, Miss Dalton."

"Why thank you, Mr. Calloway."

I wanted to do a hundred dirty things to her on that conference table. Bend her over and hike up that pretty dress. Finger fuck her until she was wet, then sink my cock in deep. I could lay her down and bury my face between her legs. Lick her beautiful pussy until she came in my mouth.

Someone walked in behind me, once again snapping me back to reality. I was doing far too much fantasizing lately. But I couldn't help it. This woman was consuming me.

The development team filed in and took their seats. I sat next to Everly, casually letting my leg brush against hers while we listened to the presentation.

Above the table, we were all business. Below, I slid my hand along her leg. Her face didn't show even a hint of a reaction—at least not that I could see—but she gently tipped her legs apart. It made my heart pound, my blood running hot. I barely resisted the urge to lean in and breathe the strawberry scent of her hair. I couldn't reach much without moving closer to her, so I settled for caressing the soft skin of her thigh.

Without losing her attentive posture, she gently nudged her pen off the table with her elbow. Her eyes flicked to me and she gave an apologetic shrug before leaning over to pick it up.

On her way down, she swiped her hand over my dick. Instead of reaching for her pen, she grabbed my cock through my slacks and gave it a good, firm squeeze.

I grunted at the pressure—holy fuck, that felt good—then cleared my throat to cover. Everly sat up, set her pen on the table, and went back to her note-taking.

I didn't hear another word of the presentation. It was as if all the blood in my body had rushed south, leaving only enough in my brain for autonomic functions like breathing and keeping my heart pumping.

The meeting ended and I decided to go straight back to my office. I was so keyed up, I was ready to pounce on her. I couldn't exactly do that in the middle of the conference room.

Plus, my office door locked.

I waited a few minutes for her to get back to her desk, then sent her a message.

*Me: Come here.*

*Everly: Oh, do you need something?*

*Me: You know what I need.*

*Everly: Coffee?*

*Everly: Should I bring a notepad?*

*Everly: Do you want the meeting notes? I think you might have missed some of it.*

*Me: Get your ass in here. Now.*

She came in and shut the door, leaning back against it, a wicked smile curling her lips.

"Lock it," I said, my voice low.

With her tongue darting out over her lips, she reached behind her and locked the door.

I looked her up and down, trying to decide what I

wanted. So many possibilities. I hit the remote to close the blinds and her cheeks flushed pink.

Before I could give her any commands, she came over to my desk. The fire in her eyes filled me with curiosity. Wondering what she was about to do, I stayed silent. Watching.

She licked her lips again and sank down to her knees in front of me. Just the anticipation, the way she traced a finger down my zipper, her eyes never leaving mine, had me achingly hard. She took her time, slowly unfastening my pants. Lowering my zipper.

"Mm," she said, pulling my underwear down. "What could I do with this?"

Grabbing me at the base, she drew her tongue up the outside of my shaft. My eyes rolled back and I groaned, low in my throat. She licked me a few more times, slowly dragging her tongue up my cock. Tracing the tip.

"Fuck, Everly."

"Shh." A quick flick of her tongue made me groan again. "We have to be quiet."

I'd have happily done just about anything in that moment to get her to suck my dick. If quiet was what she wanted, quiet was what she'd get.

I was going to make her pay for it later, though.

She swirled her tongue around the tip and I nodded, keeping my mouth closed.

"Good." She wrapped her fingers around the base again and slid my cock into her mouth.

Fuck, that felt good. She started shallow, squeezing me at the base while she sucked on the tip. Her mouth was slick and warm, her tongue sliding against the shaft each time she plunged down.

Swallowing back another groan, I let it out as a low

growl. I couldn't help it. Just the sight of her mouth around my hard length was fucking amazing.

She moved faster, taking in more of me each time. Plunging down on me. Deeper.

I slid my fingers in her hair and her eyes fluttered closed. Her soft moan reverberated through my body. I watched, playing with her soft tresses, while she worked my cock with her mouth. The pressure mounted, heat and tension building.

My hips moved with her rhythm, thrusting my cock into her mouth. She slid a hand beneath my shirt, splaying her palm across my ribs. Her fingers curled and I felt the sharp bite of her fingernails as she dug them into my skin.

Jerking my hips, I barely stifled a groan. My hand tightened in her hair and she clawed at me again, still plunging down on my cock. I watched it slide out of her mouth, glistening wet, my vision going hazy at the edges.

This was torture of the best kind. She took me deep into her wet mouth, the friction of her lips and tongue driving me crazy. Her hand slid higher, to my chest. Finding my nipple, she grabbed it between her finger and thumb and tugged—hard.

"Fuck," I growled, unable to contain myself.

She picked up the pace, her head bobbing as she plunged down on me, over and over. I held her hair, mesmerized, on the brink of losing control. Right as her eyes lifted to meet mine, she grabbed my nipple again, tugging harder this time.

And I lost my fucking mind.

I exploded into her mouth, my cock pulsing as I came. It was so sudden, and so strong, it overwhelmed my senses. The waves of pleasure crashed through my body, leaving me helpless—totally at her mercy.

After I finished, she slid my dick out of her mouth while I blinked at the ceiling, utterly intoxicated. My head swam with endorphins. I could hardly think.

I took a deep breath and the world snapped back into focus. She was still on her knees, her hands on my thighs.

Her turn.

I cupped her chin and traced my thumb across her bottom lip. "That was fucking incredible."

"Yeah, you—"

"Take your panties off."

There was no room in my tone for anything but obedience. Eyes locked with mine, she stood. She didn't try to take her skirt off first, just lifted it and slid her panties down her legs.

Good girl.

I unbuttoned her blouse and opened it just enough to get a taste of her tits. I nuzzled them, rubbing my thumbs across her nipples through the thin fabric of her bra. Pulling one side down, I flicked her nipple with my tongue a few times while I slid my hand up her inner thigh.

Her slit was wet and I felt her tremble as my fingers teased her soft skin.

"Shepherd—"

Swiping my thumb over her clit, I shushed her. "Shh. We have to be quiet."

She bit her lip, whimpering softly.

I pushed all the shit on my desk to one side—I was glad it was so big—and laid her down. She tipped her legs open and I hiked her skirt higher.

"Look at that pretty pussy." I licked up her slit. "God, you taste fucking good."

She whimpered again. I loved hearing her make that sound.

With my hands on her thighs, I went to work on her clit with my tongue. I started slow, teasing, torturing. Long drags of my tongue against her soft folds. The tension in her body built, her back arching, fingers clutching at the surface of my desk.

I slid two fingers inside her and she barely stopped a moan from escaping her lips. Flicking her clit with my tongue, I curled my fingers, giving her the friction she needed. Her body writhed and she grabbed my hair while she bucked her hips against me.

I was relentless, never letting up. I licked and sucked her clit while I worked her pussy with my fingers. Still high from my own orgasm, I was intoxicated by her taste. By the feel of her wetness on my fingers.

This sweet, gorgeous woman was laid out on my desk, her pussy all mine. I'd never felt so fucking powerful.

She took short, sharp breaths and her pussy clenched around my fingers. I gave her more, lapping my tongue against her clit. Her pussy was hot around my fingers. God, she was so close. I could feel it, almost like I was about to come again.

Her back arched and she clapped a hand over her mouth, her pussy throbbing. I rode out her orgasm with her, still licking and driving into her with my fingers.

She relaxed, still gasping for breath. "Oh my god, stop. I can't take anymore."

I planted a last kiss over her clit and slid my fingers out.

"Holy shit, Shepherd," she breathed. "I think I just died."

I helped her sit up on the edge of my desk and she blinked a few times. Her hair was a mess, her clothes disheveled.

"You look sexy as fuck right now." I held her hips and

leaned in to kiss her. "Now get your ass out, I have work to do."

Giggling, she grabbed my nipple through my shirt and twisted, making me grunt. "You ass. You can't give me an orgasm like that and not let me recover."

I kissed her again. "Let's clear my schedule and you can take all the time you need."

The crazy thing was, I meant it. I'd have happily taken the rest of the day off, just to spend it with her. It was so unlike me.

Everly was addicting, and not just because she knew how to make me come harder than I ever had in my life. I liked her—a lot. And I still wasn't sure how to handle that.

## 26

# SHEPHERD

$\mathcal{I}$n order to keep the engagement party from getting terribly out of control, I'd convinced my dad to hold it here, at my condo. I had plenty of space for a small, intimate gathering—and not enough space for a huge guest list. After some gentle prodding from Everly—*oh, Richard, wouldn't it be adorable to have it here?*—he'd agreed.

Which meant the morning of the party, I came home from the gym to chaos.

People were everywhere. Moving furniture, hanging up decorations, stringing lights. There was a caterer in the kitchen, a woman standing on a stepladder in the living room, apparently changing light bulbs, and what looked like a small construction crew assembling a portable stage where my dining table used to be.

And in the middle of it all was my father.

He looked good, I had to admit that. His cancer treatments had left him pale and fatigued, but today he seemed healthier than I'd seen him in weeks. Color in his face, straight back, energy in his movements. He had a clipboard tucked under one arm and was talking to someone on his phone.

I waited, hands in my shorts pockets, while people bustled around me, transforming my home into... well, it was hard to say at this point what it was turning into. At the moment, it looked like a party store had exploded in the penthouse.

Dad hung up and pocketed his phone. "Oh good, Shep, you're home. What do you think so far?"

I glanced around. "I'm sure it'll be great when it's ready."

"I think so too." He smiled, and damn if there wasn't that gleam in his eyes that Everly had mentioned. She was right, it was hard to resist. "By tonight, you won't recognize the place. It'll be completely transformed."

Two men walked by, carrying a tall piece of plywood.

"What's that?"

Dad watched them take it out to the balcony. "Oh, that must be for the photo booth."

"Photo booth?"

"Of course. But you should go or I'm going to spoil all the best surprises."

I tried not to groan. Surprises? "Um, Dad, what surprises? I thought we were keeping this low-key."

He patted me on the back. "Don't worry. You and Everly are going to love it."

"You didn't plan a fireworks show, did you?"

"No, nothing like that." He flipped through the pages on his clipboard. "I couldn't get the permits on such short notice."

"Wait, what? You mean you *tried* to plan a fireworks show?"

"You should really make yourself scarce, Shep. You can come back when it's party time."

"I live here. Where am I supposed to go?"

He shrugged. "Go shower and just stay in your room. Or your office. We aren't using it."

I looked around at the mess of decorations, boxes, and packing material. It was probably best if I stayed out of the way.

"All right, Dad. I'll see you later tonight."

He was already distracted, wandering off to direct someone setting up a table.

I went back to my bedroom and checked my messages. Everly was with her girlfriends for the day. Something about getting ready together. I didn't know why they needed seven hours to get dressed for a party, but I knew better than to question it.

After a shower, I got dressed and went to my office. I shut the door to dampen the noise from the party crew, and got to work.

Shortly before the party was set to begin, I emerged from my office. I'd barely been out all day. Dad had brought me takeout for lunch to keep me from coming out and seeing the decorations. Now, there was a thick black curtain hanging in the entrance to the hallway that led to my office, guest room, and master suite. It was there to keep guests from coming into the more private spaces of my home—a gesture I appreciated—but it also kept me from seeing what my dad had done.

I went back to my room to change, unsure as to how I felt about this whole thing. I'd been pushing the reality of the lie I was living to the back of my mind—forcefully. Justified the charade by telling myself this party was a harmless distraction for my father.

But guilt jabbed at me, poking holes in my logic. He'd gone to a lot of trouble to celebrate an engagement that wasn't real. Not only that, he'd put in the effort because he was genuinely excited about my supposed upcoming marriage.

Coming clean to him was not going to be easy. And this party was making it worse. I hadn't counted on that when I'd agreed to it. Which really just meant I'd ignored the truth.

Plus, I'd never been a fan of parties. Especially when I was at the center of them. It was the sort of attention I preferred to avoid. Standing at the head of the boardroom or in front of investors was one thing. I was no stranger to being a leader. But I'd never particularly enjoyed social attention, and as one of the guests of honor at tonight's party, I was about to be subjected to a great deal of it.

Everly texted to say she was on her way over. An inexplicable jolt of excitement ran through me. What was she wearing? I'd let her talk me into a vintage-style suit with a double-breasted vest and a dark gray fedora. It fit my dad's theme without looking like a cheap costume. Hell, I made this look good.

There was a knock at the bedroom door. I adjusted my hat, then answered the door to find my dad—or a nineteen-twenties mobster version of my dad. He wore a pinstripe suit with a white tie, a vintage timepiece in his breast pocket. He had a black fedora, a fat cigar pinched between his teeth, and a cane that he tapped against the floor a few times.

"What do you think?" he asked, grinning at me around his unlit cigar.

"You look great, Dad."

He smoothed down the front of his jacket. "Thanks, son. You look fantastic. Ready to go down to the lobby?"

"The lobby?"

"You're meeting Everly downstairs. And don't look when you come out. I want you to get the full effect when you come back."

"All right. I won't look."

He led me down the hall and through the curtain. I kept my eyes down as I made my way quickly to the front door, only catching glimpses of black and gold.

"The first guests will be here any minute, but take your time," he said, ushering me out the door. "The couple of honor should make an entrance."

"Right. We'll be up in a little bit, then."

I went downstairs to wait for Everly, wishing my building had a bar in the lobby. Sitting on a leather couch, I crossed one ankle over my knee and swiped through my emails. People came through the lobby—other residents as well as party guests—but I didn't pay attention to them. There was only one person I really cared about seeing tonight.

The doors opened again and three women walked in, all dressed for the party. Everly's friend Nora was on the left, in a deep red fringe dress and a sequined headband in her long dark hair. Hazel was on the right, wearing a similar dress in black, with long black gloves and a pair of glasses perched on her nose.

Between them, dressed in a stunning silver fringe dress, was Everly.

Her blond hair was curled in a vintage wave and her sequined headband had white feathers on one side. Thin straps showed her graceful shoulders and her lips were painted deep red.

I stood, awestruck. She looked incredible. It reminded me of the surprise I'd felt the night of the gala. She'd stunned me in that red dress, and here she was, doing it again.

She was so fucking beautiful.

Her smile was radiant, those red lips begging to be kissed. She stopped, her eyes landing on me, and her smile grew.

"There you are," she said, breaking away from her friends. She touched the lapels of my jacket. "Don't you look handsome."

"You're stunning," I said, my eyes sweeping over her. Glancing over at her friends, I nodded. "Ladies."

"Hi, Shepherd," Nora said with a little wave.

Everly looked over her shoulder. "You can go on up. We'll be there in a few."

"Great. See you up there."

Her friends headed for the elevator, arm in arm. I turned my attention back to Everly.

"Do you like it?" She twisted her hips a little, making all the silver fringes swirl around her.

"You're both insanely sexy and adorable as hell in that thing."

"Thank you. I love this suit on you. It's very debonair."

"I actually don't hate it."

She patted my chest. "You're a good sport. Let's go have some fun."

*Fun* might be a stretch, but I didn't object to spending the evening with this gorgeous woman at my side.

We rode the elevator up to the top floor. I traced my thumb along the back of her neck, feeling her soft skin.

She tilted her face up. "How's my lipstick?"

Looking at those bright red lips made me want to kiss the lipstick right off them. "Perfect."

With my hand on the small of her back, I led her into what had once been my condo. Now it looked like a glamorous nineteen-twenties speakeasy. Black tablecloths with gold accents. Vases with plumes of black feathers. Shimmering lights draped across the ceiling. A jazz trio played on the stage in the dining room and a guy in costume tended the bar that now stood in my living room.

My dad seemed to appear out of nowhere. He was still in his suit and hat, but had left his cane and cigar somewhere. "Everly, look at you. I knew this theme would be perfect. You look beautiful."

"Thanks, Richard. This is incredible. I love your suit."

He draped a white feather boa around her shoulders. "There. Perfect. I have one for all the ladies."

A waiter approached with a tray of champagne. Dad handed us each a glass, then took one for himself. I was going to need something stronger, but for now, I held my glass while Dad beamed at us.

"A toast," he said, raising his glass. "To my son and his beautiful bride."

Everly's eyes met mine, mirroring the hint of guilt I felt. We clinked our glasses with Dad's, then drank.

"You two go have fun," he said. "I'll stay here and greet the guests. I have more boas to hand out."

Everly slipped her hand in mine, then downed the rest of her champagne. I liked where she was going with that and finished mine too.

"Bar?" she asked.

"Yes."

Guests mingled amid the sparkling décor, drinking champagne—there was a champagne fountain next to the bar—or prohibition era cocktails. Ethan and Grant were already here, dressed in matching pinstripe suits. They stood talking to Everly's girlfriends. Some old friends of my dad had come—people I'd known since I was a kid. He'd also invited some of our neighbors here in the building—people either he or Everly had made friends with. They were so much more sociable than I was. Before they'd moved in, I hadn't known any of my neighbors.

I handed Everly her sidecar and took a sip of my old fashioned. The bartender was good. Everly glanced toward the door and smiled. "My sisters are here."

Dad was draping feather boas—a red one and a blue; apparently he had multiple colors—around the necks of two women. One had long wavy hair and wore a bright red dress. The other had to be Everly's sister. There was a strong family resemblance, although this woman's hair was darker and cut shorter.

Everly waved them over, then hugged them both. "I'm so glad you came. Shepherd, this is my sister, Annie, and her wife Miranda."

"Nice to meet you." I shook hands with both of them, then slipped my hand around Everly's waist to draw her closer.

"It's wonderful to meet you," Annie said. Her eyes flicked back and forth between me and Everly a few times.

Ethan approached with a smile. I could see Grant from the corner of my eye, still chatting—laughing, to be specific —with Everly's friends.

"Nice party, Shep." He patted my shoulder.

"Dad outdid himself."

"He always does."

I introduced Ethan to Annie and Miranda. After some small talk, Ethan realized he and Grant lived just a few streets away from Everly's sister, on Queen Anne. When Annie and Miranda mentioned they'd remodeled their house, the three of them launched into an animated conversation about home renovations.

Everly and I wandered around for a while, sipping our drinks and chatting with guests. Dad had either run out of boas, or had decided all the guests were here, because I saw him dancing with Svetlana in front of the stage.

I wondered why she was still pretending to date my father. It had been over two months. Whether or not she believed Everly and I were a real couple, she had to have realized by now that I wasn't remotely interested in her. If revenge was her motive, she was certainly taking it to an extreme. And if it was money she was after, my dad hadn't been treating her to the finer things. He couldn't. They spent more of their time together here than going out, and as far as I knew, he wasn't buying her gifts. She wasn't flaunting new jewelry or designer handbags. No fancy getaways.

Was it possible I'd been wrong about her? Maybe she'd been interested in my dad for who he was from the start. Or perhaps it had started as a way to get to me—or get back at me—but she'd developed real feelings for him along the way?

The idea was both disturbing and oddly comforting. I hated the idea that she'd been using my father this whole time. If she hadn't been, if the two of them had actually found something together, it would save him from getting hurt.

Everly dragged me into the photo booth. I thought my hat was enough of a prop, but she shoved a giant mustache on a stick at me and insisted I hold it up. She grabbed a gold and black fan and a cardboard cutout champagne bottle.

We looked ridiculous. But by the third photo, we were both laughing.

A strange thing happened as the party wore on. I realized I was having fun. We tried cocktails we'd never had, posed for more silly photos, joked and laughed with our siblings, and danced together to the admittedly very good jazz trio. As I spun Everly around on the dance floor, her silver dress twirling, I felt a freedom I'd only ever experienced on stage.

Playing with my band, I hid behind anonymity. I let the other guys work the crowd. I was just there to let go. To lose myself in the music. But here I was, in my own home, surrounded by people who knew me as Shepherd Calloway, billionaire CEO. And I felt that same sense of freedom. I laughed and smiled and danced.

The band started a new song and I pulled Everly close. I lifted her chin and leaned down, kissing her. Not because we were supposed to. Not to sell everyone in the room on the veracity of our relationship. I kissed her because, in that moment, there was nowhere else I'd rather be, nothing else I'd rather be doing. And no one else I'd rather be doing it with.

## 27

## EVERLY

*I* read the email for probably the tenth time, a potent mix of feelings swirling in my tummy. It was from Cameron Whitbury, entrepreneur and self-made billionaire. And she wanted to talk to me about a job.

Cameron was in the process of starting a charitable foundation. Her email talked about social responsibility and using her wealth to help people. How she needed a more organized approach to charitable giving. She could be doing so much more, but her schedule was already full. A charitable foundation would allow her to support organizations doing good work, start scholarship programs, and fund causes and research.

And she was considering me for the executive director position.

She'd found my profile online and spoken to a few local contacts about me. Apparently, I had a great reputation. I hadn't even realized I *had* a reputation. But Shepherd did, and I'd worked with a lot of people both inside and outside his company. That had been enough for her to approach me about her new venture and ask if I'd consider an informal phone interview.

It did sound like an incredible opportunity. I liked my job—and I was good at it—but this would be amazing. I handled all of Shepherd's charitable giving, and it was the one of the best parts of my job. This would be a huge challenge, but I knew I could do it.

The question was, did I want to?

A new job would mean not working for Shepherd anymore. I had such mixed feelings about that. On the one hand, it was hard to imagine changing jobs. Shepherd and I had a good routine. On the other, this new opportunity had so much potential.

Of course, I might not get it. She just wanted a phone interview. An informal one at that.

I'd started and deleted a reply several times already. A phone interview wasn't a commitment. There was nothing wrong with me talking to her, just to get more information.

But I didn't feel good about agreeing to an interview without talking to Shepherd first.

He was in his office—the door open a crack—and he didn't have anything on his schedule for the rest of the day. I got up and took a deep breath, smoothing out my dress, and went to his office.

I tapped my knuckles on the door a few times. "Hey. Can I talk to you for a minute?"

He looked up from his laptop and his mouth turned up in a subtle smile. "Of course."

I clicked the door shut behind me. He watched me come in and take a seat on the other side of his desk, a look of curiosity on his face.

"I'm a little disappointed you're all the way over there."

God, why was he so sexy? That little grin. Those

dimples. That perfect jaw and delicious mouth. He sat back in his chair, his posture all calm confidence.

"Sorry, I'm just... I think we should be..." How should we be? This was certainly a work issue—boss and assistant. But it also touched our personal relationship, whatever that was now. Should I approach this as his employee? His friend? As the woman he was currently living and sleeping with?

His brow furrowed. "Is everything all right?"

"Yes. Fine." I brushed my hair back over my shoulder. "I got an email recruiting me for a job. It's an executive director position for a charitable foundation. It's new, and they're looking for someone to run it, and somehow they found me. And the email just asks if I'd be open to an informal phone interview. Who knows, they might have a hundred candidates at this point, so chances are I wouldn't even make it to the next round. But I didn't feel right about responding without telling you first."

He looked straight at me, his expression so hard to read. I shifted in my seat, my tummy fluttering with nerves.

"Are you interested in the position?"

"Well, yes. At least, I'm interested in finding out more."

"Then you should take the interview."

My lips parted and I blinked a few times. "Really?"

"If it's what you want, yes."

I looked down at my hands. I could feel the immaturity of what I was about to say. The silliness of pouting when he was clearly being supportive. "That's it? You'll just let me go?"

He shook his head slightly, pressing his lips together as if trying not to laugh. "Everly, you're the best assistant I've ever had. You're amazing and I have incredible respect for you as a professional. I don't want to lose you. But I'm also a realist, and I know you won't work for me forever. That email you got was inevitable. You're amazing, and everyone you come in contact with knows it. If it isn't this opportunity, it'll be something else. And I'm not going to hold your career back. If this turns out to be the right move for you, then I'll be nothing but happy for you."

Tears. I had stupid, unstoppable tears running down my face, right here in Shepherd's office. Fighting a sudden wave of embarrassment, I swiped them away. "Wow. That was... Thank you. I don't know what to say."

"Come here."

I couldn't quite look him in the eyes as I walked around his desk. He swiveled his chair and scooped me into his lap, wrapping his arms tightly around me.

Leaning my head against his shoulder, I closed my eyes and breathed him in. He was so amazing, and I was so stupidly in love with him. For a second, I thought about telling him. Right here, in his office. Confessing to these very real feelings I had for my fake fiancé.

But I didn't. This was such a nice moment. And what if he couldn't say it back? I didn't want to ruin it when things were fine.

Okay, mostly fine.

"Just promise me one thing," he said.

I sat up and brushed more tears off my face. "What?"

"If and when you get a new job, help me find your replacement. I'm trying to be the mature professional here, but I'm actually not sure how I'd ever live without you."

My silly little heart soared at that comment. I knew he meant at work. Of course he meant at work. He wasn't saying he literally couldn't live without me, or that he wanted to make this whole thing real.

*Calm down, Everly.*

"I promise. I'll find you someone great."

He touched my chin and brought his lips to mine for a soft kiss. "Thank you."

I slid off his lap and stood, smoothing down my dress. "I should get back to work."

"Dinner tonight?" he asked. "Anywhere you want."

"Really? Anywhere?"

"Absolutely. What would make you happy?"

I couldn't do dinner tonight. I had plans with my sister. But I also couldn't resist messing with him. "There's this taco truck that's usually parked somewhere up in Shoreline. It's a little bit of a drive, and they only take cash, and sometimes they don't actually let you order, they just tell you what you're getting. And one time I ordered a Diet Coke with my meal, and the can kind of smelled like raw meat, which probably wasn't good. But it's like five dollars for this huge plate of tacos, and they're delicious."

He stared at me, unblinking. Silent.

I laughed. "I'm kidding. Although I have been there, and it's really good. But I can't, I'm having dinner with my sister tonight."

He let out a breath and shook his head. "Right. I forgot about dinner with your sister. Tomorrow?"

"I'm free tomorrow."

He smiled again, and as usual, I got all melty inside. "Perfect. It's a date."

"Yes. A date."

I turned for the door.

"Everly?"

"Yeah?" I glanced over my shoulder.

"I meant to ask, who would you be working for?"

"Cameron Whitbury."

He raised an eyebrow.

"Why? Do you know her?"

His expression softened. "Her? Cameron's a woman?"

"You've never heard of her? She's one of the richest women in America."

"I don't know every wealthy person in the world."

I grinned at him. "Were you worried some rich man was trying to take me away from you?"

He shook his head again and turned back to his laptop. "Have fun with your sister."

"I will."

I went back to my desk, feeling both better and worse. If I got this new job, and didn't work here anymore... and Richard broke up with Svetlana... would I see Shepherd anymore?

But if our fake engagement ended, and I still worked here, how would I handle seeing him every day?

I opened the email again. I really was interested. Maybe it wouldn't work out—and maybe things with Shepherd wouldn't work out either—but I was nothing if not an optimist. I clicked reply, wrote a friendly and professional response indicating that I would love to chat about this opportunity, took a deep breath, and hit send.

With that resolved, for the moment at least, I felt a bit better. I'd see where this went. But there was another issue in my life—a big one—that still needed resolution. But I was going to put that to rest tonight.

THE DINNER ANNIE and Miranda served was amazing. No surprise there, since my sister was basically perfect. Grilled salmon with lemon and dill. Roasted vegetables with fresh herbs. A delicious Salishan Cellars chardonnay.

I was feeling a little run down and my throat tickled,

making me cough. It was probably just the stress of everything lately. The party, contemplating a new job, plus the worry over how I was going to break the news to Annie that they needed to find a new potential donor. I took a drink of water to see if it would help.

"I can't wait to get the photos from the party," Miranda said. "I think we went into the photo booth ten times."

"I loved those giant cat eye glasses," Annie said. "The black and gold ones?"

"They were very fetching on you," Miranda said with a laugh.

"I'm glad you guys had fun," I said. "I think Richard missed his calling in life. He should be a party planner."

"Shepherd has such a nice family," Annie said.

"You sound surprised."

"I am, a little. The way you always talked about Shepherd, I didn't expect his dad to be so fun and friendly."

"I was surprised the first time I met him, too."

"Although, to be fair, Shepherd wasn't what I expected either," she said. "He's a great dancer."

I almost sighed at the memory of Shepherd twirling me around on the dance floor. "Yeah, he is. Which was also a surprise."

"Well, he certainly wasn't a robot, like you always said." Annie refilled Miranda's wine. "He seems like he has a great personality."

*He does, he just doesn't always let people see it.*

I stifled a cough—why wasn't that tickle in my throat going away?—and took a sip of wine. She'd just given me the perfect opportunity to bring up the elephant in the room.

"Listen, Annie, I need to talk to you about the sperm donor thing. I can't ask Shepherd to be your donor. In fact, I have to ask you not to ask him at all. I know it seems like he's basically perfect, and god, he really is, you have no idea. And I know you had your heart set on him, and I really want to help, but I just can't. I don't feel right about it."

Annie laid her hand over mine and smiled. "It's fine. You're absolutely right, we can't ask Shepherd to be our donor."

"Really?"

"No. After seeing you two together at the engagement party..." She trailed off and glanced at Miranda. "Well, don't worry. We're going to find someone else."

I let out a long sigh. "Oh, thank goodness. Wait. After seeing us together? What does that mean?"

"You two make an amazing couple."

"Fake couple," I said. Sort of. Were we?

"Everly, you can't fake that much chemistry."

Miranda nodded. "The way he looks at you? There was nothing fake about that."

I loved my sister, and Miranda, but they'd never been the ones I confided in, especially about relationships. Or sex. And right now, I didn't really feel like explaining what was happening between me and Shepherd. Because the truth was, I wasn't sure.

So I just shrugged off their comments. "We work well together. Thanks again for being there. And for finding a new donor."

"Yeah, of course," Annie said. "The perfect someone is out there. We'll find him."

"And you'll be the best two mommies ever."

I declined another glass of wine and left shortly after dinner was over. Why was I so tired? Of course, I had a lot on my mind. Shepherd. My job. At least I didn't have to worry about telling Annie I couldn't ask Shepherd to be their donor anymore. I was relieved they'd taken it so well. Hopefully they'd find the right person soon.

I stopped by my apartment on the way home, just to check on things. The air was stuffy, and the furniture a little dusty, sending me into a painful coughing fit. I really didn't feel well. But otherwise, nothing was amiss. After giving the place a once-over, I left. Went home. Or at least, my home for now.

An odd feeling of familiarity stole through me when I got back to Shepherd's condo. This place felt more like home than my apartment did, now. It was probably just because I'd spent the last couple of months living here. It was more immediate.

But Shepherd was here. And I realized as I shut the door behind me, that *he* was starting to feel like home.

Which was probably going to get me into trouble. But at this point, I was a goner for that man.

## 28

---

# SHEPHERD

With Everly gone for the evening, I went straight to my other condo instead of going home. I spent some time practicing. By the time I decided to go upstairs, I was relaxed, my mind clear.

I felt good.

Even the sight of Svetlana lounging on my couch didn't bother me. I nodded to her, then went into the kitchen to pour myself a glass of whiskey.

"That was a great party the other night," she said.

I hadn't heard her approach, but I tried not to react. "It was. Where's Dad?"

"He went out to get dessert."

There was something in the tone of her voice that set off a warning in my mind. I put the cap back on the bottle, keenly aware that this was the first time she and I had been alone together since she'd started seeing my dad. Moving Everly in had worked well in that regard.

"Enjoy your evening." I picked up my whiskey and turned to go to my office.

She stretched her arm across the entrance to the

kitchen, blocking my way. There was fire in her eyes—a smoldering mix of desire and anger.

I met her gaze, keeping my expression blank. "Excuse me."

"Shepherd, why don't we both admit to what's happening here."

"How about you move out of my way."

Her lips curled in a smile. "I know your engagement is a farce."

I didn't reply. Just took a sip of my whiskey.

"Aren't you getting tired of this game we're playing?" She dropped her arm and took a step forward.

Damn. She *was* using my father. Of course she was. I'd known it from the beginning.

"I'm tired of you taking advantage of my father."

"Oh, Shepherd, don't be silly. I'm doing no such thing. He's not serious about me. I'm just a pretty distraction."

"Indeed, although I doubt he sees you that way."

She moved closer. I stayed where I was, refusing to give her any ground. This woman was not going to back me into a corner.

"Don't worry about Richard." She ran a finger down my chest.

"I don't understand what you're trying to accomplish. Have you been using my father as a way to get revenge? Or is this all a twisted attempt to get me to take you back?"

She splayed her hand on my chest. "A bit of both."

I grabbed her wrist and removed her hand. "Don't touch me."

"Shepherd," she purred. "I know you still want me. I can see it in your eyes."

"Are you delusional?"

She surged in, invading my personal space. "Stop fighting it."

I leaned away and backed up but ran into the refrigerator. My whiskey slipped from my hands, falling to the floor with a crash of broken glass. She pressed her body against me and grabbed the back of my neck. Popping up on her tiptoes, she slammed her lips against mine.

"Svetlana? Shepherd?"

At the sound of my dad's voice, she pulled away. I dropped her wrist and wiped my mouth with the back of my hand.

"Damn it," I muttered.

Dad stood a few feet away, a paper grocery bag in his hand. He stared at us, his brow furrowed. "What's going on here?"

"Dad—"

"He kissed me," she said.

"What? You just threw yourself at me."

She crossed her arms. "How dare you. I did no such thing."

"Yes, you did. I certainly didn't want you to."

"Then why did you say all those things?" she asked. "You're a terrible person, Shepherd Calloway. You know I'm in a relationship with your father. How could you betray him like that?"

I rolled my eyes. "For fuck's sake. Enough of this bullshit. Dad, Svetlana is my ex. When you met her in Hawaii, I'd paid for her trip to soften the blow after breaking up with her."

Dad's eyes widened, moving between me and Svetlana. They came to rest on her. "Is this true?"

She blinked a few times, her face draining of color.

She'd probably figured since I hadn't outed her yet, I wasn't going to. "I can explain."

"You lied to me?" he asked.

"This isn't what you think," she said.

"No, it's exactly what you think," I said. "She's been using you to get back at me for dumping her."

Svetlana recovered quickly—she was good, I had to give her that. Her features smoothed and her shoulders relaxed, the guilt disappearing from her countenance. "Shepherd is sadly mistaken. Yes, he and I did date for a short time. But the truth is, I was ready to end things when Shepherd did. I knew it wasn't going to work out between us. When I met you, everything changed. I knew you were different. You were special."

"Then why would you keep the fact that you'd been dating my son from me?"

"I was afraid you'd reject me. I didn't realize the connection until later, and by then, I already knew I wanted to be with you. And then we saw Shepherd at the gala, and he pretended not to know me. I didn't know why, but I went along with it. I was afraid you'd leave me if you knew."

My dad was a softie, but he wasn't a complete idiot. Not even when it came to beautiful women who were far too young for him. He straightened, his back going stiff. "You expect me to believe that?"

"Yes, of course. Richard, I care about you. I'd never do anything to hurt you."

"Interesting, considering I just caught you trying to seduce my son."

"He came on to me," she said, feigning shock.

I stared her down, my gaze hard. "I wouldn't come on to you if you were the last woman on earth and the fate of humanity rested on us perpetuating the species."

Dad took a deep breath and cleared his throat. "Well, that's it, then. Svetlana, it's been nice knowing you, but it's time for you to leave."

"You're going to take his word over mine?" she asked, the pitch of her voice rising.

"In this case, absolutely," he said.

She balled her hands into fists, her lips pressing together. Her eyes darted between me and my dad a few times, her nostrils flaring. Without another word, she stomped into the other room, grabbed her things, and slammed the door behind her.

I let out a long breath and wiped my mouth again. Fucking gross.

Dad didn't say anything. He turned and went to his room.

Fuck.

I decided to give him a little time to process, so I took a shower to wash off any trace of the harpy. When I finished, I dressed and went back to the kitchen to clean up the broken glass. Then I poured two whiskeys and went to face my father.

I rapped a knuckle against his partially-open door. "Can I come in?"

"Sure."

He took the glass of whiskey I offered. I lowered myself onto the corner of his bed.

"I'm sorry I lied to you," I said.

"What I don't understand is why. Why would you keep that from me?"

I stared down into the amber liquid in my glass. "When I saw her with you at the gala, you were receiving an award. It was your night. I didn't want to ruin it."

"And after?"

"Come on, Dad. Then you dropped the bomb on us that not only were you facing the worst financial crisis of your life, you'd been diagnosed with cancer. Ethan and I figured Svetlana was just another fling. Maybe your way of dealing with the fact that you were facing your own mortality. We decided to let it run its course. It's not like you haven't had short relationships with younger women before."

He sighed, turning his whiskey glass in his hand. "You're right. I have."

"I hoped you'd realize she wasn't right for you and we could all move on. And you wouldn't have to get hurt."

"You were trying to protect me," he said. It wasn't a question.

"Yeah."

"I knew something wasn't right with her. I ignored it because... well, because she was very beautiful, let's be honest. And because I'm an idiot. Here I am, sixty-three, and I'm chasing women more than thirty years younger."

"You're not an idiot."

"It's ironic. My first day in Hawaii, I'd resolved to stop dating. I decided I was better off alone. I guess I didn't really believe that. Twenty-four hours later, I met Svetlana, and I threw that out the window."

"You don't need to give up. But if you're dating women for the wrong reasons, you'll attract the wrong women. Trust me, I know a thing or two about that."

He nodded slowly and took a sip. "I suppose being with a younger woman isn't going to make me live any longer. Probably the opposite."

"You need a woman who wants to be with you because she wants to share a life together. Not because she's good at being arm candy and wants to live in luxury."

His mouth turned up in a grin. "Like Everly."

That hit me like a punch to the gut. Fuck. "Dad, there's something you need to know about Everly."

"What?"

Damn it. I didn't know what was worse. Having to confess to this, or telling him he'd been unknowingly dating my ex. "She's my assistant."

"I know that."

"No, what I mean is, when you met her at the gala, she wasn't my girlfriend. I saw Svetlana with you, and I had Everly come down to pose as my date. Then when you moved in, I asked Everly to keep up the ruse. I didn't want Svetlana thinking I was available."

His brow furrowed. "Are you saying you and Everly aren't getting married?"

"No, we're not."

"And you're not actually a couple? You've just been pretending?"

I glanced away. "Yes."

He chuckled. I'd just told him I'd been lying to him. That made him laugh?

"What are you laughing about?"

"Oh, son." He tossed back the rest of his whiskey. "If you haven't figured it out yet, you will soon."

"Figured what out?"

"You're in love with that girl."

I stiffened, feeling the emotion drain from my features. This was hitting far too close to the mark. Right in the center of the bullseye, actually.

He chuckled again. "Maybe your relationship started off as a fake, but it's real now. There's no doubt in my mind about that."

I wanted to steer the conversation back in the right

direction. "I'm sorry I let you go through with the party. I thought it might be a good distraction for you."

"Don't be sorry. You're absolutely right, it was. I had a lot of fun putting that party together. Besides, now I don't have to throw you another one when you and Everly actually get engaged."

"Dad—"

"Denial doesn't look very good on you, son. Trust me, the sooner you accept that you're in love with her, the better things will be for both of you."

I cleared my throat. "Don't blame her for this. It's not her fault. I talked her into it. She'll feel terrible if you're upset with her."

"I'm not, and I'll make sure she knows that. I probably should be upset with you. I was half an hour ago, and I wish you would have told me the truth in the beginning. But Svetlana was a mistake, and I knew it all along."

"I'm sorry, Dad."

"It's all right. I'll recover. I always do."

I stood, still holding my whiskey. "Night."

"Goodnight, son."

I went to my office and sat down. Sipped my drink. It was over. No more Svetlana. That part was an enormous relief.

But what did it mean for me and Everly?

I heard the front door open and close. She was home. Her footsteps came closer and she coughed a few times.

She pushed the door open. "Hey, you."

Did she seem pale, or was it just the light? "Hi. How was dinner?"

"It was good. I had a nice talk with Annie." She turned and coughed again.

I stood. "Are you okay?"

"I'm fine. I stopped by my apartment to check on things and it was a little dusty. I'm sure that's all it is." She coughed again.

"That cough doesn't sound good. Let's get you to bed."

"I'm okay, really. It's still early."

Despite her protests, I gently steered her into the bedroom. She kept insisting she was fine, but it looked to me like she was getting worse by the minute. Her skin was pale and warm to the touch. I helped her out of her clothes and into a pink tank top and pair of shorts, then waited while she finished getting ready for bed in the bathroom.

"I'm sure I'll be fine by morning." She paused to cough again. "Maybe I just need some sleep."

"We'll see how you feel, but if you're sick, you're staying home."

She crawled into bed and I helped pull the covers over her.

"I never get sick." Her eyes were already closed.

I sat on the edge of the bed and brushed the hair back from her face. "I'm sure you don't."

She curled into a ball, her brow creased with tension. I rubbed slow circles across her back until her body relaxed and her breathing evened. When I was sure she was asleep, I got ready for bed. It was early, and I wasn't tired, but I wanted to stay with her in case she got worse or needed anything.

I'd break the news about Dad and Svetlana later. And then we were going to have to have a serious talk about us.

## 29

# SHEPHERD

*E*verly coughed all through the night. When I got up to shower and get ready for work, she mumbled something about not being late. But when I came out of the bathroom, she was still in bed.

I sat on the edge of the bed and caressed her back. "How are you feeling?"

"I'm fine," she croaked.

"You're not fine. You're sick."

As if her body wanted to prove me right, she curled up with a coughing fit. "It's just allergies."

"Do you have allergies?"

"No, but I never get sick."

I kept rubbing her back. It seemed to help relax her. "You're still staying home today."

She groaned and turned to face me. "I can't stay home. I've never taken a sick day."

"Yes, you can. There's nothing at work that's more important than you getting better."

Tucking her hands beneath her cheek, she gave me a

weak smile. Even with red-rimmed eyes and no color in her cheeks, she was adorable.

"Fine, I'll stay for now. But if I feel better this afternoon, I'll just—"

I touched my finger to her lips. "No. You're not allowed to get out of bed today, except for physical necessities or food. Otherwise, I want you here."

"I like it when you're bossy. You should keep me in bed all day more often."

A day in bed with Everly sounded like heaven. "We'll do that when you aren't coughing up a lung."

"Fair enough. But call me if you need anything."

*No, Everly. I will not be calling you about work today.* "Don't worry. Don't think about work. Just rest."

She nodded and I kissed her forehead.

Before I went in to the office, I brought her breakfast, a big glass of water, and a box of tissues. I found her Kindle, and a few magazines she'd left in the other room, and made sure she had the remote to the TV. I wished I could stay here with her, but I had meetings I couldn't miss.

I caught my dad in the kitchen on my way out.

"Morning. Listen, Everly's sick. Keep your distance, you can't afford to get sick right now. Your immune system is already stressed."

"Is she okay?"

"I think so. It's just a cough. She felt warm last night, but I don't think she has a fever. I'll check on her later and try to get home early."

"All right. Thanks, son."

"And Dad, I haven't had a chance to talk to her about Svetlana."

"I'll leave that to you," he said. "Is there anything I can do to help her? Get her some soup or something?"

"Maybe bring her some lunch later, but don't get too close and don't let her cough on you. And don't touch anything."

"I've got it. I'll be careful."

"Thanks."

I still didn't like leaving her, and I was worried about my dad getting sick. His radiation treatments were over, and he was doing well. But a simple virus could be serious for him right now. I'd have to call the housecleaners and have them make a special trip out today to disinfect everything.

Work was busy enough to keep my mind off Everly for most of the day. I texted her a few times in between meetings and conference calls. She assured me she was fine and didn't need anything, but I was still anxious to get home to her.

I walked by her empty desk, feeling the tug of missing her. Which was so odd. I'd seen her this morning. She'd be there when I went home tonight.

But it wasn't the fact that she was home sick today that was bothering me. We were at a crossroads. Our reason for living together was gone. Svetlana was out of the picture. And chances were, Everly wasn't going to work for me much longer. I wasn't the least bit surprised that someone else was recruiting her. She was amazing. Cameron Whitbury would be crazy not to hire her. And if it wasn't Cameron, it would be someone else.

I went into my office and shut the door. Sat down and rubbed my chin. My dad's words kept echoing in my head. *You're in love with that girl.*

Was I? Had I fallen in love with Everly?

The problem was, I'd never been in love before. How were you supposed to know?

I picked up my phone and called Ethan.

"Hey, Shep. Everything all right?"

"Yeah, fine. Do you have a minute?"

"Sure."

I took a deep breath. "How do you know when you're in love with someone?"

"Oh. That's... okay, that's unexpected."

"This is fucking with my head, Ethan. I'm basically dead inside. I don't know how any of this works."

He laughed. "You're not dead inside, Shep."

"Don't be so sure. I'm too much like Mom."

"Are you, though?" he asked. "You're not bitter. I know you're not exactly effusive with your emotions. You're not a hugger like dad."

"Or you."

"Yeah, or me. You keep things to yourself, but I've never thought you don't feel things. Keeping it on the inside isn't the same as not having feelings. Can I ask what brought this on?"

"Dad broke up with Svetlana last night after he caught her trying to paste herself to me in the kitchen."

"Oh god. How is he?"

"Surprisingly, he's okay. He didn't realize she was using him to get to me, but he knew she wasn't right for him. He just hadn't admitted it out loud yet."

"Thank god that's over. I was starting to worry we'd made a mistake by not telling him immediately."

I rubbed my chin again. "Me too."

"So now you're wondering what to do about Everly."

"Yes."

"It doesn't have to be complicated, Shep. Does being with her make you happy?"

"Yes, it does, but of course it's complicated. I convinced

my assistant to move in with me and pretend to be my girlfriend. And then..."

"And then pretending wasn't so hard because it started to feel real."

"Exactly."

"What are you really worried about? That her feelings aren't real? That she's faking it so well she has you convinced too?"

Letting out a long breath, I stared down at my desk. This was so hard to admit, I wasn't sure if I could say it out loud. "I'm afraid once our reason for being together is gone, none if it will have been real. And I'll..."

"You'll get hurt."

I cleared my throat. "Yeah."

"That's the thing about love, though. If you never open yourself up to the risk of being hurt, you'll never give someone the chance to get close enough to love you back. And honestly, I don't think you need to worry about this. Anyone who's seen you two together can tell you're crazy about each other."

"Yeah. Okay, thanks Ethan."

"Anytime. Let me know if you need anything. And I'll call Dad and invite him to dinner tonight. See if he needs to talk."

"Sounds good. He'll appreciate that."

I said goodbye and put my phone down. This was such unfamiliar territory. I'd faced financial risks, made huge business deals, and dealt with millions—even billions—of dollars. None of that had ever fazed me. I was used to being all cool confidence. Untouchable.

Everly had broken me wide open and I felt the raw edges of my exposed nerves. I'd already trusted her with so much. Why was I worried now?

Maybe Ethan was right. It didn't have to be complicated. Being with her made me happy—happier than I'd ever been. I loved spending time with her, and I missed her when we were apart. She made me laugh—which I didn't do all that often. She saw through right to the heart of who I was, as if she had the power to reach inside past all my barriers.

I did love her. I'd fallen a little bit in love with her every day, since that night at the gala. Since I'd opened my eyes and finally seen the incredible woman I'd been working with for the last few years.

And just like that, I knew what I was going to do. Ask her to stay.

With that settled, I felt immensely better. As much as I wanted to rush home to talk to her, I had more work to do. It could wait. I knew she'd be there waiting for me. And not just because she was sick. Because despite the fact that neither of us had acknowledged it out loud, we both knew. She was mine. I just needed to make it official.

I clicked my laptop to bring the screen back up. Once I reviewed the sales reports, I could get out of here.

Everly hadn't sent them to me yet, but she probably had hard copies at her desk. I didn't want to bother her, so I decided to check myself. If I didn't find them, I could give her a call. But I didn't want to make her think about work if I didn't have to.

Her desk was neat and tidy, as usual. There wasn't anything sitting out, so I checked in the drawers. I didn't see anything in the first two, but when I opened the third, a folder caught my eye. The label said *Shepherd Calloway Donor Contract.*

Donor contract? That was odd. Was it a charitable thing? I donated money to a number of organizations, but those didn't require contracts.

I flipped open the folder. It was indeed a legal document, and I was named multiple times just on the first page. And so were Everly's sister and sister-in-law.

Picking it up, I read it more carefully. A sick feeling grew in the pit of my stomach as I realized what this was. It was a sperm donor agreement—a contract for me to become the biological father of Everly's sister's potential child.

There were provisions for giving me photos and updates on the child, as well as the option for me to opt out of any and all contact. I could have the records sealed for complete anonymity if I chose. It spelled out my responsibilities, which amounted to nothing more than providing up to five ejaculatory samples for the purposes of fertilizing Annie's eggs in a lab. No financial support or parental duties were expected.

I took the contract into my office and tossed it onto my desk. This must have been why Everly had agreed to my proposal. She wanted leverage so she could ask me to be her sister's sperm donor.

Why hadn't she told me? Was she waiting to spring it on me after her end of the bargain was fulfilled?

I'd dated a lot of women who'd only been with me for my money—because they wanted something from me. But I'd thought Everly was different. She didn't want my money.

But she did want something a lot more personal.

As I stared at the folder lying on my desk, I wished it had been money. Because this hurt a hell of a lot more.

## 30

## EVERLY

*A*fter a rough start to the day, I was feeling a lot better. I guess Shepherd had been right, I did need to stay home. I'd spent most of the morning in bed, and Richard had brought me some chicken soup for lunch. I didn't want to get him sick, so I'd shooed him out of the room right away. I'd taken a long nap this afternoon and woke up feeling refreshed.

I didn't want to spread my germs around the house, so I stayed in the bedroom. Now that I had some energy again, I was restless. I sat in bed, idly searching Netflix for something to watch, wondering when Shepherd was going to get home.

I settled in with a cooking show. It sounded like someone was home, but I couldn't tell if it was Shepherd or his dad. I hoped it was Shepherd. He'd texted me throughout the day to check up on me—which was so sweet; I knew how busy he was—but I hadn't talked to him since this morning. I missed him.

He peeked in the door and I smiled, reaching for the remote to turn off the TV.

"Hey. I'm glad you're home."

"How are you feeling?"

"So much better. I'm still coughing but not as much as this morning."

"Good." He came in and set down a stack of paperwork. There was something about his body language that bothered me. Why wasn't he looking me in the eyes?

"How was work?" I asked.

"Busy."

"Is everything okay?"

Without a word, he went to the stack of paperwork he'd set down and pulled out a folder. He tossed it on the bed. "No."

The coldness in his voice made my shoulders tense and a knot of worry uncurled in my stomach. I reached for the folder and before my fingers touched it, I realized what it was.

Oh no.

"I was looking in your desk to see if you had hard copies of the sales reports. I found that."

I flipped it open, then closed again. The donor contract. "I wasn't going to give this to you."

"Then why do you have it?"

I took a deep breath. "Annie and Miranda want to have a baby, and they hoped I could get you to be their sperm donor. I told them I'd ask but it's not like I promised them anything."

"Well, thank fuck for that," he snapped. "Although they seemed confident enough to have this contract drafted."

"They just wanted to be prepared. And I told you, I wasn't going to give it to you."

"Then I'll ask again. Why do you have it?"

"Well, originally I was going to, but I decided I couldn't. I don't want them to ask you at all. I felt wrong about it, and I told them so last night."

He looked away. "So up until last night, you were still planning to go through with it."

"No, not up until last night. I decided a while ago that I couldn't. Actually, I had mixed feelings about it from the start, but then you asked me to move in and I thought—"

"You thought you'd do me a favor and get a favor in return."

I stared at him for a beat. "Shepherd, this was your idea. You asked me to pose as your girlfriend and move in with you. It's not like I wormed my way into your house."

"But you had an ulterior motive that you kept from me."

"That isn't something you can just ask your boss. Hey, Mr. Calloway, it's been great working for you, and sure I'll upend my entire life to help you get rid of your gold-digging harpy of an ex-girlfriend. Oh, and by the way, can you be the sperm donor for my sister's genetically perfect baby? Thanks, I'll see you at work in the morning."

"Right, because I'm just your boss."

"At first you were. Come on, Shepherd, neither of us knew what was going to happen. I'd worked with you for three years, but I barely knew you. So yes, at first, I thought if I moved in with you, I'd have a good reason for asking you to do this for my sister. But I was never going to lord it over you or try to guilt you into it. And like I said, I decided not to. I told them they have to find a new donor, and they agreed."

"My dad ended things with Svetlana last night."

My mouth popped open but the tickle in my throat came back. I turned to the side to cough a few times. "He did?"

"And I told him everything."

"Is he okay? How did he take it?"

Shepherd still wasn't looking at me. "He's fine."

"Are you sure? That must be a lot to process."

"I said he's fine. And now our reason for this," he said, gesturing between the two of us, "is over."

I flinched away, like I'd just been slapped. "That's it? You want me to leave?"

His voice was cold. "Every woman I've ever dated has wanted something from me. Every single one. Usually it's just money."

"Shepherd, no—"

"You can stay until you're better, but I won't be here."

"Wait. Don't walk away. Please."

But he was already out the door. A few seconds later, the front door closed, hard enough that I could hear it all the way back here.

Shock left me motionless for a long moment. What had just happened?

I gathered up the contract. I wanted to burn this stupid thing. I never should have agreed to ask him in the first place. And now he thought...

He thought I'd been using him. He thought I was no better than Svetlana, or any of the other gold-diggers he'd dated.

My shock and hurt were quickly replaced with a hot streak of anger. Is that what he thought of me? That everything I'd done had been to butter him up to get him to agree to donate his sperm? That I would go so far as to sleep with him to get what I wanted?

I pushed the covers aside. There was no way I was staying here. I'd go back to my stuffy, dusty apartment.

The ring on my finger caught my eye, feeling suddenly

heavy. I hated this ring. It was too big and flashy and it didn't mean anything. A stupid, expensive reminder of why I was here.

I pulled it off and tossed it onto the bed.

Sniffing and coughing a few times, I shoved some things in a bag. I'd have to come back for the rest of my stuff. Anger fueled me, but I could feel the crash coming. The tidal wave of emotion that was soon to overtake me.

For now, I clung to anger like a lifeline. Stuffed my clothes in a bag. Hauled dresses out of the closet. Tears stung my eyes as I took a load down to my car, but I swallowed them back. Refused to let them fall.

I packed what I could and before I left, I wrote Richard a note. I wanted him to know I was sorry for lying to him and that I hoped he could forgive me. He was a good man. I hated to think that what I'd done had hurt him.

I put the note on the desk in Richard's room. And then I left.

By the time I got to my apartment building, I was struggling to hold back the tears. What had I done? My entire life had just blown up in my face.

Nora and Hazel had called it. They knew me too well— knew I'd fall for my boss. And I hadn't just fallen. I'd tumbled over the side of a cliff. But now I realized there wasn't anyone at the bottom to catch me.

I'd had some shitty experiences with men. Awful first dates. A couple of relationships that had ended badly. But I'd never been this devastated. Not once.

Because I'd never loved someone like I loved Shepherd.

I shuffled into my apartment and tossed my stuff on the couch. There was more in my car, but I'd get it later. My throat hurt from coughing, but worse was the pain in my chest. It had nothing to do with my lungs, and everything to do with my heart.

It was completely broken, shattered into a million pieces on the rocks at the bottom of the cliff.

## 31

## SHEPHERD

*I* slept in my condo downstairs and when I came back in the morning, I knew she was gone. She hadn't just gone to work. Half her stuff was missing and there was no sign that she'd slept here last night.

A glint of light on the bed caught my attention. Her engagement ring—fake though it was—sat on top of the rumpled covers, as if she'd carelessly tossed it aside. I picked it up, pinching it between my thumb and forefinger. It was over. She was gone.

Fuck.

I felt like shit. I put the ring in the top drawer of my dresser and went out to the kitchen. It wasn't even seven in the morning, but I poured myself a glass of whiskey. And then I did something I hadn't done in years.

I took the day off.

It wasn't just to avoid Everly, although I was man enough to admit that was part of it. But I doubted she'd gone to work today anyway. She was probably going to quit. I tried to tell myself it was for the best. I'd unceremoniously kicked her out last night. I certainly didn't expect her to still work for me.

But really, I stayed home so I could do nothing but get royally fucking drunk.

I was feeling too many things—a confusing jumble of emotions. I'd been up half the night, wrestling with what to do. Had I made a mistake? Should I have listened to her? I was sick of second-guessing myself. That wasn't me. I was firm. Decisive. I never let feelings get in the way.

Now I was drowning in feelings. So I'd drown those fuckers in whiskey.

Hours later—I was too trashed to have any concept of time—Dad peeked into my office. My head was down on my desk, the bottle near my elbow.

"Shepherd? Are you okay? Why aren't you at work?"

I lifted my head and slowly blinked. "Day off."

"What happened?"

Sitting up, I raked my hands through my already-messy hair and poured more whiskey. "Everly wanted me to donate my sperm."

"Excuse me?"

"She had a contract and everything. For her sister."

He pulled the glass away from me before I could pick it up and take a drink. "Shep, I'm not following."

"Doesn't matter. She's just like the rest of them." I leaned forward, intending to put my forearm on the desk, but it slipped off the edge. I swayed in my seat, but managed to recover. "I thought she was different, but she's not."

He regarded me through narrowed eyes for a moment. "Have you eaten recently?"

"No. Food soaks up the alcohol."

"Exactly." He took a deep breath. "Okay, Shep. Stay here. I'll be back."

"Don't bother." The room kept spinning, so I laid my head on the desk again. "I'm fine."

I wasn't sure if he answered. The next time I opened my eyes, he was gone. Good. I didn't want his pity.

But when I reached for more whiskey, it was gone.

"SHEPHERD?"

I cracked an eye open. Had the room stopped spinning yet?

"Hey, Shep." Another voice. Who was here?

Where was I?

Sucking in a deep breath, I sat up. Blinked my dry eyes open. I was still at my desk. I must have fallen asleep—or passed out—with my head on my arm. I had a red mark on my forearm and probably a matching one on my face.

I was still too drunk to give a shit.

The people in the room came into focus. Dad. Hadn't I told him to leave me alone? I was mad at him for something. Right—he'd taken my whiskey. I was about to ask him where he'd put it, when I realized who else was here.

Ethan and Grant stood next to my dad. They both looked like they'd just gotten off work, wearing similar button-down shirts and slacks. Grant had his arms crossed and Ethan stood with his hands in his pockets.

"He's been in here all day," Dad said.

"Thanks for letting us know," Ethan said.

"I'll get dinner going," Grant said. "Need help moving him?"

"You don't move to need me," I said. "I'm fine."

"Clearly." Ethan's voice was laced with sarcasm. "Dad

and I can handle it. But I think we should feed him first anyway."

"Not hungry. I'm fine."

Ethan chuckled. "You're not fine, you're drunk off your ass. I'd call Everly but I have a feeling she's the reason you're shitfaced right now."

"Why didn't she tell me?" I asked. Or at least, that's what I meant to say. I was slurring too much to make a lot of sense.

"I don't know, man, but let's get you sobered up." Ethan shoved some water at me. "Drink this and we'll get some food in you. You look like hell, by the way."

I took a long swallow of water.

Food and water started to clear my head, which was exactly what I didn't want. But no one would let me near the whiskey again.

Eventually, as if I were a helpless child, my brother helped me to my room. I fell into bed, my head still too fuzzy to argue. Vaguely, I was aware of Ethan and Dad talking. Something about letting me sleep it off. I ignored them. Just kept my eyes closed and sank into drunken oblivion.

I WOKE UP FULLY DRESSED, sprawled out face down on my bed. My mouth was dry, my eyes gritty, and I had a splitting headache. I hadn't been this hungover in a very long time.

This was why I preferred to keep myself—and my life— under strict control. The consequences of letting go were never worth it.

"Fuck." I brought a hand to my forehead. I had no idea what time it was. Or how I'd gotten here. The last thing I remembered, I'd been sitting at my desk, pouring whiskey down my throat.

A hazy memory of food came back to me. I had the sense that Ethan and Grant had been here, but maybe I'd imagined it.

Groaning, I hauled myself out of bed. There was still a hint of Everly's strawberry scent on these sheets. I needed to get away from it.

The glimpse I caught of myself in the bathroom mirror was nothing short of horrifying. I was a goddamn mess.

A shower helped. Someone had left me water and ibuprofen by the bed, so I took those. The water helped, too. I was dehydrated as fuck. My stomach was raw, but I figured I should try to eat, or at least have some coffee.

I shuffled to the kitchen, wincing at the light. Ethan and Grant were drinking coffee in the living room with my dad. Was it the same day? Or had they spent the night? I still hadn't figured out what time it was.

"Morning," Ethan said, his voice bright.

"Is it?" I fumbled for the coffee.

"Yeah, you slept all night. But you still look pretty rough."

I grunted as I poured myself a mug. "Did you stay here?"

"Yeah."

Grant stood. "I have to get to work. Are you sure you've got this?"

Ethan nodded. "Yeah, we'll handle it. I'll see you at home tonight."

"There's nothing to handle," I said.

They ignored me. Grant squeezed my shoulder on his way to the front door.

I went into the living room and sank down into an

armchair. Everly's ugly bean bag chair was still in its place, mocking me with its hideous yellow fuzz.

"Don't you have to work, too?" I asked, glancing at Ethan.

"I took the day off."

"Why?"

His brow furrowed, as if I'd just asked a stupid question. He pointed at me, tracing his finger up and down. "Because this."

I hunkered down in the chair and took a sip of coffee.

"So, all we could get out of you last night was something about Everly, and being a sperm donor, and some mumbling about gold-diggers," Ethan said. "What the hell happened?"

I told them about the contract I'd found in Everly's desk. How she'd agreed to be my fake girlfriend so she could hit me with a sperm donor request—and she'd kept that detail from me.

"So, you broke up with her," Ethan said.

"No, I couldn't break up with her because our relationship was fake. I told her our arrangement was over."

"That's the same as breaking up with her."

I groaned, pinching the bridge of my nose. "Are you here to argue semantics?"

"No, I'm here to help because you're a fucking mess."

He wasn't wrong. For the first time in my life, I'd totally fallen apart. It was pathetic. "I just drank too much. I'll finish my coffee and go into the office."

"Don't go to work today," Dad said.

"I was already out yesterday. I have to go in."

"No, you don't," he said. "Give yourself a break."

I rubbed my forehead with my fingertips. "I don't need a break. I just need some caffeine and to go to work."

"Shepherd." Dad's voice was uncharacteristically sharp. I hadn't heard that tone from him in a long time. "You're hurt. You need to deal with that, not bury it and pretend it didn't happen."

"There's nothing to deal with."

"He's doing it again," Ethan said, as if I wasn't sitting right here.

"I know," Dad said.

"I'm doing what?"

"Bottling everything up," Ethan said. "I can practically see you doing it. It's like you're shoving every emotion you've ever had into the deepest, darkest recesses of your psyche. You did the same thing when Mom left."

I didn't reply. Just took a sip of coffee, keeping my eyes anywhere but on my dad and brother.

"It's not healthy," Ethan said. "Come on, you can talk to us."

I didn't want to talk. I wanted to go to work where I could focus on something else—anything but Everly. I had a company to run. I couldn't wallow in hurt feelings because my fake girlfriend had been keeping a secret.

"There's nothing to talk about. We had an agreement. It's over."

"I don't know how she put up with you," Ethan said, rolling his eyes. "If Grant was this emotionally stunted, I'd have gone crazy a long time ago."

"She doesn't have to put up with me at all, because it's over."

"And clearly you're fine with that." Ethan's voice was full of sarcasm.

I took a deep breath. "No, I'm not fine with it. I feel like shit and not because I'm hungover. I was going to..." I paused, shutting my eyes for a moment. "I was going to ask her to stay. But it turns out, she's no different than any of the other women I've dated."

"Have you *met* Everly?" Ethan asked. "Because I've met a few of the women you dated. They were all... well, like Svetlana. Sorry, Dad."

"It's all right," Dad said. "I should have known better."

"Do you remember when Dad had the heart attack scare, about five years ago?"

My brow furrowed. "When it turned out to be severe acid reflux?"

"Yes. Who were you dating at the time? What was her name?"

I thought back. "Ava Sinclair."

"And where was she while you were in the hospital, waiting for news?"

I cleared my throat. "At the spa. Or getting her hair done. I don't remember."

"What about when Grant got a promotion and Dad threw him that big party. Hadn't you been dating that woman, Megan something, for a year? But you came to the party alone."

"I remember her," Dad said. "Vaguely."

"Yeah, I'd been dating Megan for about a year. And she didn't come with me to Grant's party because she was getting Botox. Paid for with my credit card."

"See?" Ethan leaned forward, resting his elbows on his knees. "Everly showed up for you when I was in the ER. She'd never even met me."

I couldn't deny that. She had.

"And she went above and beyond with this whole fake girlfriend thing. I have a hard time believing it was all a maniacal plot to get you to jizz in a cup for her sister."

"I trusted her," I said. "I trusted her with a lot, and she kept this from me."

Ethan opened his mouth to reply, but he was interrupted by a knock at the door.

Dad stood. "I'll see who it is."

I waited, straining to listen while Dad answered the door. A moment later, he led two men into the condo. They looked familiar, but I couldn't place them.

Why were they glaring at me?

Dad cleared his throat. "Movers. Here for the rest of Everly's belongings."

That was why they looked familiar. They were the same guys Everly had hired when she moved in.

Groaning, I leaned my head back against the chair. "Fuck."

"I'll take care of it," Dad said.

"Did I drink all the whiskey?" I asked.

"No, and I'm tempted to let you spike your coffee at this point," Ethan said.

One of the movers came in and picked up the bean bag chair.

"Careful with that," I barked at him. "It's her favorite."

He glared at me again.

"Are they friends of hers?" Ethan asked, lowering his voice.

I shook my head. "No, they're just the guys she hired when she moved in here. But basically everyone Everly meets becomes her new best friend, so..."

"Of course they do," Ethan said. "Everly's delightful."

I shot him a look.

"Sorry. Not helpful."

I got up and shadowed the movers as they packed Everly's things and took them out of my condo. Neither of them spoke a word to me. Dad kept Ethan company in the kitchen while he cooked breakfast, and I acted like a lunatic, barking at the guys moving my former fake-fiancée's belongings.

This wasn't me. I didn't pace. I didn't yell at people. I wasn't intimidating because I was loud. It was my silence that made people jump to do what I wanted. I was precise, disciplined, and cold.

Or I had been before Everly turned me inside out.

After the movers left, Ethan wanted to talk more. But I was done talking. I thanked him for his concern, and his help, and went back to my office. Cleaned up the mess I'd made getting plastered in there the day before.

Then I got to work. It was what I did. What I'd always lived for.

It was all I had left.

## 32

# EVERLY

"*E*verly?"

I heard Nora's voice through the door, followed by three sharp knocks.

"Everly, are you in there?"

"Come in."

The door opened, but I couldn't see Nora. There were too many boxes in the way. The movers had dropped off my stuff yesterday and I still hadn't lifted a finger to put anything away.

She peeked around a stack of brown boxes. "Ev—oh god. Hazel, it's worse than we thought."

Nora tiptoed into the room, like she was afraid to touch anything. Hazel was right behind. They both looked around my apartment, vague expressions of horror on their faces.

"Stop judging me," I said.

It was a ridiculous thing for me to say. They should definitely be judging me. I was in an old pair of pajamas that I'd been wearing since I got home two nights ago. My hair was in a messy knot on top of my head—and not the cute kind of messy. I hadn't put any makeup on in days, but somehow I still had mascara flecks on my cheeks.

I was surrounded by the shameful evidence of my post-breakup pity-fest. A box of chocolates, a bite taken out of each until I found the two that I liked. A half-empty ice cream container, the remnants a soupy mess. A litany of sad love songs played from my Bluetooth speaker—I'd found a breakup playlist on Spotify—and I'd started at least five poems in a spiral notebook I was now calling my poetry journal.

Nora pinched the top of a pizza box and looked inside, wincing. "Everly Dalton, what the hell?"

"How long have you been home?" Hazel asked, eying a stack of self-help books I'd dug out of the depths of my dusty bookshelf.

"I came back Tuesday night."

"You did all this in less than seventy-two hours?" Nora asked. "Why didn't you call us sooner?"

"I wasn't ready to face you yet."

"Oh honey." Nora picked up a box of pink hair dye. "Really?"

"I didn't use it."

"Thank god." She tossed it over her shoulder.

"Not yet. I'm waiting until after my hair appointment."

Nora made a pained noise. "Hazel, do you mind taking notes? I don't want to forget to cancel Everly's hair appointment."

She already had her phone out. "I'm on it. Which salon, Everly?"

"You're not canceling my hair appointment."

"Of course I am," Nora said. "I don't trust you to do it, and I would be a terrible friend if I let you go through with a breakup haircut. I fell down on the job when it was Hazel and we all know how that turned out."

"It took me a year to grow out those bangs," Hazel said.

"Trust me, Everly, now is not the time for rash hairstyle decisions. You'll only wind up with a lot of pictures that you'll regret. And they'll be on social media where they never, ever go away."

"I barely even use social media."

"Doesn't matter," she said. "Tell you what, if you want to go pink, we'll do something temporary, like some clip-ins or chalk."

I groaned, pulling my knit afghan around my shoulders. "I don't care about the pink."

"Okay, but we need to make some progress here," Nora said. "Otherwise, you're going to be in the wallowing stage for months."

"It's been less than three days," I said. "I can still wallow."

She sat down on the edge of the couch near my feet and squeezed my leg. "Yes, you can. And we're all going out to get breakup drunk tonight. But maybe let's wallow in clean clothes."

"Everly, I still need the name of the salon," Hazel said.

"Red X on Capitol Hill," I mumbled.

Nora rubbed my leg. "Do you want to tell us what happened now, or should we go get drinks?"

"It's morning," I said.

"Do you remember who we are?" Nora asked. "Breakfast drinking is why they invented bloody marys and mimosas."

"Good point. But I drank some wine last night and I don't think I'm ready for more alcohol yet."

"How much wine did you drink?" Hazel asked, picking up the empty bottle.

"Yeah, that."

"Just the one?" Nora asked.

I nodded. "But I didn't use a glass."

"Oh lord," Nora said. "Okay, honey, just tell us what happened."

I took a breath. "Shepherd found out about Annie wanting me to ask him to be her sperm donor. She'd given me the contract and I still had it in my desk. He found it."

"Ouch," Nora said. "But, hold on, I thought you'd already decided you weren't asking him."

"I did. A while ago."

"Thank goodness. There was no way that wouldn't have been weird."

"I tend to agree," Hazel said.

"I know, it would have been weird. Worse than weird. And I already told Annie and Miranda, and they're fine with it. But Shepherd found out and he was really upset. And then he announced that Richard broke up with Svetlana and said that meant our reason for being together was over."

"He did not," Hazel said.

Nora lifted her eyes to the sky. "Oh, Shepherd."

"He did. He told me I could stay until I felt better, but he wouldn't be there. I tried to explain, but he said every woman he's ever dated was only with him because they wanted something, and he thought I was different. Then he left."

"And you came here, obviously after a trip to the store to get supplies." Nora held up a bottle of self-tanning lotion. "Please tell me you didn't use this yet."

I held up my hands. "Do my palms look orange? No. You're supposed to exfoliate first."

"Oh, Everly," Nora said. "Honey, you're a mess."

"Should we check her internet history?" Hazel asked.

Nora pointed. "Absolutely. Everly, there better be nothing but porn from the last few days."

"What? Why?"

Hazel grabbed my phone and turned off the music.

"Because if you're looking at porn, at least you're doing something that'll help. Your body could use some orgasm endorphins."

"I don't even like porn."

"That's because you need to find some good lady porn. I can help with that." She turned to Hazel. "What's she been googling?"

"Meditation retreats, solo travel for women, world's saddest love songs, and egg freezing services."

"Egg freezing?" Nora asked.

I crossed my arms. "On the off chance I do get married someday, it's probably going to be well after I'm fertile. What if I still want kids and I can't have any by then?"

Nora lifted the bottom of my pajama pants and rubbed my leg. "Woman, did you stop shaving?"

"Why bother? I'm just going to keep going on an endless string of awful dates until I give up and accept that I'm doomed to be alone forever. I might as well save myself the agony and quit now. I might try again in another twenty years, in which case I'll be very glad I froze my eggs."

"Okay, that's it." Nora grabbed my hands. "We're going out. Mimosas for breakfast. Martinis for lunch. And then, I don't know, we'll see where that takes us. But we're getting you out of the house. After you shower, obviously."

"I can't go out. I have a phone interview this afternoon."

"Already?" Hazel asked. "Did you quit your job?"

"No, although I'm probably fired. I haven't been there in days. But the interview doesn't have anything to do with breaking up with Shepherd. Is it breaking up if we were fake-together? Anyway, I got an email about a job opportunity and they asked if I'd be interested in a phone interview. Shepherd knew about it. I told him before everything blew up in my face."

"What did he say?" Nora asked.

I fiddled with the holes in my afghan. "He said that if it seemed like a good opportunity, I should go for it. That he didn't want to lose me, but he'd support me if it was what I wanted."

Hazel and Nora shared a look.

"What was that for?"

"Nothing," Nora said. "But if you have a phone interview this afternoon, we need to get you cleaned up."

"Why? It's over the phone."

"Unless you find out at the last minute it's a Skype call and you have to show your normally pretty face," Nora said.

She had a point. If Cameron Whitbury saw me like this, the interview would be over before it started. And now it looked like I needed a new job.

My eyes filled with tears. New job. No more Shepherd.

Hazel and Nora turned me so they could sit on either side. Then they put their arms around me and let me cry.

I sobbed for a while, knowing I was making myself look worse. But I had to get it out. My friends hugged me and stroked my hair. When I calmed down, Nora got me water and tissues while Hazel pressed a cold washcloth to my forehead.

Sniffing, I wiped my eyes. "You guys, there's a part I haven't told you."

"What's that, honey?" Nora asked.

"It wasn't fake. I fell in love with him. I know I wasn't supposed to, but I did."

They both squeezed me again.

"That was actually clear to both of us a while ago," Hazel said.

Nora rubbed my back, murmuring her agreement.

"Why did I let this happen? Why did I have to go and fall in love with someone who doesn't love me back? I should have known better."

"Shepherd acted like a dick, but that doesn't mean he doesn't love you," Nora said.

I tossed a used tissue on the mess that used to be my coffee table. "Um, yes it does. He basically kicked me out as soon as his dad dumped Svetlana."

Nora and Hazel gave each another look—one of those *we're secretly communicating something* looks.

"Will you two stop that? I'm not done wallowing."

"You can keep wallowing after your interview," Nora said. "You go shower. We'll clean up out here. Then we'll go get some brunch and coffee to perk you up so you're ready."

"But you and I are still drinking mimosas, right?" Hazel asked.

Nora nodded. "Naturally."

I grabbed another tissue and wiped my nose. "All right, I'll pull it together, but just for the interview. Then I'm wallowing again."

"Breakup pity party, table for three is on the agenda for tonight." Nora leaned closer and sniffed me. "After you shower."

Hazel and Nora stood up and each grabbed one of my hands to help peel me off the couch. I shuffled into the bathroom, avoiding the mirror, and turned on the shower. I still felt awful—the ache in my chest refused to go away—but having my friends here to help me pick up the pieces of my heart and glue them back together was priceless.

# 33

## SHEPHERD

*I* clicked away from the report I was supposed to be reviewing, and went back to my email. The photographer from the engagement party had sent a link to our photos. I'd already seen them. I hadn't been able to resist. At this point, I was basically a masochist, considering I'd gone through them at least a dozen times today.

There were candid shots of guests smiling, holding up drinks, dancing. Ethan and Grant in matching fedoras, lifting champagne glasses. Dad with his ridiculous hat and cigar between his teeth. Everly with her girlfriends, posing like a twenties version of *Charlie's Angels*. Annie and Miranda laughing with Ethan and Grant.

I'd purposely skipped the ones of my dad and Svetlana. Those still made me cringe.

The next photo was me and Everly on the dance floor. The photographer had caught her mid-spin, one arm above her head, her hand in mine. The tassels on her dress swirled around her, but it was her face that drew the eye. Bright red lips parted across her perfect teeth in a bright smile.

It didn't escape my attention that I was smiling too, my gaze intent on her.

The photo booth pictures were just as bad. Silly props held up to our faces. We'd gone in multiple times and never managed to keep from laughing.

In the final one we'd taken, I'd grabbed her and planted a hard kiss on her mouth. Nothing about that kiss looked fake. Our lips were molded together, her bottom lip disappearing between mine. Her body was relaxed, arms draping down, as if she were melting against me.

She had been. I remembered how good it felt.

Someone knocked and my office door opened. I shut my laptop quicker than a guy watching porn at work.

Nora stepped in, her hand still on the door handle. "Do you have a minute?"

That was odd. Why was Everly's friend here? My brow furrowed. "Sure."

It wasn't just Nora. Her other friend, Hazel, came in behind her. Nora's dark hair was up and she wore a white sleeveless blouse and tan cropped pants with heels. Hazel wore a navy dress belted at the waist and a pair of dark-rimmed glasses.

"Can I help you?" I asked.

Nora ushered Hazel in and shut the door. Uh-oh. This couldn't be good.

"Mind if we sit?" Nora asked, pointing at the two chairs on the other side of my desk.

"Please."

Hazel sat, her back stick straight. The way she regarded me, her expression impossible to read, made me feel like a subject in a lab experiment.

Nora lowered herself more slowly and set her handbag down at her feet. "Shepherd, we have a problem."

I knew *I* had a problem. An Everly-shaped problem, right in the center of my chest. But *we* had a problem? Were they here to chew me out on Everly's behalf?

"We?"

"Yes, we," Nora said, and Hazel nodded so hard she had to fix her glasses. "Do you have any idea where Everly is right now?"

"No, she took all her vacation time," I said. "Why? Don't you know where she is?"

"Oh, we know exactly where she is," Nora said. "Miami."

A sense of dread hit me in the pit of my stomach. "Why is she in Miami?"

"Remember her phone interview last week?" Nora asked, and I nodded once. "It went well. So well, in fact, that they invited her to come for an in-person interview. In Miami. She left this morning."

My eyes widened. Miami? As in, Florida? "What the fuck?"

"Exactly," Nora said. "I'm glad we're on the same page. We need to do something about this."

"We want what's best for Everly," Hazel said. "And there's a slim chance that moving to Miami is what's best for her."

Nora waved a hand. "Maybe, but I doubt it. Hazel and I agreed that if she really has her heart set on Miami, and the job is a once in a lifetime opportunity, we'll support her even though we'll be devastated to lose our bestie. After all, Miami is a great place to visit."

I gaped at her, still too shocked at the notion of Everly moving to the opposite corner of the country to say a word.

"However," Nora continued, "I'm not even remotely convinced this is what's best for her."

"Neither am I," Hazel said.

Nora pointed to her friend. "If Hazel agrees with me, you

know I'm right. That's how this works. The job might be fantastic, but all three of us know what's really important here."

"What?" I managed to croak out.

"You," Nora said, her tone matter-of-fact. "You're obviously her true love and if there's anyone in this world who deserves to spend the rest of her life in blissful happiness with her true love, it's Everly."

"Precisely," Hazel said.

"Believe me, I'm as surprised as you are." Nora re-crossed her legs. "I don't even believe in true love. But Everly was made for it. She's like a princess in a fairy tale. A sunshiney, overly-optimistic princess with terrible dating luck, but a princess nonetheless."

I had no idea what to say to that. But Nora wasn't finished.

"Let me level with you, Shepherd. You messed this up, and you messed it up badly. But I'm still on your team, mostly because Everly genuinely loves you and I've decided to channel my inner Everly and try to see the best in you. So we're here to help."

"Help?"

Hazel sighed. "Help you, of course."

"You need to fix this," Nora said.

"Why is this my fault?" I asked, knowing full well it was my fault. Mostly, at least.

Nora's brows knitted together. "Is that a serious question?"

Hazel glanced at her. "I think he's serious."

"Maybe I was too harsh with her, but she kept the sperm donor thing from me."

"*Too harsh* is an understatement," Nora said. "Did you

really expect her to tell you about that, especially after she'd already decided she wasn't going to go through with it?"

"It's an uncomfortable topic to begin with," Hazel said. "And the dynamic of you being her employer made it particularly awkward."

"She had an ulterior motive that she kept from me. I trusted her and..." I trailed off. I didn't want to get into all the ways I'd trusted Everly. How hard that had been for me.

"You feel a sense of betrayal because you discovered information that changed the way you viewed your relationship with Everly," Hazel said.

"Yes, exactly."

"It's natural to need some time and space to process that information," Hazel said.

"But now we need you to get your head out of your ass so you can fix this and bring our girl back," Nora said.

"Excuse me?"

Nora sighed. "Shepherd, you know her. You know what a big heart she has. She'd do just about anything for the people she loves."

I rubbed my chin, my eyes on my desk. Everly had the biggest heart of anyone I'd ever met.

"Maybe we were wrong about you," Nora said. "But answer me one question."

"What?"

"Do you love her?"

"Yes." The answer rolled off my tongue so fast, I blinked in shock that I'd admitted it to them.

Nora and Hazel glanced at each other, smiling.

"We thought so," Nora said. "Everyone who saw you together at the engagement party could tell."

"And the fact that you supported her accepting an interview for another job speaks to both your character and your feelings for her," Hazel said.

Something was dawning on me as I listened to Everly's two best friends. It wasn't so much what they'd said—other than the interview in Miami, they hadn't really told me anything I didn't already know—but what they *hadn't* said that struck me.

Everly hadn't told them about the band.

I wasn't sure how I knew. It was possible they were avoiding the topic because she'd made them swear to keep it to themselves. But as I listened to them talk, I knew she hadn't. She hadn't told her best friends my secrets. She shared everything with them—I remembered her saying so —but she hadn't shared this.

She hadn't betrayed my trust at all.

"Oh fuck." I stood and started uncharacteristically pacing around my office. "I told her to leave instead of listening to her and now she's at an interview in fucking Miami."

"Oh good, he's catching up," Nora said.

"What if she takes the job and leaves?" I was muttering to myself, no longer paying attention to her friends. "Damn it, she thinks I don't want her. She doesn't know it was real, because I never fucking told her."

"This is good," Hazel said quietly.

"Wait for it," Nora said.

"I need to go to Miami."

Nora held up a finger. "There it is."

"When did you say she left?"

"This morning," Hazel said. "They sent a private jet for her."

"When is the interview?"

"Tomorrow," Nora said.

"Thank fuck." I went back to my desk to get my phone. Started scrolling through my contacts. "I have time to get there."

Nora stood and patted my shoulder. "Atta boy. We'll come if you want, but I have a feeling you've got this."

I looked up. "Yeah. Thanks."

They left, but I was too busy trying to find the right contact to notice. I didn't own a private jet, although I could have. I hated to fly commercial, but I found it easier to just charter a plane when I traveled.

But what was the guy's name? Everly always made the arrangements, so I rarely spoke to him. Which meant I was probably shit out of luck getting him to do me this big of a favor. A last-minute cross-country flight was a tall order, even with what I was willing to pay him.

However, if he knew Everly...

Finally, I found him. Tom Nguyen, owner Blue Streak Charters. Hoping for a miracle, I called.

"Blue Streak Charters, this is Tom," he said.

"Tom, this is Shepherd Calloway. I need your help."

"Okay..."

"I think you know my assistant, Everly Dalton?"

"Of course," he said, and I could practically hear him smile. Good. That was a good sign.

I took a deep breath. Here went nothing. "I'm in love with her, but I'm also an idiot and I screwed up. And now she's in Miami interviewing for another job and I need to get there before tomorrow morning, otherwise I risk losing her forever."

"Is this a joke?"

"I'm not known for my sense of humor, Mr. Nguyen."

He chuckled. "Fair enough. So you need a last-minute flight to Florida."

"Yes."

"I just have one question."

"Sure."

"Does Everly love you back, or am I going to get in trouble for this?"

"I think she does. I hope. Her best friends were just here trying to convince me to go after her."

"Nora and Hazel? If they're on your side, I'll do it."

How the hell did he know about Nora and Hazel? I shook off the question. "I'll pay whatever you ask."

"Standard rate will be fine, Mr. Calloway," he said. "This is for Everly. If I didn't have to pay for the fuel, I'd do it for free."

## 34

## EVERLY

*M*y heart beat like a hummingbird's—a rapid flutter, sending too much blood to my face. I stood in the restaurant lobby, wishing my cheeks weren't so hot. Wondering if I'd worn the right outfit. Trying not to fidget or fan myself.

Nora had helped me choose the perfect interview attire —a breezy cream blouse and charcoal knee-length skirt, paired with yellow and white polka dot heels. I'd balked at the shoes, but Nora had insisted. She'd said they showed my personality, and if Cameron Whitbury didn't want to hire a girl who could rock yellow polka dot heels, it wasn't the right job for me anyway.

In a weird way, I saw her point.

But now that I was here, in a gorgeous restaurant in Miami waiting for this interview, I wanted to vomit from nervousness. And maybe change my shoes.

The phone interview had gone well. It hadn't been over Skype, which had turned out to be a very good thing. Even after a shower, clean clothes, a good meal, and Nora's makeup and hair treatment, I'd still looked like a girl who'd just been dumped and was ready to chop all her hair off and dye it pink.

Which, to be fair, I had been.

But I'd pulled myself together for the interview. It had been with Cameron herself, and I almost hated to admit it, but we'd really connected. It hadn't felt much like an interview at all. More like catching up with a friend. She'd told me about her plans for the foundation, and what she was looking for in an executive director. And although she'd asked me questions about my work experience and future goals, the feel of our conversation had been easygoing and casual.

Right then and there, she'd invited me to come meet with her in Miami. And I'd said yes.

Afterward, I'd descended into the depths of despair again, and this time I had something new to lament about. I'd liked Cameron Whitbury, and I could see myself taking this job.

Nora and Hazel had been extremely confused by my angst. I was interested in the position, and the interview had been great. Why had they found me in a puddle of my own tears?

I'd been forced to admit that I'd secretly hoped to discover the job wasn't for me, or that I disliked Cameron, or some other compelling reason for me to turn it down.

Logical? Not even a little. It wasn't like passing on this job would mean Shepherd would suddenly come to his senses, apologize—with an appropriate amount of groveling —and declare his love for me. It would just mean I'd either have to suffer the horrific awkwardness of working for Shepherd until I found another job or deal with being unemployed for a while.

The only potential problem was the location. Nora and

Hazel had gone very quiet when I'd told them I was being flown—by private jet, no less—to Miami for the next interview. They hadn't said I shouldn't go, nor had they reminded me how difficult it would be for the three of us to live on opposite sides of the country. I appreciated that they'd held back. I'd seen the concern in their faces, and I'd heard them frantically whispering when they thought I couldn't hear. But they hadn't tried to sway my opinion.

Not yet, at least. They would, if it came down to it. But I appreciated that they were letting me explore this option on my own.

The hostess seated a party of three and I smoothed my skirt. I'd gotten here too early. Not being late was one thing, but twenty minutes of standing in the lobby was making me a little bit crazy.

The truth was, I didn't know if I was willing to move all the way to Miami. Did I really want to uproot my life? Move away from Nora and Hazel? From Annie and Miranda? If they had a baby—and I was sure they would, somehow—it would be a lot harder to be the cool aunt who came to every birthday party, Little League game, and school play. I'd fly home to visit as often as I could, but how often would that really be?

And it would mean closing the door forever on whatever I'd had with Shepherd.

I took a deep breath. I couldn't think about Shepherd right now. The only thing I needed to focus on was nailing this interview.

Cameron came into the plush lobby. She was stunning. I'd seen plenty of photos of her online, but they didn't do her justice. She had thick auburn hair and a light dusting of freckles across her nose. Flawless skin, and I'd have killed for those cheekbones. She wore a blue sleeveless blouse that made her eyes pop, high-waisted slacks, and a pair of silver stilettos I'd covet until the day I died.

She gave me a warm smile. "Everly?"

"Yes." I held out my hand and she shook it. "Everly Dalton. It's so nice to meet you in person, Ms. Whitbury."

"It's nice to meet you, too. And please, call me Cameron." She glanced at my feet. "I love your shoes."

Kudos to Nora. "Thanks."

"Are you ready to be seated, Ms. Whitbury?" the hostess asked.

"Yes, thank you."

I nearly gasped as one of the largest men I'd ever seen seemed to appear out of nowhere behind Cameron. He must have been six and a half feet tall. But it wasn't just his height that almost made me jump out of my cute yellow heels. He was practically two people wide. Huge shoulders, thick tattooed arms bulging out of his tight black t-shirt. Thighs the size of tree trunks. How had I not noticed him there?

"I'll go first," he said, his deep voice monotone.

A flash of irritation crossed Cameron's features. She gestured for him to go ahead of her, then she and I followed.

The hostess led us to a private terrace. The man held up a hand and raised his eyebrows at Cameron before going outside. He searched the entire area. For what, I had no idea, but he looked beneath the table, under the chairs, and over the railing.

"Clear," he said, then stood off to the side, arms crossed over his thick chest.

Cameron cleared her throat as we walked outside onto the terrace. "Sorry. Jude is... security."

"I suppose someone like you needs a bodyguard," I said.

She pulled out a chair. "My friends seem to think so."

We both sat and I crossed my legs at the ankles.

"I'm glad you could come out on such short notice," Cameron said. "I appreciate you taking the time to meet with me in person."

"Absolutely."

The waitress came and asked for our drink orders. I was about to order a very sensible glass of water, when Cameron spoke first.

"Mimosas?" she asked, a hint of a smile on her face. "Or a bloody mary, perhaps?"

A drink? Yes, please. "A mimosa sounds great."

She ordered two mimosas and we made small talk until the waitress came back with our drinks and took our breakfast orders.

"I already gave you the details on my plans for the foundation," Cameron said. "I need someone who can hit the ground running. And I know your background is in a different area, but you have the set of skills, and the personality, that I'm looking for."

"Wow, thank you."

"Plus, if you've worked for Shepherd Calloway this long, I know you're tough."

I covered the sudden surge of emotion by taking a sip of my mimosa. "Do you know Shep—I mean, Mr. Calloway?"

"No, we've never met, but his reputation precedes him."

"Of course it does. Although he's not really what people think."

We chatted for a while longer. The waitress brought our breakfasts, and the food was delicious. Thankfully, she didn't stay on the topic of Shepherd. We talked more about the foundation, and how it would be structured. What she needed from an executive director. I already had ideas, and she listened to me intently as we ate.

I loved this opportunity. It filled me with a sense of excitement and purpose. I liked Cameron even more in person than I had on the phone, and it wasn't just the mimosa breakfast. She was direct, but personable. We had a good rapport, and I could easily see myself working for her.

But there was one big problem.

"There's just one issue I wanted to talk to you about," I said. "I'm not sure how I feel about relocating. Miami is beautiful, and this sounds like such an amazing opportunity. But my entire life is in Seattle."

"I thought that might be an issue after we talked the other day. If you don't want to relocate, I have no problem opening the foundation's headquarters in Seattle."

"Really?"

"Absolutely. I won't need to be there in person on a daily basis, and technology makes communication simple. If you want the job, we'll open the office in Seattle."

Saying yes was right. I knew it, deep in my soul. This wasn't about Shepherd. It was about me, and reaching out and grabbing a fantastic opportunity.

"Then I want the job," I said.

Cameron smiled. "I was hoping you would."

I put a hand to my chest and let out a breath. "I can't believe that just happened. Did you really just hire me?"

"I sure did." She raised her glass and I followed suit. "Here's to doing some good in the world."

I clicked my glass against hers. This was a milestone moment in my life. I could feel it. The future suddenly stretched out before me, full of promise.

It made me want to call Shepherd to tell him the news. I had a momentary fantasy of coming home to his condo. Bursting in the door to find him waiting for me. I'd run into his arms and he'd scoop me up and hug me tight. Whisper in my ear that he was proud of me.

I finished my drink and set my glass down, trying my very best to keep the sadness off my face.

"Excuse me, sir, you can't go out there."

A commotion inside the restaurant drew my attention. A man was hurrying toward our terrace, followed by the hostess.

I blinked in disbelief. It was—

Jude moved with shocking speed, especially considering his size, and before I could fathom who I was seeing, he blocked the door.

"Sir, that's a private dining area," the hostess said from inside. "You don't have a reservation."

"Everly."

That voice. Oh my god, it really was him. I stood. "Shepherd?"

"Jude," Cameron said, her tone annoyed. "Let him by."

Jude shot Cameron an irritated glance but stood aside.

I gaped at the man who walked out onto the terrace. It was Shepherd. Sort of. The only time I'd seen him like this was at the bar when he was playing bass.

Plain t-shirt, although white this time. Jeans. No suit. No tie. Messy hair. Even his facial hair had grown in thicker than usual.

He looked a little bit forlorn, and utterly and completely delicious.

"Sorry to interrupt, Ms. Whitbury." He came to the table and held out a hand to Cameron. "Shepherd Calloway."

"Cameron," she said, shaking his hand. She seemed both awed and slightly amused.

"I need to ask you not to offer Everly the job," Shepherd said. "Not yet, at least. Don't get me wrong, you should absolutely hire her. You'll never meet someone who's as smart, kind, hard-working, diligent, and passionate about everything she does. As her boss—or former boss, I suppose—I give her my wholehearted, unequivocal recommendation. But as a man, I'm asking you to do me an enormous favor and give me a few minutes to talk to her first."

"I'm sorry, Mr. Calloway, I've already offered Everly the position. And she accepted."

The stricken look on his face as he slowly closed his eyes took the breath right out of my lungs.

He nodded once, then looked at me. "Of course. As she should have."

Cameron picked up her purse. "I just remembered, I have another meeting to get to. Everly, thank you so much for coming. We'll connect later and work out the details. Mr. Calloway, it was nice meeting you. I hope you both enjoy your visit to Miami."

She glanced at Jude, who gestured for her to walk ahead of him. She smiled at me, then left, her giant hulking bodyguard moving with surprising grace behind her.

"Oh my god, Shepherd, what are you doing here?" I hissed at him when they were gone.

"Everly, I'm so sorry." He covered his mouth, then ran his hand down his chin. "I never did figure out what I was going to say when I got here."

"How did you know I was here?"

"Nora and Hazel."

My mouth dropped open. "What?"

"They came to my office yesterday and said you'd gone to Miami for a job interview."

"Those meddling little vixens. But how did you know I was at this restaurant? They didn't know where I was meeting Cameron."

He winced. "That was them, too. Nora, to be specific. She guessed your email password."

"Damn, I knew I should have changed it."

"I'm sorry. This is the craziest, most unprofessional thing I've ever done. Also, you might want to let Cameron know she can ignore all the messages I left at her office."

"You called her office too?"

"I was desperate," he said. "I don't know what I'm doing. I've lost my mind, and I've never felt this way before."

"How did you get here so fast?"

"I called Tom Nguyen at Blue Streak Charters. He says hello, by the way."

I couldn't help but smile. Tom was the nicest man. "Aw, I love Tom."

"Luckily for me, he feels the same about you."

I glanced into the restaurant, but no one seemed to care that we were out here. "You might as well sit down."

He took Cameron's seat and I sat in my chair.

"So, you took the position," he said.

"I did."

His eyes were on the table. "That's... great. I'm glad for you. You'll be amazing."

"Shepherd, why are you here?"

He took a deep breath, his chest rising and falling against that crisp white shirt, and his disheveled hair fell across his forehead. "I hoped I'd get the chance to talk to you before you made your decision."

"Why didn't you just call me?"

"I know. I'm sorry. I'm sorry for everything. I didn't call because I needed to do this in person."

"Do what?"

He looked up, meeting my eyes. "Tell you that it wasn't fake. Not for me."

"What?"

"I love you. I think I've loved you since the moment you stepped out of that car in that goddamn red dress. And I've fallen a little bit more in love with you every day. I should have told you a hundred times, but I'm an emotionally stunted robot."

I laughed softly. "No, you're not."

"I really am," he said. "From the very beginning, I was fighting my attraction to you. Do you remember the first night we slept in bed together?"

"Yes."

"I barely slept because all I could think about was how beautiful you were. How good you smelled. I kept wondering how I'd worked with you for years, but I'd never really seen you. But I know exactly why. I didn't let myself see you. Not because you worked for me, although that was part of it. But mostly because deep down, I knew if I did, I'd fall for you. And that fucking terrified me."

He glanced away again and rubbed his jaw. It seemed like he had more to say, so I waited, my heart in my throat.

"I'm sorry I overreacted when I found the contract. I should have listened to you."

I nodded. "I'm sorry too. I'm sorry you found out the way you did. I never wanted to hurt you."

He reached across the table and traced the back of my hand with his fingers. "I know you didn't. Everly, thank you for everything. I asked you to turn your life upside down for me, and you did it. Regardless of whether you thought it might get me to agree to something else, you did it because you care so much about the people in your life. Even me, and I'd never done anything to deserve it. Thank you for your kindness to my dad. For coming into my world and injecting color. Maybe this sounds stupid, but your sunshine warmed my cold soul, and I'll always be grateful for that."

"Shepherd, I'm not moving to Miami."

"What?"

"You sound like you're trying to say goodbye, but I'm not staying here. I told Cameron I wasn't sure about relocating. She said the foundation can be headquartered anywhere. We're opening the office in Seattle."

He stared at me for a long moment, his mouth slightly open, brow furrowed. Without saying a word, he rose and took my hand, gently pulling me to my feet. He tilted my chin up and looked down at me with those gorgeous blue eyes.

"Everly," he said, his voice soft and low. "I love you. Please come home."

My eyes stung with tears and I squeezed them shut. Relief poured through me. He'd said it. It was real. Shepherd Calloway loved me.

"I love you, too."

And there it was. That smile. The one that showed his perfect teeth and puckered his adorable dimples. The smile he never gave anyone else. The one he saved for me.

"I wasn't trying to say goodbye," he said, caressing my cheek. "Not exactly. I was formulating a plan B. Wondering how long it would take to buy a private jet. I wasn't going to let you get away so easily."

I smiled and he leaned down to seal his lips over mine. I melted against him, tossing my arms around his neck. He wrapped me in his strong arms and lifted me off my feet.

"Congratulations," he whispered into my ear. "I'm so proud of you."

## 35

---

## EVERLY

*I* already knew Sophie was perfect.

Shepherd and I had interviewed several other candidates for my replacement, but from the moment Sophie had walked into the room, I'd known. Why? The fact that she hadn't balked when Shepherd stared at her, like a scary unblinking robot, while she introduced herself said a lot.

We'd interviewed a guy this morning who'd wilted so fast under Shepherd's gaze, we hadn't even gotten to the questions before he'd excused himself. His hands had been shaking so badly, he'd barely been able to get the door open. And he hadn't come back.

I'd almost told Shepherd to tone it down—he was scaring away the good applicants. But I'd thought better of it. Whoever we hired was going to have to face those cold blue eyes on a regular basis. If they didn't have the spine to stare him down in an interview, they'd never last as his assistant.

Sophie was holding her own.

Her dark blond curls were pulled up in the cutest bun,

and she wore a tasteful blue dress with a cream cardigan that looked great on her curvy frame. She smiled pleasantly and quickly adjusted her glasses.

"I think that's all the questions we have for you," I said. "Shepherd, do you have anything else?"

"No." He pushed her resume toward me, picked up his phone, and started checking his messages.

I resisted the urge to roll my eyes. But Sophie didn't seem fazed. She reminded me a little bit of—well, me. I had a feeling she was the type of girl who came across as *nice* and *sweet*, which made people underestimate her.

I also had a feeling she'd be the one who could handle Shepherd Calloway.

Being with me hadn't changed who he was. He was still stoic and serious. Still appeared cold and unfeeling, especially at work. Not many people got to see the Shepherd on the inside. The guy who could shred on a bass, whose rare smiles made my knees weak, and who loved it when I left bite marks on his chest.

He had four right now. I'd counted them this morning as I kissed them better.

"Thanks for coming in." I stood and shook Sophie's hand. "We'll be in touch soon."

"Thank you for your time, Ms. Dalton," she said. "Mr. Calloway."

Shepherd's eyes flicked to her, but he didn't reply. Just gave her the tiniest of nods, then went back to his messages.

Sophie turned to leave and the door flew open, hitting her right in the head. She stumbled back, clutching her forehead. Shepherd stood, and I grabbed her shoulders to steady her.

"I'm so sorry." It was Nina, the front receptionist. "I

thought you were interviewing in Mr. Calloway's office. I didn't know anyone was in here. Are you okay?"

"Yes, I'm fine," Sophie said, and I could hear the dejection in her voice as she rubbed her forehead. "It's probably my fault."

"No, it was totally me." Nina seemed to realize Shepherd was still in here. Her eyes landed on him and she paled. "I have to get back to the front. I'll find another conference room for the marketing team."

Nina scurried away. I still had my hands on Sophie's shoulders. I felt her take a deep breath and straighten her spine.

"Are you sure you're okay?" I asked.

"Yes." She took a step and turned. "I'll be fine. Thanks again for your time."

I leaned a little closer and lowered my voice to a whisper. "Don't worry. That didn't ruin it."

She gave me a bright smile. "Thanks."

"We'll be in touch."

Sophie left and I gathered up the resumes we'd collected.

"That was the last one. What do you think?"

"We'll hire Sophie."

I agreed, but I was surprised he'd made the decision so fast. "Really?"

"She's the obvious choice. Don't you think so?"

"I totally do, I'm just surprised you decided that fast."

"She's experienced and well-qualified. She interviewed well. And I don't hate the sound of her voice."

I laughed. "That's your criteria? Is that why you hired me? You didn't hate the sound of my voice?"

Pocketing his phone, he looked me in the eyes. "No. You

were the best for the job *and* I didn't hate the sound of your voice."

I slipped my arms around his waist. It didn't matter that the door was still open and anyone walking by could see. In fact, Steve walked by, right then. He paused and gave me a dramatic wink. I had no idea why. Shepherd and I were no secret. Everyone knew that we were dating and I'd moved in with him. People probably thought I'd taken a new job because of our relationship—which was both true and false. But it didn't matter what they thought.

The corner of Shepherd's mouth hooked in a little grin and he leaned down to kiss me. I caught his lower lip between my teeth and bit down, just hard enough to get him to grunt.

"I'm going to fuck you so hard for that later," he growled in my ear.

"Promise?"

The last couple of weeks, since we'd come back from Miami, had been busy. I was still working for Shepherd, just until we could get a replacement up to speed. Cameron was anxious to get moving on her new venture, so I'd been scoping out office locations, pricing furniture, and putting together a preliminary budget.

Thankfully, it was Friday. It looked like we'd just found his new assistant. I had a few options for office space to send to Cameron. Nora had been helping me with office décor ideas, and Hazel had given me a lead on a potential office assistant.

Things were coming together.

Reluctantly, I dropped my arms and stepped back. "I have a few more things to do, then I'm heading home. Are you going to the Office early?"

"Yeah."

The way he looked away, not quite meeting my eyes, made me feel all squishy inside. I'd caught that rare display of emotion. Shepherd Calloway was nervous.

I squeezed his arm. "I'll see you there. And it's going to be great."

As usual, the Office was packed. Dahlia Marlow was on first, regaling the crowd with her sultry voice. I loved that the same bar that rocked out to Incognito was mesmerized by a woman in her late fifties singing folksy music and playing an acoustic guitar.

To be fair, she was amazing.

"I still don't believe you," Nora said. She stood next to me in a ripped Jack Daniel's t-shirt showing little peeks of her lacy red bra, with distressed jeans and shiny black stilettos. Somehow Nora knew how to dress perfectly for every occasion, even a rock show at a dive bar.

Hazel sipped her bourbon. This wasn't exactly a martini kind of place, so we'd all opted for Maker's Mark, neat. "I think you're trying to play a joke on us."

I shrugged one shoulder. "Think what you will. You'll see."

The other day, Shepherd had surprised the heck out of me—and his dad and brother—when he'd unceremoniously invited them to see his band. He hadn't bothered to set up his invitation with any explanation. No *by the way, I play bass in a band, and I've never told you.* He just casually told them he was playing Friday night and said they could come if they wanted to.

I'd given Richard and Ethan more details. Then Shepherd had mentioned, just as casually, that if I wanted to invite anyone else, it was fine.

Obviously, I'd taken him up on that. Show off my hot bass player to my friends? Yes, please.

His secret guitar lair, however, was still just that—a secret. I think we both liked it that way. We'd meet down there sometimes and pretend to be strangers. At least, I'd pretend. Shepherd's version of role-playing was mostly letting me do all the talking and then ravaging me on every available surface.

I loved it.

Richard made his way through the crowd, followed closely by Ethan and Grant. Shepherd's brother and brother-in-law looked around, bewildered, like they were wondering the same thing as Nora and Hazel—when we were going to drop the punch line and let them in on the joke. Richard, however, almost walked right into me. His eyes were locked on the stage.

"Who is that?" he asked, his voice awed.

"Dahlia Marlow," I said. "She's amazing, isn't she?"

"She's incredible."

If a man could have actual stars in his eyes, or maybe little red hearts appearing around his face, Richard would have had them now. He always wore his heart on his sleeve, but I'd never seen him like this. I wondered if there was a way I could introduce him to Dahlia after her set. I didn't know her well, but I'd chatted with her once on a night I'd come to see Shepherd play.

Annie and Miranda arrived, looking just as skeptical as everyone else. We all exchanged hellos and hugs—except for Richard, who was still too busy mooning over Dahlia to notice anyone else existed.

Her last song ended and she smiled at the enthusiastic

applause. Richard whistled. I could have been imagining things, but for a moment, it looked like their eyes met. Dahlia's face registered a hint of surprise, and she seemed to pause before continuing to smile and wave at the crowd.

The bar owner came out and thanked her for her set. Excitement swirled in my tummy. This was it.

"And now, let's give it up for Incognito," he said.

The crowd roared as the band took the stage. The lead singer and the guitarist came out first, taking their places in front. The drummer waved his drumsticks at the crowd and sat behind the drum kit.

And then there was Shepherd.

Dressed in a dark t-shirt that showed off his toned arms and a pair of jeans that made me want to take a bite out of his cute butt, he walked out on stage and picked up his bass. He was all cool, casual confidence. No swagger. Shepherd didn't need swagger. Not in a tux at a fancy gala, or in a plain t-shirt on stage in a dive bar. He wasn't here for the attention, and that made him infinitely more sexy.

"Holy shit," Nora said.

He slung the strap over his shoulder and fingered the bass strings. He knew we were out here, but I didn't see a hint of that nervousness I'd caught earlier today. His eyes swept the crowd, finally landing on me. The corner of his mouth twitched and he winked.

My knees buckled and I had to grab onto Ethan to stay standing. Oh my god. That man.

"Hey, Seattle," the lead singer said into the mic. The crowd cheered again. "Thanks for hanging out with us tonight."

The drummer beat out a quick intro, and they launched into their first song.

Richard beamed at his son. Ethan and Grant still looked shocked, but they smiled and moved to the music.

Nora gaped at the men on stage. "I can't believe you didn't tell us."

"It wasn't my secret to share," I said.

"They're very good," Hazel said, raising her voice to be heard above the music.

"Yeah, they are," Nora said. "The drummer is exquisite. Do you know if he's single?"

I shook my head. "Nope. They're all married. Sorry."

"Damn," Nora said.

We all stood together, moving, swaying, clapping, and cheering as they played through their set. We hollered and punched fists in the air during the fast songs. Held our phones up like lighters for the slow songs. Watched as Shepherd played his heart out, lost in his music, letting the people closest to him get just a little bit closer.

They finished their set and the crowd roared. Richard cheered so loud Shepherd probably heard him all the way up on stage. Instead of staying back in the shadows, he came to the front with rest of the band. Lifted his arm in a wave.

"Thank you so much," the lead singer said. "Until next time, good night."

The stage lights went dark, leaving just the band members' silhouettes. Music came on the speakers and the hum of conversation grew as the crowd around the stage broke up.

Richard touched my elbow. He was looking at something—or someone—near the bar. "Excuse me for a minute."

He made his way to a small table. Dahlia turned and smiled. They shook hands and she gestured, inviting him to sit with her. He did, and I could practically see the sparks.

The way they smiled at each other was the most adorable thing I'd ever seen.

A pair of cute guys had struck up a conversation with Nora and Hazel. This kind of fun, casual flirting was Nora's catnip. She was clearly enjoying herself. Even Hazel looked interested. It made me wonder if she would decide her no-dating days were over.

"I'm glad you two are here," Ethan said to Annie. "Grant and I need to talk to you."

"What's up?" Annie asked.

Ethan and Grant shared a smile. "I know this is personal, but we wondered if you were still looking for a donor."

Annie's lips parted and she blinked at him a few times. "We are."

"Grant and I have been talking about it, and I'd like to volunteer," Ethan said. "We've already decided we're not having kids. We've always known that. But we thought this would be a good thing to do."

"Plus, if it's the physical traits you're after, he looks a lot like Shepherd," Grant said. "And Ethan is a brilliant architect. He's smart and caring, not to mention gorgeous."

Ethan shook his head, grinning. "Stop."

I touched my fingers to my lips. They knew I was standing here, but this moment felt so personal. I didn't want to ruin it by squealing with joy.

"There's no pressure at all," Ethan said. "I won't be offended if you decide to go with someone else. I just wanted you to know, I'm willing if it's what you want. And if this works out, we'd love to be around as the cool uncles, if you're okay with that."

Annie's eyes glistened with tears. She glanced at Miranda. "I shouldn't answer you without talking this over with Miranda first, but that's the most amazing gift."

"Yes," Miranda said, clutching Annie's arm. "We accept."

"Are you sure?" Annie asked.

"I'm positive." She stepped forward and wrapped Ethan in hug. "Thank you. I don't even know how to thank you for this. Saying it isn't enough."

Next thing I knew, everyone was hugging everyone else. Grant hugged Annie. They swapped and Ethan hugged Annie while Grant wrapped Miranda in an embrace. Tears wet everyone's eyes, including mine.

Especially mine.

We were turning into one big family. Maybe a quirky, slightly non-traditional one, but a family nonetheless. And somehow, that made it even more special.

Shepherd came out, a little sweaty, his hair a mess. Without a word, he wrapped his arms around me and captured my mouth in a soft kiss.

He rubbed his nose against mine. "Hey, you."

"Hey. You guys were great tonight."

"Thanks for coming."

I wound my arms around his waist and smiled up at him. To most people, Shepherd Calloway was a focused and unemotional businessman. But I was the lucky girl who got to see the real Shepherd. The guy on the inside.

That guy was all mine.

# EPILOGUE
## EVERLY

*T*he night air was fresh as we walked across the Seattle Center grounds, my hand tucked in the crook of Shepherd's arm. We'd had a nice dinner at a bistro up the street. Nothing fancy, but the food had been excellent. Since the night was so nice, we'd decided to take a little walk.

People strolled by on the paved path and a few still lounged on blankets on the open expanse of grass. The low hum of the city surrounded us, and streetlights twinkled in the darkness.

It had been six months since Miami. Since Shepherd had said those six magical words. Not three. The *I love you* had been important, but only half of what I'd needed to hear. The second half, *please come home*, had meant just as much.

I had come home. And we hadn't spent a night apart since.

I'd spent this morning planning Annie and Miranda's baby shower over brunch with Richard. He'd moved out shortly after I'd started my new job and was well on his way to financial recovery. Last week, he'd been given a clean bill of health. He was officially cancer-free. He still needed to be cautious and take good care of himself. But now that he had Dahlia in his life, he was healthier than ever.

They'd been dating since the night they'd met at the Office, and Richard had never been happier.

Annie and Miranda had successfully conceived a baby girl, with Ethan as the donor. Some people might consider it strange, or even awkward, to have the brother of the man you're dating donate sperm to your sister so she could have a baby. For us, it wasn't weird at all. We were all just family, now. Their baby would be raised by the two best mommies ever, and have two awesome uncles in her life. She wasn't even born yet, and she was already one lucky little girl.

The fountain was on tonight, its huge jets of water streaming from the large silver dome. A ring of lights illuminated the water, making the whole thing glow.

We paused to watch. The fountain's bursts were choreographed to classical music, the rise and fall of the water matching the cadence of the song.

"It's beautiful," I said.

Shepherd rubbed slow circles across my back. "It is."

The song grew soft and the fountain went down to nothing but a trickle. A loud clash of cymbals and horns seemed to send the water bursting from the top in a huge stream. It reached for the sky and crashed to the ground, sending out a cloud of mist.

We were too far away to get wet, but it made me laugh just the same.

"Everly," Shepherd said, his voice strangely soft.

"Were you watching?" I asked. "Did you see how high the water went?"

His eyes flicked to the side, in the opposite direction.

"What?"

The corner of his mouth twitched, his dimple almost puckering. With his hand on the small of my back, he gently turned me around. "Look."

For a second, I didn't see anything. Just an open expanse of lawn, cloaked in darkness. Even the late-night picnickers seemed to have packed up and left.

A figure dashed out, crouching low, and paused. I saw a spark, like the tiny flame of a lighter. Then more sparks.

The tiny flashes grew, one spark growing into several, each lighting the next. They moved fast, lighting up the night with their soft glow. They looked like large sparklers, each one placed in the grass just close enough to light the next. A bright, flashing domino effect.

In seconds, the lawn was lit up with silver and gold sparks, their lights winking and flashing in the darkness.

As I stared at the display, wondering who on earth had done such a thing and how we'd gotten so lucky that we'd witnessed it—and how had Shepherd known to tell me to look?—I realized it spelled something. Four words.

*Will you marry me?*

It even had the question mark.

I looked at Shepherd, my mouth open. But I'd suddenly lost the ability to speak.

His lips turned up in that heart-melting smile and he slowly lowered to one knee. He took my hands, his eyes never leaving mine.

"Everly, you have the biggest heart of anyone I've ever known. And I'm about to ask you to give it to me, forever. All I have to give you in return is mine, which, to be perfectly honest, isn't enough. But I love you with every bit of it— with every piece of my soul. Will you marry me?"

"Yes, Shepherd. Yes. Oh my god, yes."

Before he could do anything else—he probably had a ring, but I wasn't thinking very clearly—I threw my arms around him. Still on one knee, he pulled me lower and held me against him. Leaned his face into my hair and took a deep breath.

"I love you, Everly," he whispered.

"I love you too."

I sniffed, letting the tears trail from the corners of my eyes.

After a long moment, he rose and helped me stand. He produced a small box from the inside pocket of his jacket and opened it. Inside was a rose gold ring with a center stone surrounded by a halo of diamonds. It wasn't large—nothing like the fake-engagement ring I'd worn. But it was beautiful. Perfect, even. In fact—

"Shepherd, this looks like the ring I tried on when we bought the fake ring."

He pulled the ring from the box and held it up. "It is the ring you tried on."

"You found one just like it?"

"No, this is the same ring. May I?"

I nodded, holding out my hand. He slipped the ring on my finger.

"I can't believe it was still there."

He took my hand in his and ran his thumb across my knuckles. "Actually, I bought it at the same time as the other one."

"You bought this when we were faking? Why?"

"I honestly don't know. It was a whim. And I never have whims; I always think things through. But I saw this ring on your finger that day and I had to buy it. So I did."

"Thank you. It's perfect. And were those sparklers? How did you do that?"

His lips turned up in a grin and he nodded toward the lawn. "I had a little help."

Richard stood on the path near the now-burnt-out sparklers. He waved.

I grabbed the lapels of his jacket and leaned closer. "You're a little bit crazy, Shepherd Calloway."

"You bring out the best in me."

I melted into his strong embrace, throwing my arms around his neck as he kissed me. Happy tears trailed down my cheeks and it was almost hard to kiss him back. I couldn't stop smiling.

He was smiling, too.

As it turned out, Shepherd Calloway wasn't the only person on the planet who was impervious to my sunshine. All it had taken was a gold-digging ex-girlfriend, a parent in crisis, a sister looking for a sperm donor, a fake relationship, some awkward bed-sharing, a stupidly huge diamond, and some strawberry shampoo to crack that man open.

Oh yeah. I knew about the shampoo. I ordered it in bulk now, just in case they stopped making it someday.

Once upon a time, I'd thought I was cursed. But my happily ever after had been there all along. The road we'd taken to find it had been winding, filled with surprises neither of us had seen coming. But it was impossible to imagine things turning out any other way. Shepherd and I had been made for each other. And now we were going to spend the rest of our lives together. Happy. Loved.

And a little bit kinky.

After all, who could resist biting her brand-new-not-fake-fiancé's bottom lip when it made him growl like a predator? Not this girl.

WANT MORE SHEPHERD AND EVERLY? Turn the page for a special (HOT) bonus epilogue with an extended look at their happily ever after.

# BONUS EPILOGUE
## SHEPHERD

*A* cool breeze came off the water, easing the tropical heat. I adjusted my sunglasses and took a sip of my drink. It was fruity, served in an actual coconut shell, and had a little paper umbrella sticking out the top. It looked ridiculous. But I had to admit, it was good.

Everly wandered down by the edge of the water, dipping her cute little feet in the surf. Her yellow bikini—of course it was yellow—looked fantastic against her sun-kissed skin. She glanced over her shoulder and smiled. The sun had nothing on Everly. She lit up the entire fucking world.

My world in particular.

She wiggled her fingers at me, then waded out a little further, the water splashing around her ankles. Made for a great view. The enormous sky touching crystal blue water. Pale sand. And my wife in a tiny bikini, shaking her ass at me.

Perfection.

The feel of my ring was already familiar, not even a week after our wedding. I rolled it around my finger with my thumb, feeling the smooth metal. It felt good. It belonged there.

I hadn't expected much to change when I married Everly. Why would it? We'd already been living together. A wedding was just a formality.

But something had changed. As we'd stood in front of our friends and families, saying our vows, I'd felt it. That moment had done something to me, deep inside. Bound me to her in a way I didn't really understand. But like the ring on my finger, it felt right.

My phone buzzed next to me, so I tore my eyes away from the view—the beach was great, but god, my wife's body was delicious—and checked my messages.

It was from Nolan, my CFO. I'd left him in charge while I took the first ever vacation of my adult life. I hadn't been away from work for more than a day... ever. Everly wanted me to check out entirely, insisting I'd left the company in good hands. That I had nothing to worry about and they could live without me for a couple of weeks. She was right, but old habits die hard.

I read his text. It started with *this is just an FYI, no need to respond*. But I wondered if I should just schedule a conference call. I should really check in with everyone, anyway. It wouldn't take more than an hour. I started typing my reply.

Everly cleared her throat. I hadn't realized she'd approached.

She put her hands on her hips. "You're working again, aren't you?"

I lifted my eyes to meet hers, letting my gaze trail slowly over her curves.

"I can tell you're working," she said.

"It's nothing. Just a quick message. And maybe a conference call later."

She rolled her eyes. "We're on our honeymoon. You're allowed to take actual time off."

"I am taking actual time off."

"A conference call later?"

I stared her down, my gaze hard. The way she challenged me was such a turn-on.

Her eyes narrowed and her lips twitched in a tiny grin. Then she snatched my phone out of my hand and darted toward the water.

"Everly."

I stood, but she was already at the water's edge. She stopped, her feet on the wet sand, and threw my phone into the ocean.

She walked back, brushing her hands together, a smug smile on her face. "There."

"You just threw my phone in the water."

"That's very observant of you, Shep." She brushed the sand off her feet with a towel before lying on the large blanket we'd set out on the sand. She patted the spot next to her. "Now come relax with me."

I scowled at her, but I wasn't mad. I'd get a new phone when we got back. But I'd take it out on her ass later.

She reached over and pulled her phone out of her bag.

"Why do you get to check your messages?" I asked.

She playfully rolled her eyes. "Well, one of us needs to have a phone. And yours is in the ocean."

I gestured to the water. "Because you threw it."

"Details. Besides, I'm not working."

"Nora?"

"Yeah." Her eyebrows drew together. "Do you mind if I call her? I have no idea what she's talking about."

"Not at all." I got comfortable and took another sip of my

ridiculous fruit thing. At least it had a healthy amount of rum.

"Hey, sweetie," Everly said into her phone. "No, it's fine, of course you're not bugging me. Hazel did what?"

She paused for a long moment, listening.

"Wow. You totally did the right thing. And call Sophie. She's my proxy in the circle of trust until I get back."

I raised an eyebrow. Everly had become friends with my new assistant—because of course she had—but I wasn't sure what it meant that she'd drawn her into her little circle with Nora and Hazel.

Wasn't my issue. Sophie was competent at her job. That was all I cared about.

"That's a good idea," Everly said. "I'm sure it'll be fine. Okay, love you too. I will. See you next week."

She hung up and tossed her phone back in her bag.

"Everything okay?"

"I think so. Minor crisis with Hazel. She's being very... un-Hazel-like. Nora and Sophie will handle it."

I reached over and slid my hand across the smooth skin of her stomach. "Good. Because as amazing as you look in this bikini, you'd look better naked."

Her cheeks flushed pink and she glanced around. "Here?"

"It's a private island. We're completely alone."

"What if the staff is still here?"

I shifted closer and palmed her breast, feeling her nipple harden through the thin yellow fabric. "They're at the villa. No one's watching. And if they are, I'll just fire them."

She laughed softly, her eyes drifting closed while my hands roamed over her body. I turned her onto her stomach and pulled on the string to unfasten her bikini top. She let it drop to the blanket and glanced at me over her shoulder, biting her bottom lip.

I smacked her ass and she gasped. "Bottoms off."

She rolled over again and slid her bottoms down her legs. With a flick of her foot, she tossed her last scrap of clothing aside.

"Good girl."

This was heaven, right here. The warm sun shining down on my wife's beautiful body. The soothing rhythm of the ocean waves. A gentle breeze. This vacation thing was proving to be pretty fantastic. I was definitely bringing her here again.

Leaning down, I captured her mouth in a kiss. Ran my hand along her delicious curves. She raked her fingernails across my chest, the light scratch making my blood run hot.

Splaying her palms against my chest, she pushed against me. "You still have clothes on."

I moved onto my back and watched, a hint of a smile on my lips, while she took off my shorts. My dick was hard and ready for her, but I loved to watch her play. She kissed up one thigh, then nudged me onto my side.

"God, this ass. It's so cute, I want to bite it."

Meeting her eyes, one corner of my mouth turned up and a low growl rumbled in my throat.

She giggled and kissed her way across my hip. Then she sank her teeth into the tight flesh of my ass, biting hard.

I groaned. Fuck, I loved it when she did that.

Her hand moved to my erection and she gave it a good squeeze while she leaned over me and bit my ass cheek again.

"Fuck," I growled. "Get your ass over here."

I manhandled her onto her back and climbed between

her legs. Her eyes sparkled with her smile and her cheeks flushed pink. Holy shit, I loved her so much.

She raked her hands through my hair as I thrust inside her. God, that pussy. So hot and wet. I groaned, sliding in and out. Her hips tilted to meet my thrusts and she let out a breathy sigh.

"Shepherd."

I loved hearing my name on her lips. Leaning down, I kissed her sweet mouth. She tasted like summer. Her teeth caught my lip and she nibbled, teasing me with a light scrape.

Growling again, I drove into her harder. She ran her hands down my back, letting her fingernails trail over my skin.

"You feel so good, baby." I kissed down her neck, feeling the pleasant pressure of her tits against my chest.

"Harder," she murmured.

Her fingernails sank into my back and it was like a spark flaring to life, the sharp sensation rushing straight to my groin. With a low grunt, my muscles clenched, and I drove into her, hard and fast. Over and over, slamming my solid cock into her sweet, wet pussy.

Burying my face in her neck, I was surrounded by her strawberry scent. I fucked her hard, my cock driving deep. She clawed at my back, moaning into my ear with every thrust.

Her pussy was hot and tight around me, pulsing with her impending orgasm. My balls drew up tight, heat and tension rising.

Still fucking her hard, I growled low in her ear. "I love you."

"I love you t—ahh—" Her last word cut off as her pussy

pulsed around my dick. She rolled her hips to my rhythm and clutched at my back, moaning as she came.

It was enough to set me off, but I held back. With my cock buried deep inside her, I kissed her deeply, my tongue dragging across hers.

"Good?" I asked.

She sighed, her eyes rolling back. "So good."

"On your knees."

I pulled out, the aching pressure almost painful. She turned over and got on her knees, arching her back. I gave her ass a good smack.

She giggled as I grabbed her hips and thrust inside. This view was amazing. Her round ass in my hands, her hair falling across her back. She glanced back at me over her shoulder.

"You're so fucking sexy," I said.

Holding her hips tight, my back burning from her nails, I pounded her hard. My muscles flexed and my fingers dug into her skin. The tension built fast. I was ready to fucking explode.

I leaned back enough to pull out and grabbed my cock. She watched over her shoulder while I stroked my solid length. Grunting, I burst, my dick pulsing. Thick ropes of come spurted out onto her luscious ass. I kept stroking, groaning as I came all over her.

With one last pulse, I was done.

She giggled again. "That was fun."

My heart hammered in my chest and an intoxicating mix of endorphins swept through me. I grabbed a towel and wiped the mess off her ass, then leaned in to kiss the pink spot where I'd spanked her.

"Oh, poor baby, did I scratch you?" she asked. "Do you need me to kiss it better?"

Smiling, I lay on the large blanket and closed my eyes while she kissed my back. She even kissed the spot on my ass where she'd bitten me.

"Oops, I left a mark down here."

I took a deep breath. "You know you can't hurt me."

As if to test me, she smacked my ass cheek.

I rolled over, grabbing her, and hauled her down on top of me. She melted into me, her body draping over mine, her head resting on my chest. I traced my fingers over the smooth skin of her back.

"Best honeymoon ever," she said.

I couldn't have agreed more.

This sweet girl had bathed my cold and sterile life with her warm summer sun. I'd appreciated and respected her as my assistant, but this was so much more. I loved her. I loved her with every piece of my heart and soul, but I wasn't sure if that was enough. She had more love to give than anyone I'd ever met. And somehow I was the lucky man who got to spend the rest of his life basking in her sunshine.

∼

# AFTERWORD

Dear reader,

This book was a long time coming.

Almost two years ago, an editor at one of the "big five" publishing houses had a conversation with my agent about me. She asked if I might be interested in pitching a book to them. They liked what I'd been doing with the Book Boyfriend series, and were interested in something along those lines.

I thought, what the heck! Let's see where this goes. So I came up with the concept for what eventually became this book. I outlined most of it, and wrote the first six or seven chapters.

The editor loved it, and they did offer me a book deal. As much as I liked the editor on a personal level, I had to look at it from a business standpoint. For various reasons, I wound up turning them down.

At the time, I was working on the first couple of Miles family books and in the planning stages of Bootleg Springs with Lucy Score. I already had a very full editorial calendar.

So Shepherd and Everly had to wait.

When I started looking at my calendar for this year, I really wanted to include this book. I'd worked on it a little more here and there because I just couldn't help myself. These characters were speaking to me, and I wanted to dive into a book that was straight up sexy and fun.

I nudged things around, and squeezed it in. It's made for a busy first half of the year, with some tight deadlines. But I'm SO glad I was finally able to finish this book.

Everly was such a fun character to explore. Sometimes characters who are very sweet or nice wind up being doormats. They're too nice, and although that can make for a great character arc, I didn't see Everly that way. She is a bright, sunshiney optimist, but she's also tough. And let's be honest, she'd have to be to handle Shepherd Calloway.

Shepherd was all about the layers. On the outside, he's brusque and cold. He's civil at best, and definitely not friendly.

But beneath that exterior, there's a lot more to him. And I loved watching Everly peel those layers back and start to see the man on the inside.

I hope you enjoyed Shepherd and Everly's story. I set out to write a book that was hot, fun, and would leave you with a big smile on your face.

And if you're wondering about Hazel and Nora, yes I definitely plan to write books about each of them. You also got a peek at someone else you'll see more of. Just saying.

Thanks for reading!
    CK

P.S. Did you catch the Easter egg? If you've read the Miles Family series, you've seen Shepherd before. #hotbassplayer

# ACKNOWLEDGMENTS

A huge thank you to everyone who was a part of bringing this story to life.

To Elayne, my fabulous editor, for cleaning up the messy parts.

To Kari, for creating this gorgeous cover.

To my beta readers, Nikki and Jodi, for taking time out of your busy schedules to offer feedback.

To David, who once again gave me a fantastic concept to run with. (And for ALL the other things.)

To my unicorn mermaid queen of a PA, Nikki, for keeping me from losing my mind. (That's basically her job description).

And to all my readers for your love and support. Thank you! I love your faces!!

# ALSO BY CLAIRE KINGSLEY

For a full and up-to-date listing of Claire Kingsley books visit
www.clairekingsleybooks.com/books/

For comprehensive reading order, visit www.
clairekingsleybooks.com/reading-order/

## The Haven Brothers

Small-town romantic suspense with CK's signature endearing
characters and heartwarming happily ever afters. Can be read as
stand-alones.

Obsession Falls (Josiah and Audrey)

The rest of the Haven brothers will be getting their own happily
ever afters!

## How the Grump Saved Christmas (Elias and Isabelle)

A stand-alone, small-town Christmas romance.

## The Bailey Brothers

Steamy, small-town family series with a dash of suspense. Five
unruly brothers. Epic pranks. A quirky, feuding town. Big HEAs.
Best read in order.

Protecting You (Asher and Grace part 1)

Fighting for Us (Asher and Grace part 2)

Unraveling Him (Evan and Fiona)

Rushing In (Gavin and Skylar)

Chasing Her Fire (Logan and Cara)

Rewriting the Stars (Levi and Annika)

## The Miles Family

Sexy, sweet, funny, and heartfelt family series with a dash of suspense. Messy family. Epic bromance. Super romantic. Best read in order.

Broken Miles (Roland and Zoe)

Forbidden Miles (Brynn and Chase)

Reckless Miles (Cooper and Amelia)

Hidden Miles (Leo and Hannah)

Gaining Miles: A Miles Family Novella (Ben and Shannon)

## Dirty Martini Running Club

Sexy, fun, feel-good romantic comedies with huge... hearts. Can be read as stand-alones.

Everly Dalton's Dating Disasters (Prequel with Everly, Hazel, and Nora)

Faking Ms. Right (Everly and Shepherd)

Falling for My Enemy (Hazel and Corban)

Marrying Mr. Wrong (Sophie and Cox)

Flirting with Forever (Nora and Dex)

### Bluewater Billionaires

Hot romantic comedies. Lady billionaire BFFs and the badass heroes who love them. Can be read as stand-alones.

The Mogul and the Muscle (Cameron and Jude)

The Price of Scandal, Wild Open Hearts, and Crazy for Loving You

More Bluewater Billionaire shared-world romantic comedies by Lucy Score, Kathryn Nolan, and Pippa Grant

### Bootleg Springs

#### by Claire Kingsley and Lucy Score

Hot and hilarious small-town romcom series with a dash of mystery and suspense. Best read in order.

Whiskey Chaser (Scarlett and Devlin)

Sidecar Crush (Jameson and Leah Mae)

Moonshine Kiss (Bowie and Cassidy)

Bourbon Bliss (June and George)

Gin Fling (Jonah and Shelby)

Highball Rush (Gibson and I can't tell you)

### Book Boyfriends

Hot romcoms that will make you laugh and make you swoon. Can be read as stand-alones.

Book Boyfriend (Alex and Mia)

Cocky Roommate (Weston and Kendra)

Hot Single Dad (Caleb and Linnea)

~

**Finding Ivy** (William and Ivy)

A unique contemporary romance with a hint of mystery. Stand-alone.

~

**His Heart** (Sebastian and Brooke)

A poignant and emotionally intense story about grief, loss, and the transcendent power of love. Stand-alone.

~

**The Always Series**

Smoking hot, dirty talking bad boys with some angsty intensity. Can be read as stand-alones.

Always Have (Braxton and Kylie)

Always Will (Selene and Ronan)

Always Ever After (Braxton and Kylie)

~

**The Jetty Beach Series**

Sexy small-town romance series with swoony heroes, romantic HEAs, and lots of big feels. Can be read as stand-alones.

Behind His Eyes (Ryan and Nicole)

One Crazy Week (Melissa and Jackson)

Messy Perfect Love (Cody and Clover)

Operation Get Her Back (Hunter and Emma)

Weekend Fling (Finn and Juliet)

Good Girl Next Door (Lucas and Becca)

The Path to You (Gabriel and Sadie)

# ABOUT THE AUTHOR

Claire Kingsley is a #1 Amazon bestselling author of sexy, heartfelt contemporary romance and romantic comedies. She writes sassy, quirky heroines, swoony heroes who love their women hard, panty-melting sexytimes, romantic happily ever afters, and all the big feels.

She can't imagine life without coffee, her Kindle, and the sexy heroes who inhabit her imagination. She lives in the inland Pacific Northwest with her three kids.

www.clairekingsleybooks.com

Made in the USA
Middletown, DE
01 February 2024